THE HESPERIAN DILEMMA

To Ian,

Wishing you abundant joy and success !

Colin Waterman
03/04/19 .

THE HESPERIAN DILEMMA

A SCI-FI ADVENTURE AND LOVE STORY

COLIN WATERMAN

 First published in 2019 by by Fabulahula, a
division of E & Q Services Ltd, Gloucester, UK.

ISBN: 978-1-9160519-0-4

For Linda, with all my love.

Ay me! For aught that I could ever read,
Could ever hear by tale or history,
The course of true love never did run smooth.

From *A Midsummer Night's Dream*
by William Shakespeare.

Part One
New World

New Arrival

11.30 Central Hesperian Time (CHT), June 2135
Europa, second moon of Jupiter

Dr Geoff Kirby was lying on the lawn in the garden, the only place in the Unidome where there was real grass. He was waiting for his com-phone to ring and, not having anything urgent to do, he relaxed and surveyed the scene above him. It was like a transparent termite mound, its occupants scurrying in all directions, many of them flying through the air.

The scene of constructive purpose changed abruptly to one of confusion, as flashing lights and wailing sirens filled the dome's air space like an electric storm. Geoff leapt up and ran to join the crowd gathering around the Securopa viz-box in the concourse. The screen showed a girl standing near the top of the roof. She looked puzzled, teetering at the edge of the maintenance platform, her emerald green Pinna 7 sports-aerofoils spread wide. Long, chestnut hair, parted in the middle – he'd seen her photograph only that morning. She was the girl who was supposed to call him. He unslung his wings, flapped hard in a steep climb to the apex of the dome, and dropped down next to the Oceanography Department's latest recruit, Dr Maura O'Hara.

'Come on,' Geoff shouted. 'We've got to get out of here.' He launched himself into space and circled until he saw Maura gliding down. The cacophony of alarm signals stopped, and Maura joined her companion on the ground. 'Welcome to Europa,' he said. 'You've just set off the main alarm.'

'God between us and all harm!' said Maura, waving her wings to keep her feet on the deck.

'Okay, calm down. I've called the control room. We'll go and say we're sorry. That platform is a maintenance area. You have to get permission to land there. Did you forget? Prof should have explained it when you did your induction.'

Maura shook her head, her long hair swinging in the low gravity. 'The professor fast-tracked me through that. I think he missed some bits out. But what's the big deal anyway?'

'You'll see,' said Geoff, with a tight-lipped smile. 'But let me do the talking, okay?'

Geoff began to apologise but the Securopa man told him to shut up and listen carefully. Geoff wondered why he was standing with his feet so far apart. But there was no mistaking his jutting chin and squinting eyes, nor the rasp in his voice. It was hard to tell if the officer was naturally malicious or simply inflating his own ego. But, for whatever reason, he was clearly intent on giving them a hard time. He would force them to listen to his droning voice as he recited the formal regulations. No one was allowed to land on the platform without a permit. Failure to obtain security clearance was gross negligence. Every precaution had to be taken against possible Khitan infiltrators. The platform could be used by terrorist snipers. They should never approach the prohibited areas without proper authorisation.

Geoff leant forward to disguise his height, made himself look serious and kept nodding in apparent agreement. He knew as long as they appeared to be sufficiently apologetic, the officer's tirade would eventually fizzle out. Maura's face had flushed red. Geoff covered her hand with his as she drummed her fingers on the control room desk.

Eventually Geoff's tactics had the desired effect, and the officer began to run out of things to say. He concluded by admitting that Maura had some excuse, being a new arrival. However, he said he viewed Geoff's breach of regulations to be more serious, and he would ensure that Human Resources would register a formal warning in Geoff's personnel file. Maura opened her mouth to object, but Geoff's sudden look told her to stay silent.

An hour later, Geoff spotted Maura sitting at a table in the Unidome coffee bar, looking glum. Everything on Europa was less than a seventh of its weight on Earth. Geoff bought two coffees and carried them over, rotating the tray slowly on one finger. Maura rewarded his trick with a smile, but then looked serious again.

'I guess it was you I was supposed to contact to get shown round. I'm sorry, Dr Kirby, once I got my wings I completely forgot to call you.'

'That's normal,' said Geoff, smiling his forgiveness. 'Newcomers are always excited when they get their wings. It's amazing how the low gravity changes the feel of the air in the Unidome. It's like being in breathable water – and call me Geoff, by the way.'

'Thanks, and you're right about flying. It's brilliant. I do breaststroke arms and waggle my feet to go up. Then I spread my wings and just glide down. It's so easy.'

'It's great, isn't it,' said Geoff. 'I used to dream about flying when I was little.'

'Sure, but I'm sorry I got you into trouble. I thought the platform was a viewing gallery.'

'Don't worry, I don't work for anyone here. The Unified Nations sent me.'

'I know,' said Maura. 'I read your bio-notes during the trip from Earth. You're a consultant on the Committee for Peaceful Uses of Outer Space.'

'You've certainly done your research. Yes, we call it COPUOS for short. I'm only attached to the Oceanography Department for administrative purposes. So, what's brought you to this ice ball?'

'My tutor in Massachusetts told me there was a vacancy for an oceanographer on Europa, and I jumped at the chance.'

Geoff had guessed as much. Maura had taken a step into the unknown. She was way out of her depth and he longed to help her if he could. It was his duty as an older, more experienced man, he told himself. But then, she was rather attractive.

'You were at MIT then?' said Geoff. 'It's a great uni.'

'I was researching extremophile microbes,' said Maura, her green eyes shining brightly as Geoff nodded his interest. 'You know

Jupiter's gravity kneads Europa like a lump of dough. It heats up the ocean under the ice. For years, people thought there could be life here. If there's even the simplest living cell, I want to find it.'

⊱⊰

Geoff was finishing work when he noticed Maura storing her wings in her locker. In fact, he couldn't fail to notice her because she slammed the locker door with such violence that it bounced without latching. She had to slam it again. He left his briefcase and walked over to her quickly, but not so fast as to make it appear he was concerned.

'Everything okay?' he enquired casually.

Maura shook her head, her earrings flying out horizontally. 'Janey Mack! I don't know whether to laugh or cry.'

'You're not still worried about Securopa, are you? They knew you were no threat.'

'No, it's Professor Mitchell who's upset me. He called me into his office and gave me a right lashing for setting off the alarms. He said it gave the department a bad name.'

'Come on,' said Geoff, nodding towards the pathway around the dome. 'Let's go for a walk.'

Since his early teens, Geoff had been aware he often misunderstood other people's emotions. He could tell if someone's mood was congenial, unpleasant or neutral but, beyond that, he was unable to recognise how someone was feeling. He had been told it was a form of alexithymia but, as he could identify his own emotions, there was no exact diagnosis for his condition. He'd realised that, to live a normal life, he had to compensate using logic, and he'd studied body language and facial expressions as if learning a foreign language. He could now interpret visual and audible signs which, when considered in sequence, he could read as clearly as a sentence. Now, as he observed Maura's behaviour, he was in no doubt she was exhibiting the classic signs of disappointment. He raised his arm to put it round her shoulder, but then let it drop again to his side. *Too soon,* he told himself.

The outer corridor offered the colonists the opportunity to experience a change of scene after they'd worked an extended day in the Unidome's artificial environment. Viewed through the radiation-resistant windows, the landscape was hostile, but beautiful. In the foreground, a smooth annular ring of ice reflected the radiance of the dome, while the tiny sun shining on the landscape beyond revealed a criss-cross of ridges and chaotic, fractured surfaces punctuated by shiny hillocks.

Maura fell into step beside him. 'You know, I had no idea it would be like this here. Once Prof had finished raving about how careless I'd been, he told me the Oceanography Department only did research to support the OPDEO naval base. Would you believe it, he's ordered me to do temperature surveys? He wants a complete map of the isotherms over the complete feckin' surface of the moon.'

'He hasn't got any choice,' said Geoff. 'He has to do what OPDEO says because they fund the whole colony.'

'I thought he'd want to know if there was any life in the ocean, but he told me not to waste my time looking for flora and fauna. Actually, I'm so pissed off, I'm thinking of taking the next transport back to Earth.'

'Cheer up, Maura, we're pioneers on a new frontier. Doesn't that get your adrenalin flowing?'

'So far it's the eejits who control this place who've done that for me, and not in a good way.'

'Well, the truth is that OPDEO is more interested in military supremacy than science. It's the Hesperian Federation's armed force in space. They've set up a base here to get an advantage over our enemy.'

'You mean because the Khitan Empire built a command centre on Mars?'

'Exactly. That was an escalation of the arms race against the Federation. Now we've built the means to destroy the Khitan's base. Whoever's furthest from the sun can fire missiles at their enemy with gravity to help. Here, the Federation can do it from submarines under the ice. It's the ultimate deterrent because their subs are impregnable.'

'But they advertised for research scientists,' said Maura, arching her eyebrows.

'Right, but as Prof said, it's only research to assist OPDEO's navy.'

'So why are you here, Geoff?'

'Call me cynical if you like, but I think OPDEO wanted someone from the UN as window dressing. It helped them disguise their true ambitions.'

'But OPDEO's just a deterrent. It was set up to protect us. You've just told me that.'

'I'm sorry to disillusion you, Maura, but OPDEO's name is deliberately deceptive. It's nothing to do with "Outer Planets Defending Each Other". It's really an aggressive organisation. That was one reason the UN sent me here.'

'You work for the UN, but you're not on their payroll. You're a consultant, right?'

'You really did do your homework.'

'I had a long time to kill coming here. Your committee employs you to write papers about ANN.'

'Sorry, I don't know anything about neonatal nursing, or its academy,' said Geoff, keeping his face expressionless.

She pulled at his sleeve to stop him walking. 'I'm talking about artificial neural networks,' she said, laughingly articulating each word with exaggerated clarity. 'I understand you're an expert on the subject.'

'I know it's more predictable than human intelligence. It has extraordinary possibilities.'

'But how safe is it really? I know you'll say all programs have built-in safeguards to protect us. But artificial minds more intelligent than us. Won't they get their own ideas?'

'Oh, Maura, I think you've read too much science fiction. But finding life under the ice here is a definite possibility. That's science fact.'

'Maybe, but Prof doesn't want me to look for it. I've wasted nineteen months travelling a billion kilometres to a place that's a complete jacks.'

She stopped to look out through the windows. Geoff was afraid for a moment she might kick the glass. 'Don't give up,' he said quickly. 'Sometimes it's best to bend with the wind, if you know what I mean.'

'I don't . . . tell me.'

'You could collect Prof's data and do your own scientific study at the same time.'

'How would that work?'

'Well, the best bathyscaphes ever constructed are here on Europa. They can go deeper than the Mariana Trench. Once you're inside one of those bathtubs, you could collect any data you like.'

⟵🐟

Maura had almost completed her training as a bathyscaphe hydronaut. She'd dealt successfully with the score of random fault conditions created during simulator exercises, and had carried out supervised practice dives in an actual 'bath' down to one kilometre depth.

Standing in the Unidome sky gallery, she looked out across the Solar System. The sun was directly overhead, but in the thin atmosphere of Europa, the sky was black. The starscape was magnificent, dominated by two of Jupiter's moons – the giant crescent of Ganymede and dark Callisto in its gibbous phase. She couldn't see Jupiter itself, nor its innermost moon, Io, because the Unidome was situated on the side farthest away from the giant planet. But the sun was still the brightest star in the sky. Just to the right, a tiny disc of light was visible, tinged blue by the oceans that covered two-thirds of its surface. Maura heard the click of magnetic soles on the walkway. She turned and greeted Geoff with a smile.

'How did you get on with the bathyscaphe theory exam?' he asked. 'It was today, wasn't it?' he said, slightly emphasising the word 'today' in acknowledgement that days were an artificial concept on Europa. The colonists chose to maintain their natural biological rhythms in synchronism with CHT.

'It was, and I did okay, I think,' said Maura. 'As soon as I realised piloting a bathyscaphe was like flying a powered air balloon, I knew what the theory must be.'

'So, when will they let you take command?'

'Soon, I expect. D'you want to come with me? I'm looking for an assistant.'

Difficult Question

It was the hardest question Kai had ever tried to answer. 'Which fish cannot swim to the end of the ocean?' It was illogical, and it was meant to be. Kai Yongze had wrestled with the problem for the last six months, during periods of sitting meditation, walking meditation, carrying out his duties at the monastery, and even during his dreams. He'd looked at the conundrum from every point of view: scientifically, spiritually, and poetically – but without success. He had failed again, just as he'd failed to perform the role he'd been given by his birthright. As the son of a rich Khitan deputy, he could have enjoyed a lifetime of leisure. His unearned riches and the opulence of his surroundings had shackled him with chains of gold.

He'd broken free, run away to a city in the outlands, and spent his personal wealth in brothels and gambling dens, trying to escape his inner emptiness. After his money had run out, he'd joined the beggars in the street. Some passing monks told him about a monastery in the mountains where he could find peace. The Abbot, Wu Jiu Li, had taken him in and given him both hospitality and a goal for his life. But the path set by the Abbot had been difficult to follow. Kai shaved his head, donned the simple robe of a novice monk and began to meditate, following a regime intended to reshape his mind. He had to reject all he'd ever known, to answer a question that made no sense.

Kai was no nearer the solution. He had not slept for two days, nor eaten for three. During the last meditation practice he'd been unable to sit upright, and a monk had been forced to correct him, striking him eight times across his back. He wandered through the grounds looking for a place where he could find peace of mind.

Since Wu had put him on light duties, he was now responsible for feeding the fish in the ornamental pond at the end of the rock garden. He collected a bucket of rice flakes, hoping that the task would distract his troubled mind. However, there was no peace to be found in the formal garden where the high midday sun provided no shade. A few severely pruned bushes were interspaced between randomly spaced boulders, all set in a sea of white marble chippings. The fragments of stone dazzled his eyes and burnt his bare feet. He sat by the edge of the ornamental pond and dangled his feet in the water while his reflection gazed up at him, the image of a stranger.

The carp gathered around, jumping and diving in anticipation of food. Kai got up, scattered the rice flakes on the surface of the water and watched a shower of golden fish dart towards the morsels. He looked for the Great Fish, rumoured to be some hundred years old, but he didn't really expect to see it. All the monks knew it preferred to find fragments of food later, flakes of rice caught on the water-lily leaves. But, on this occasion, the ancient carp rose to the surface, lifted its head from the water, and fixed Kai with a misty eye. Then it spoke, clearly enunciating a single word: 'Thiosh.' Kai promptly fell over backwards and dropped his bucket in the water. The shoal erupted in turmoil, gorging themselves on their unexpected second helping.

All the novices had their own personal riddle. Every day, they knelt before Wu in turn, and chanted the illogical question their master had given them. Wu would say, 'Well?' Sometimes the novice would offer a response, and sometimes he said nothing. In either case, Wu would frown and wave him away.

Kai picked himself up from the edge of the pond and hurried over to the hall where Wu sat on his wooden throne, serenely resplendent in a carmine toga. He wore a helmet surmounted by a golden coxcomb, a sign he was an enlightened one. Wu signalled with his finger, and Kai chanted, 'Which fish cannot swim to the end of the ocean?'

'Well?' said Wu.

'Thiosh,' said Kai, and Wu roared with laughter, rocking on his throne, his helmet askew.

'That's very good,' said Wu, 'I'll tell the authorities. Pack your things. You'll be going to the Dongfeng Aerospace City in Gansu Province. There's much for you to learn there.'

'It is a long way to Gansu,' said Kai, feeling obliged to say something.

'Yes, but Jupiter is so much further,' said Wu. 'So much further.' He cackled and chortled until tears ran down his face and onto his robes. His echoing guffaws transfixed the monks in the midst of their activities, as if they'd been caught in a photograph.

꙳

Nearly three years had passed. Kai had completed basic celestonaut training and was now seeking a qualification as a pilot captain. He'd done well in the written examinations but he still had to demonstrate leadership skills. Previously he'd had his evaluation interviews with his commander. But this time Kai's line manager, Tang Linto, had asked Kai to see him. Tang was Director of Operations, in charge of all launch missions. However, Dongfeng Aerospace City was a notorious hotbed of political intrigue. Kai suspected Tang spent most of his energy expanding his power base, rather than dealing with technicalities.

Even though Kai was five minutes early, he knocked on the Director's door. Tang called him to come in and Kai entered.

Tang was leaning back on his leather-bound chair, his hands clasped over his considerable girth. He smiled broadly. 'Thank you for coming early, but there's no rush. I've told my secretary to make sure nobody disturbs us.'

'Sir, I am honoured you have chosen to do my training evaluation yourself,' said Kai. 'But have you time to counsel me, a mere trainee?'

'To tell the truth, I'm curious about you, Kai. It's unusual to have such a variation in grades.' Tang tapped the screen of his com-pad and displayed Kai's assessment matrix on a wall-mounted screen. Kai studied the evaluation data, dozens of performance parameters, each with as many possible attainment levels.

'Your practical skill as a pilot is outstanding,' Tang continued. 'In all our tests you have shown exceptional self-control and steadiness under pressure. But, and this is what worries me, you're way below average against other parameters. Association, for example. You appear to have made no effort to cultivate anyone with influence in Aerospace City. Why's that? Do you not know you need good contacts to succeed?'

'I have learnt to be the pioneer of my own path, sir. Do the scriptures not teach that?'

'Hm, I'm not sure that's relevant. You've scored low on Procedural Compliance too. I understand you made an unauthorised change to one of the simulator programs. According to the training supervisor, you created a new fault scenario without permission. Is that true?'

'Yes, sir. I combined a solid-fuel booster failure with a main thruster flame-out.'

'Then you left it as a random launch occurrence without telling anyone.'

'I believe we should consider all possibilities, sir. Is it not written that ignorance is the impurity that exceeds all impurities?'

'No, that's totally irrelevant, Kai. Trainees must keep to the approved programme. Such a combination of faults is virtually impossible. You've wasted everyone's time and failed to reach your scheduled targets. Team Synergy, for example. You've not filed any reports for at least six months. Team building is essential to ensure your crew all think the same way.'

'Should not everyone work out their own salvation with diligence, sir?'

'Listen Kai, you're not toeing the line, d'you hear me?' The Director's voice was beginning to crack. He paused to gulp down some water, and then lowered his tone. 'Let your crew play some team-bonding games,' he continued. 'They'll enjoy that. And don't be so damned aloof. Go down to the Tigercat Saloon and relax a little. And stop inventing new fault scenarios for the simulator. It's hard enough dealing with the ones we know about already. Next time I see you, I'll expect you to have shown an improvement!'

Kai found a free meeting room and summoned the two members of his crew.

'Gentlemen, we have been set a task by no less a person than our Director himself. Chen, please empty the contents of the box on the table.'

'*Aiya*!' said Chen. 'Jenga blocks. Are we playing game?'

'We are going to design and build a tower, and then we will measure its height.'

'*Ta ma de*!' Huang swore. 'You have not fallen for this Team Synergy crap, have you, Kai? I thought as a potential pilot captain you had more sense.'

'Think of it as a test of obedience,' said Kai, trying hard not to smile.

'I know what this is,' said Chen. 'Tang Linto, he choose best crew for next transport to Mars. Our team and Zhejiang in competition. We build biggest tower and we get countdown.'

They ran through the build options: horizontal stacks, square-based legs and platforms, bricks either flat or on edge. '2D arched pyramid is best,' said Chen. 'It have secure base and use less bricks.'

'This is just great,' said Huang. 'After three years of celestonaut training we are going to build walls with children's blocks.'

'By the way,' said Kai. 'Our final score will be tower height divided by the time taken for design and construction. And we have already had ten minutes.'

Huang swore again and began rapidly placing Jenga blocks on end. Tang Linto slipped quietly into the room, holding a tape measure.

⊱━⬤

Later that day, Kai, Chen and Huang were having dinner together in the celestonaut accommodation, dipping slices of tripe in boiling chili sauce made according to Kai's own recipe. It was usually Chen's favourite, but this time he seemed to have no appetite. Once they'd cleared the table, Huang announced he was going to take Chen down to the Tigercat Saloon. 'It might cheer him up. Why not come as well, Kai?' he asked, smiling broadly.

'I will look in later,' said Kai, enjoying Huang's look of surprise. 'I am supposed to do some "association". It could be a good place to start.'

Huang and Chen were watching a girl with Hesperian features swinging from a rope. She'd been wearing a tiger-skin bikini, but now the noisy crowd below were tossing both parts in the air. Huang bent down to shout a crude remark in his companion's ear, but Chen seemed to be thinking of something else. He downed his sixth glass of *baijiu* and staggered across to the table where the Zhejiang crew were playing cards. Tai Qiu Wu was dealing, but Chen knocked the cards out of his hands. 'Hey, baboon bollocks – I saw photo of your tower – you had more bricks. I hope your son born with no anus.'

Tai spat and, holding a bottle by its neck, smashed it against the edge of the table. For a big man Huang could move quickly. He overturned the card players' table, gripped Tai by the arm, and twisted. *Crack!* The bones snapped like brittle plastic. Huang prepared to throw Tai over the bar, just as Kai walked in. Huang froze, holding Tai by the scruff of his neck, dangling him half a metre above the floor. The music died, the girl stopped swinging, and a murmur went through the crowd, 'It's the Holy Man!'

In one coordinated gesture, Kai patted the air and beckoned with his fingers. Huang dropped Tai and steered Chen back into the street.

First Dive

It was the day Geoff had agreed to dive with Maura. The thought weighed him down. Then he calculated the relative positions of Jupiter's nearest moons and immediately felt better. In Europa's ever-changing gravitational field, his weight was actually at its maximum.

He downloaded the hazard analysis for bathyscaphe dives onto his com-pad, but quickly closed the page without reading it. It would be dangerous, but he had to go diving regardless. He boarded the maglev cage and dropped down the two-kilometre-long vertical shaft through the ice. A member of dockside service personnel helped him change into a thermal suit and led him to the airlock. Geoff squeezed down the vessel's entrance tunnel leading to the observation gondola, but he stepped into the cramped space too quickly, banging his head on an overhead valve. He thought Maura was about to laugh, but was relieved when he realised her smile was one of sympathy. He squatted down, hunched on the spare seat. Maura continued to fill in data records, relaying information to the support crew at Port Authority Control.

The basic design of a deep-sea bathyscaphe hadn't changed in two centuries. The main part of the vessel was a streamlined tube containing tanks for buoyancy and hoppers for ballast, and the gondola was a thick-walled steel sphere slung underneath. The internal diameter was no more than two metres, and the only place where Geoff could stand upright was in the centre. Maura, being petite and agile, had no such difficultly moving around.

'Just waiting for clearance to dive,' she told him. 'Prof made me plan the temperature surveys myself, so I thought we'd start with the

Cronus Rift. It's not deep by Europan standards, only ten thousand metres, but there's some volcanic activity on the seabed that causes local heating.'

'Could there be some sulphur-eating microbes, by any chance?' said Geoff, trying to sound more nonchalant than he felt.

'There could be, right enough. But it would be grand just to find an amino acid. Just think, if the building blocks are present, then the whole universe must be teeming with life.'

Geoff heard the excitement in Maura's voice and it made him smile.

'Just sit tight 'til we get to the bottom,' she said. 'Then we'll turn on the lights and see what's there.'

Geoff waited, fidgeting periodically in an attempt to get comfortable, until the Port Controller's voice broke the silence of their tiny cabin. 'Cleared to dive. Bon voyage!'

Maura detached the magnetic hooks tethering the craft to the quayside, and the dive began. Geoff felt more relaxed now they'd set off. Maura would have to pilot the craft manually – there were insufficient data on currents and other hazards for her to use auto-control. This was an advantage for him, he realised as he perched on his chair facing Maura, less than a metre away. She was oblivious to his gaze while he watched her frowning and pursing her lips as she made course corrections.

Cybernetics was one of Geoff's specialisms. He was fascinated by the way she scanned the screens, operated the controls to adjust the craft's buoyancy and drove the propulsion units. But he also studied her face, in frank appreciation of her perfect complexion, green eyes and chestnut-brown hair which cascaded in curls to the top of her shoulders. He felt certain her youth was genuine and, like him, she had never resorted to the regenerative drugs that were commonly used to reverse the effects of ageing. His own self-denial had left him, aged thirty-five, with pepper-and-salt hair and a beard to match. He wondered about her age. No more than mid-twenties?

Maura had been reporting to base at fifteen-minute intervals, but the Port Controller's voice had become increasingly distorted the deeper they dived.

'Why is the line so bad?' Geoff asked.

'We have to use acoustic signals to communicate,' Maura explained. 'No one has found a way of using radio signals in deep water.'

'It seems to be getting worse.'

'We're getting close to the volcanic activity on the seabed. It's drowning the signal.'

Geoff gave her a 'wouldn't you just know it' sort of smile. He could feel the vibration through the walls of the gondola. It was as if the whole cabin was trembling. But what with – excitement? Or something else?

'Are you sure you want to carry on?' asked Maura. 'If we go any deeper, we'll be on our own.'

Geoff had known the Cronus Rift would be dangerous before they began the dive. He'd look like a coward if he backed out now. 'It's okay,' he said. 'Let's have a quick look around and then get back up.'

'Right then, get ready with the camera and shoot anything that looks interesting.'

Geoff turned on the lights and peered out of the observation window. 'Wow!' he said in amazement. 'It's like a scene from the Industrial Revolution. I can see hundreds of chimneys belching black smoke.'

'Sure, they're on Earth's seabed too, you know.'

'Really?' Geoff felt he should have done more research.

'It happens whenever hot water from geothermal springs erupts into cold sea. The sulphides deposit out, making black smoke, and the build-up of minerals at the blowholes creates hollow towers.' Geoff lifted his eyebrows but made no comment.

They drove over vast fields of 'black smokers' and reached an area where many of the chimneys had fallen in random piles. 'What's happened here?' Geoff asked. 'Did they get too high?'

'We're on a fault line in the crust's tectonic plates. I think a seismic tremor brought them down.'

'I'm panning with the camera. There's a piece of debris that seems to be moving around.'

'Jaysis,' said Maura. 'We've hit the feckin' jackpot. There's something alive down there. I'll try to steer between the chimneys and get in close.'

A violent jolt threw Maura and Geoff across the cabin and an ear-rending crash reverberated through the structure of the bathyscaphe. The vessel had come to a dead stop and was now tilting down at thirty degrees.

'Feckin' hell, I'll check for damage.' Maura scanned the alarms on the viz-box. 'Forward buoyancy tank pressure zero. For'ard water tank zero. Port-side transverse propeller kaput. Both bow floodlights are dead. Try the infrared camera.'

'There's a chimney right across the bows,' said Geoff. 'Can we go backwards?'

'Aft propeller on full power now. Still stuck fast. I'm dumping the for'ard ballast. Nope, no change. I could ditch the aft ballast. The risk is we'll be out of control when we surface. We'll smack into the ice cap like a champagne cork. Shall I try it?'

'Just do it. We've got to get off the seabed somehow.'

'Okay, I've opened the aft ballast hopper. We're about as light as we can be, but we're still not going anywhere.'

'Can we call for help?' Geoff asked, trying hard to keep his voice steady.

Maura switched on the acoustic modem and a sound like a rocket exhaust filled the tiny cabin. She turned off the receiver. 'Any other ideas?'

⸻

After an hour of trying to free their craft from under the stone cylinder, Geoff and Maura were strangely quiet. Geoff knew ranting and raving about their fate would only use their remaining oxygen more quickly. Even so, he felt oddly composed.

All the sensory inputs to Geoff's brain had become more intense. The lights were brighter, and every creak of the damaged superstructure was amplified a thousand-fold. Ignoring his emotions, Geoff's analytical brain began to break down the smell of the gondola into its separate components: the grease on the mechanical linkages, the electrolyte used in the ultra-capacitors, the tang of his own perspiration.

Once again, he studied Maura's face. Her lips were pressed tightly together, her eyebrows were lowered, and she was glaring at the flashing alarms on the viz-box screen. *What's she feeling? It won't help if she panics. But she's not showing signs of fear. Her body language means something else.*

'You're angry,' he said.

'You bet I feckin' am!' she said. She balled her fists and looked around as if she wanted something to punch. She settled for thumping the control desk and then kicking it.

They stayed silent for a while. 'D'you know why I'm fuming?' said Maura. 'It's that feckin' fish.'

'Er, sorry?'

'The fish – for the first time ever in the history of humankind, we found extraterrestrial life. And now it'll stay secret.'

'Someone will find it again, one day.'

'If humankind doesn't destroy itself first!' She looked hard at him. 'You must regret coming with me. The only reason you're here is because you wanted to help.' She shook her head. 'I suppose I may as well tell you now. I think we would have been good together.'

Thanks, Maura, but this isn't a good time. But I'm glad she's talking. It'll calm her down and give me more time to think.

'Aren't you seeing anyone, Maura?' he said, while he scoured his brain for ideas of how to escape. *If we throw our weight from side to side, could we shake off the cylinder?*

'Not really,' said Maura, smiling sadly. 'There's been no one I wasn't happy to leave a billion kilometres away. All my relationships have been disasters.'

'Why didn't they work out?' said Geoff. *Would we float if we detached the gondola and left the main hull behind?*

'Oh, there were lots of reasons. Some men wanted to lord it over me, and I wasn't having any of that. Some accused me of trying to dominate them, which I never did, not at all. But they all seemed to want me for their own benefit.'

'Of course they did,' he said. 'You'd be a benefit to anyone.' *If we discharged our compressed air into the sea, would that shake us loose?*

'I don't mean in a good way,' said Maura. 'They wanted me just to hang on their arm, or make small talk to people they were sucking up to. I hated feeling I was being used.'

'So, none of them really cared about you?' he said. *Keep thinking. There must be a way.*

'The bastards I met were so selfish. They would have been crap fathers, I know that much.'

She's getting angry again. I'll ask her about her work. 'I thought you were a career scientist?'

'I wanted to use science to help endangered species,' said Maura. 'But I meant to settle down one day, maybe have a family.' Her hair fell in swathes across her face and she tossed it back, fixing her eyes on him. 'How about you? What's your story, Geoff?'

'Oh, I got married young, too young,' he said, forgetting for a moment his search for a means of escape.

A clanking sound resonated through the vessel and he felt the cabin levelling out. Maura was thrown out of her seat as the bath lurched again.

Geoff stooped to help her, but froze as he saw a shape on the viz-box screen – a shadowy but familiar outline.

'Something's moved the chimney,' he said, staccato tapping his viz-box screen to get the picture back.

Maura jumped up and began rapidly paging though the instrument readings. 'We're going back up, thank God. What did you see?'

'I dunno. The screen's gone blank. We've lost the infrared.'

'Something must have happened. Did the chimney just roll off?'

'Yeah, it must have done. P'raps it was a seismic tremor.'

'You saw something. What was it?'

'Nothing, a hallucination, my blood oxygen's low.'

'Tell me, Geoff. Something happened.'

'I don't know. I thought there could be something there. It was just for a second. It'll be gone by now – if there was anything.'

He checked the panel alarms. The forward searchlights had failed but the camera indicated its flash was still working. He operated the shutter. 'Hey, Maura, look! What do you make of that? That thing – it looks like a crab, doesn't it?'

'Jaysis! I think I must have died already. I don't understand anything anymore, not at all.'

'You thought there was life here. Now we know.'

'Mary, Mother of God, it must be gigantic! It's taking us back up. Look at the depth readout. At this rate we'll be under the ice again in an hour.'

'We could hit it hard. D'you want to contact Control? Say we're coming in for an emergency landing?'

She lifted a flap on the desk and hit a button. 'Okay, we're sending a mayday, but no way am I opening the voice channel. I don't want to tell anyone we're being rescued by a crab.'

'Look, I've got another photo,' said Geoff. 'It's not a crab, it's a machine. It's got a grab-arm and a rocket nozzle.'

The crab machine accompanied the bathyscaphe all the way to the ice cap, retracing the course of their descent from Port Authority quayside. During the final fifteen minutes, Geoff noticed their rate of ascent reduced, as if the machine was slowing them to minimise their impact with the ice cap.

'Glory be!' said Maura. 'We're back at quayside. Where's the crab thing?'

'It seems to have disappeared. I could only see it now and then using the flash. It's probably dived back where it came from.'

'I think we've got enough manoeuvrability to dock without help. But what in the universe was that thing?'

'It looked very mechanical to me. I think it was a robot.'

'Whatever it was, something intelligent must have made it,' said Maura.

She clutched her head with both hands and Geoff gripped her wrists to steady her. 'Listen, please,' he said, 'the crab robot – promise me you'll keep it secret for the moment. There's something I haven't told you.'

Suspicion

Maura had agreed to meet Geoff in the Unidome sky gallery. It was late morning, CHT, but the blackness of the sky had an intensity unknown on Earth. Saturn floated high, the bands on its surface and gaps in its rings clearly visible. Geoff pointed out Titan and four of the planet's other moons strung out like beads on a wire drilled through Saturn's equator. But his conversation sounded false even to his own ears. Their recent experience on the seabed weighed heavily on him. He knew he needed time to digest the significance of what had happened, both to them and between them. For long minutes they said nothing until, eventually, he asked how she was feeling.

'Actually I'm zinging, like you do if you breathe too much oxygen.'

'Well, that sounds better than too little,' said Geoff, the memory of their experience fresh in his mind. 'But, tell me, did you see Prof? What did he say?'

'Huh, it was funny. Would you believe he congratulated me? He praised me for what he thought was my skill in saving the bathyscaphe after it was damaged.'

'Good for you,' said Geoff. 'You deserve Prof's praise after being so brave.'

'Mm, maybe. He was such a gobshite previously, I decided to take all the credit myself, at least for the time being. I mentioned you in dispatches though.'

'So you didn't say anything about the crab robot?'

'I decided not to mention the crab-bot until after I'd talked to you. But, really, we've got to tell everyone. It's feckin' cataclysmic!'

'That's why we've got to tread cautiously. We haven't got enough evidence yet,' said Geoff.

'We've got photos of that crab-bot thing. It was made by some intelligent being. It's the most brilliantly wonderful news since Adam said "Hiya" to Eve.'

'No, we can't tell anyone. We have to find the robot-masters first.' Geoff touched Maura's arm. She was young and she believed she'd made a supremely important scientific discovery, and he had to persuade her to keep it secret. 'The Federation is desperate to achieve military superiority. They only want this place as a weapons base, and they won't allow anything to jeopardise it. When they find out another life form exists in the sea, they'll try and destroy it.'

'But we can show everyone what we've seen,' said Maura. 'OPDEO won't dare annihilate a new, intelligent species.'

'Publishing some blurry pictures of a machine won't be enough to protect its makers. No matter what we say, OPDEO will claim it was their own robot that saved us. It's up to us to prove the aliens themselves exist. Until we've done that, we must keep what happened secret, okay?'

'Are you sure about all this? You're not paranoid, are you?'

'You don't know the half of it. The UN has been watching OPDEO for some time. There's no doubt they're utterly ruthless.'

Geoff waited for Maura's reaction. Rhea, Saturn's second largest moon, appeared from behind the planet, but still she remained silent, her lips pressed tight. Then at last she spoke. 'Just before we docked, you said there was something you hadn't told me.'

'Yeah, okay, I guess I'll have to come clean. For some time now, even before anyone landed here, COPUOS thought there could be life on Europa.'

'Sure, that's not news. Everyone knows life could have started here.'

'Well, not only did it start, it came a long way. In fact, it's come so far it can send messages across space.'

'Jaysis! Are you coddin' me?'

'No, at least, not if you mean what I think you mean. Now, this is important, you're the first person outside the UN to hear this. Over a long period, COPUOS has received signals we've traced back to Europa.'

'What sort of signals?' asked Maura, tilting her head to one side.

'We discovered strings of words written directly onto our computer memories. We think it's only ever happened on our network.'

'Why your computers?'

'Perhaps it was because the name of our committee has "peaceful" in it. At least, that's what I hope.'

'Okay, what were the signals like?'

'The early ones were just gobbledygook. They looked like software errors. Then we went through a phase when we thought it was hackers having a bit of fun. Our internet security is the best in the world but, whatever firewalls we put up, somebody or something cut through them, like a thermite lance slicing a ship's hull.'

'Very nautical, Geoff. But what was in the message?'

'It was in a sort of flowery English, almost like poetry. We were convinced for a long time it was a hoax.'

'Come on, for Chrissakes, tell me what the messages said.'

'It's not that easy to say. I think an extraterrestrial was trying to work out how to communicate with us. Now we've had our lives saved by the crab-bot, I'm certain the messages were an attempt to contact us. Some living being was looking for peaceful acceptance and a mutually beneficial relationship.'

'You mean it wanted to be friends?'

'You could say that.'

'D'you think the crab-bot sent the messages?'

'I don't think so. My guess is it was being manipulated by something else, either from inside or outside. Thanks to you, I've now got strong evidence that advanced aliens live on this moon, just as the UN suspected. I'll write them a coded report.'

Maura looked pensive. Then she stepped back from Geoff and stood with her hands on her hips. 'So now I know your game. You've been cosying up to me so you could go looking for aliens.'

'Hey, that's not fair,' said Geoff, thinking hard. *She's become unfriendly and she's not being rational. If I explain, she'll understand we've been sharing a common interest.*

'It was your idea, remember?' he said. You asked me to help you search for living organisms. I was more than willing to, because I was on the same search. The only difference was, I expected my organisms to have a higher IQ than yours.'

'Now you're just being a smart-arse.' Maura smeared away a tear from her cheek.

Geoff was confused. *What have I missed? What I said was entirely logical, wasn't it? I've done something wrong and it's made her unhappy.*

'Why are you upset?' he asked. 'I don't understand – you were a real hero when we were trapped on the seabed.'

Maura began strapping on her wings. 'Let me alone, I'll talk to you tomorrow.' She took off leaving Geoff staring at the icy landscape.

General Flannery returned Major Breckenridge's salute. He walked over to the drinks cabinet that stood in the corner of his office, half filled two glasses with Bourbon and added a scoop of ice. 'I heard you were good at baseball, Major. We ought to start a team. How about the OPDEO Strikers? I've been reading your report. You certainly gave that fucker what for.'

'Thank you, suh,' said Breckenridge, his face momentarily contorted by a nervous tic. 'I love them supercavitation torpedoes. They fly like rockets. The insurgent never knew what hit it.' He downed his whiskey in one gulp and the general gave him another.

Flannery shifted his overflowing in-tray and sat on the edge of his desk. 'It was a smart move defusing the explosive. You disabled the machine without wrecking it. What's the latest analysis?'

'Well, it was definitely unmanned, suh, or what the heck you call them critters that built it. Nothin' was livin' inside. It was made from some real fancy alloys, and it had steam jets for propulsion. It used a lotta technology we've never seen before.'

'What was its purpose? Was it military?'

'I don't think so. It had a hell of a big claw, and a lot of cuttin' gear. We think it was designed for maintenance, suh.'

'So, what d'you think controlled it, Major?'

'It had a lot of complicated control programs. We know that from the chips we've found, pico-arrays with awesome memories. Our geeks are checkin' 'em out right now, suh.' The major's face was looking flushed and his habitual tic had reduced to a flicker of his eyelid.

'Was it autonomous, Major? A slave drone, or could it make decisions?'

'Aw, we're workin' on that right now, suh. One of the chips looks like a receiver for external commands. We're scannin' the ocean for acoustics. That's how we think the machine gets its orders.'

'So, you reckon our oceanographers discovered the machine before us, but never told us about it?'

'It certainly looks that way. O'Hara and Kirby say they got their bathyscaphe stuck under some rocks on the seabed. But it was never just a rock that caused damage like that on the hull.'

'How d'you mean?'

'I raced a lotta stock cars in my youth, suh. Smashed 'em up and welded the good halves together. For me it's a lead-pipe cinch – that vessel's been gripped by mechanical jaws and the debris cut away with a torch. Shall I bring 'em in for questionin', suh?'

'No, not yet. I think we can use them to find out more, at their risk.' Flannery sat back, steepling his fingers. 'O'Hara clearly wasn't telling the truth. If they've had contact with aliens, they'll try it again, and I want to see what happens. Meanwhile, go and find someone who's got access to their files, and who wouldn't be averse to a career move to assist OPDEO. But don't tell anyone else, okay?'

'You mean you wanna spy. Yessuh, I get you.'

'Let's say a confidential advisor, shall we? It sounds more refined.'

'Gotcha, suh.'

Kai smiled as he read Tang Linto's message, appointing him and his crew to fly the next transport ship to Mars. The Zhejiang team had been front-runners for the task but their navigator had a broken arm. The rumour was that Tai had stolen extra Jenga bricks to help his team win the tower building contest. The eyewitnesses to what had happened suddenly acquired a vivid memory of how Tai had tripped down the steps as he'd left the saloon and broken his arm as he tried to save himself.

Shortly after, Kai heard his doorbell ring. He was surprised to find a young man with a shaven head and wearing a saffron robe standing outside his living apartment. The monk passed Kai a scroll, bowed and departed without saying a word. Kai broke a seal bearing the familiar name of his monastery and unfurled the roll of stiff paper. The Abbot's secretary had written in the old style, using brush and ink. Kai frowned as he interpreted the ancient Khitan calligraphy. It was a message to tell him Wu Jiu Li was dying.

Kai knew he had to leave immediately to visit Wu. He wrote instructions for Huang and Chen to prepare for the voyage to Mars. Then, after changing into a dress uniform appropriate for his new rank as a Celestonaut Pilot Captain, he unlocked his strongbox and took out an antique orrery dating from the Qing dynasty. Its intricate mechanism modelled the movements of the sun, Earth and the five other planets of the Solar System known when it was made. It was a treasure he'd inherited years ago, but he had been unable to take it with him when he'd run away from home. Now he had a career and status again, he was reconciled with his family. They had returned the orrery to him as a sign of goodwill. He packed it into a small case with his luggage and set off for the maglev terminal.

Kai stopped his taxi-drone some distance from his destination so he could arrive on foot, as he had on his very first visit. The monastery, set on a mountain ledge, was imposing more for its breadth and symmetry than for its height. Kai stopped to study the building from afar. He rejoiced at the sight of its stone-carved pillar gates, the doubled-tiered roof sweeping upward at the corners, and the ceramic figurines embedded in the eaves.

When Kai reached the monastery, he was met by Prior Shetani who confirmed that Wu was dying. As he was second in command, it was common knowledge Shetani expected to become Abbot after Wu's death. Kai found Wu in his tiny cell and was shocked to see how thin his body had become. He was still lying on the hard board he'd slept on every night, as long as Kai could remember. Shetani grimaced when Kai ordered him to bring Wu a soft mattress from the visitors' quarters. But, observing Kai's uniform, the Prior hastened to fetch the bedding. When Kai demanded chicken broth for Wu, Shetani brought it himself, perhaps anxious to be seen to be doing all he could for his master. Kai gently spooned the broth into the Abbot's mouth, but the old man couldn't swallow more than a few mouthfuls.

He gripped Kai's hand weakly and drew him close to speak to him. 'The Thiosh are calling you,' he whispered. 'Beware of the destroyers.'

Kai felt a sudden draught and went to close the window. 'Tell me, Father, who are the destroyers?' he asked, but Wu began a fit of coughing and could not reply immediately.

'Go . . . to . . . the . . . Thiosh,' he said finally, and then began the loud, laboured breathing that is a precursor to death.

Kai gave Shetani money for Wu Jiu Li's tomb and asked him to place the orrery in Wu's coffin. Shetani thanked Kai for coming and said it was a pity the Abbot had been delirious when Kai saw him. 'On the contrary,' said Kai, 'no one on his deathbed spoke more clearly than Wu Jiu Li.'

Kai walked around the monastery grounds and paused at the ornamental lake, near the spot where the appearance of the giant carp had changed his life. But this time the surface remained a perfect mirror.

As he left the monastery, he noticed a new crop outside the kitchen. He photographed the leaves with his com-phone and identified the plants as a type of castor bean. He knew oil could be extracted from its seeds and used for medicinal purposes, to ease stomach problems or skin conditions. But as he journeyed back to join his crew, he remembered the seeds could be used to make another product: the highly toxic poison known as ricin.

Second Dive

Geoff was desperate to talk to Maura. He called and arranged to meet her in the Unidome garden. She was sitting on a park bench watching tiny humming birds hovering over a scarlet etlingera flower. It was lunchtime, and groups of two or three people wandered around, relaxing before going back to work. Prof's office supervisor, Leona, walked by – very straight, very tall, wearing her braids threaded with blue beads. She gave Maura a friendly wave. Geoff felt the garden turning around him as the combined scents of hibiscus, frangipani and white champak saturated his senses. He caught hold of the armrest and dropped into the empty space on the bench.

'Maura, we need to talk. You said I'd been cosying up to you to hitch a free ride under the ice. And yes, that was true in a way. I admit I had an ulterior motive, but it wasn't the only reason I wanted to get to know you.' Geoff blurted his words in a rapid staccato. He thought for a moment she was smiling, but he looked again and saw she was serious.

'I would have told you earlier why I was sent here,' he continued, 'but I was afraid you'd think I was crazy.' He put his arm around her shoulder, but Maura gently removed it.

'It's okay,' she said. 'I forgive you, but no hanky-panky, okay? Actually, I need to talk to you. I think OPDEO suspect something.'

'I don't think we've done anything to upset them, have we?' said Geoff. 'Not yet, anyway.'

'Well, the bathyscaphe went in for repairs and the technicians have been photographing the damage. They've found scorch marks from something like an oxyacetylene torch. And there are indentations that look like the hull was gripped by something powerful.'

'Oh heck, d'you think they realise something helped us?'

'I don't know,' said Maura. 'But an OPDEO major has been crawling over the hull too. I had to see Prof yesterday. I thought he was going to give me the third degree about what happened on the seabed.'

'Is he suspicious too?'

'Actually, he was as nice as pie. He wants me to go diving again in the spare bath as soon as possible. He said he needed more temperature data from the Cronus Rift. He even told me to take you as my crew.'

Geoff was relieved Maura was talking to him again. But there was something very odd about what she'd just said. He sat listening to the sound of a pair of humming birds, rising and falling in volume to a regular beat. He knew the birds were flapping their wings at slightly different frequencies, making the sound increase and decrease in volume. He estimated the pitch of the humming and then rapidly calculated the difference in their rate of flapping. Then, having solved that problem, he began another train of thought.

'You know,' he said at last, 'I think OPDEO already know about the crab-bot. Earlier today, one of the OPDEO programmers asked me for advice on something he was working on. His boss had downloaded some hardware device and given him a printout of machine code.'

'Why did he ask you?'

'He shouldn't have spoken to me, but he was under a lot of pressure. He knew I had a background in artificial intelligence and he asked me what the program was for.'

'That's weird. Don't they have manuals for their software?'

'It wasn't OPDEO programming. In fact, it was in a code I'd never seen before, but it used highly developed back propagation routines.'

'Sorry, that means absolutely nothing to me,' said Maura with a dismissive wave.

'Well, what if I said there were subroutines for operating a jib with a grabbing device? What would that make you think of?'

'You mean like a crab-bot?'

'Exactly. I think OPDEO have captured our robot friend, or one of its kind. They're probably dissecting it to see what it's made of. If I'm right, OPDEO know there's extraterrestrial life in the ocean.'

'So they know that we know. Is that it, Geoff? Perhaps they'll stop us diving again.'

'Maybe, or they may have ordered Prof to send us back to the Cronus Rift, hoping the bots, or their masters, will contact us.'

'Holy Mother of God, you mean now we have to go searching for extraterrestrials after our fellow humans have taken apart one of their robots?'

'Exactly,' said Geoff. 'OPDEO could use any encounter to learn more about the aliens, without putting themselves at risk.'

'But, even if we meet the ETs, I don't understand how OPDEO will find out. There's no way they can see us in the Rift.'

'They don't need to. They could bug the inside of the observation gondola. Then they'd rerun the recordings after we've come home again, assuming that we come back. And if the aliens turn nasty, then we'll just be another tragic news item.'

Maura sat looking at Geoff, her arms crossed. 'So, according to you, we've been set up. Up to our necks in the Wicklow bog and sinking fast. What are we going do now?'

'Well, I think we'd best stick to my plan. If we can get direct proof the aliens exist, then we can tell the world. That'll make it much harder for OPDEO to destroy a whole new biological domain.'

'You're certain OPDEO are a load of heartless bastards? I thought they were ecologically friendly.'

Geoff looked Maura full in the face. Somehow, he had to get the seriousness of the situation across to her. 'I've seen secret UN reports,' he said. 'They show OPDEO plans a pre-emptive strike on the Khitan Empire on Earth. They don't care about human life, never mind aliens.'

'Mother of God! But if you're right, the aliens may not be so friendly next time we dive. Last time a crab-bot came to rescue us. It could just as easily have sawn us in two.'

'True, and I cannot guess what might happen if we dive again. But I still have one trick up my sleeve. The UN gave me something, just in case I could ever leave a message.'

'How do you know what language they speak – if they speak?'

'I don't. But what I've got is a copy of one of those plaques carried by the Pioneer spacecraft in the early nineteen seventies. You know, a diagram of the Solar System with an arrow pointing to Earth, and fundamental data about hydrogen and stuff that extraterrestrials ought to recognise.'

'With the picture of the naked man and woman? I always thought it would give aliens funny ideas.'

'At least the man was waving – with his hand, I mean – I'd better shut up.' Geoff was relieved to see Maura had given up trying to look serious, and they both laughed.

'It's on a cylinder this time,' he continued. 'I've weighted it so it'll have negative buoyancy in the Cronus Rift.'

'But we can't possibly know if the aliens have the same senses as us. And how are they going to read it? The seabed's in total darkness.'

'The cylinder's engraved with pictures. If they're as smart as I think they are, they should be able to understand it. It's also coated with gold, to resist corrosion. That should make it a rare object anywhere in the universe.'

'So, what you're saying is there are creatures we know nothing about and, unless we risk our lives again, they may not even make it to a natural history museum.'

'We don't have to do any of this, Maura. But we're on the verge of a breakthrough that could change humankind. I'm prepared to take the risk, if you are.'

'We'll be like two worms on a hook. When d'you want to go squirming?' Maura stood up and wriggled her hips. Geoff copied her, and they both collapsed back on the bench, chortling happily.

They were being reckless but Geoff didn't care. He was too excited by the prospect of diving with Maura again to worry about the consequences. He was sure she had forgiven him for their previous upset. He was ready for any adventure if he could share it with her.

'Tell Prof we'll take the spare bath down again in two days' time,' he said. 'That'll give me enough time to prepare.'

～⋖●

Major Breckenridge rapped sharply on the door of the Professor's outer office and went in.

'Major, how nice to see you,' said Leona, 'and how polite of you to knock.'

'Just to give you a heads-up. Here's a programme and a list of topics we'd like your department to research,' said Breckenridge, his face contorted into a smile.

'But you could have sent us all the documents electronically, Major,' said Leona, as if she wanted to help.

'Well, it's always nice to see all your pretty faces.' He scanned the room, his face twitching, but all the assistants continued working at their com-pads without looking up. He turned back to Leona. 'I like your tanzanite beads, by the way. Talk to you later.'

He left the office and paused outside to call his contact in OPDEO Intelligence. 'Shirl, I've got a job for you. Can you dig out some dirt on Leona Adaeze, for me? Today, if you can.'

It was 20.10 CHT and Leona was the last to leave. She'd taken her wings from the office rack, locked up, and was about to launch herself for the short flight to her accommodation, when Breckenridge appeared from behind a screen in the Oceanography concourse.

'Hi, Leona,' he greeted her, simultaneously grinning and twitching. 'I was hopin' to bump into you. I understand you're a divorcee, right?'

Leona stood rigid, taller than Breckenridge. 'That is correct information, Major,' she replied.

'You were married to Shashi Mavuto, who's now collaboratin' with the Khitan Empire, and livin' in Chenzhen?'

'I expect you know the details better than me. Shashi defected five years after our divorce.'

'Yeah, but confidentially . . . we suspect he was spyin' for the Khitans a long time before he did a runner. What did he tell you?' Breckenridge began whispering in her ear but she leant quickly away.

'We got divorced because we were incompatible,' she said. 'I knew nothing about his political activities.'

'Look, I don't wanna bring you in for questionin' or anythin'. You wouldn't like that. These truth drugs can really mess you up. It'd be good if you could do somethin' to confirm your loyalty.'

'Something for you, or something for OPDEO?'

'Oh, sweetheart, you could do a lot for me. But maybe we could just start with a little bit of consultancy, like a confidential advisor.'

'Forgive me, Major, but you don't strike me as a man who asks for advice.'

'You could be right there. But this is purely professional. These geeks you work for, they do a lot of probin' around under the ice, don't they? They find things, do tests and, when they've got chapter and verse, they write some smart paper and share it with their buddies, ain't that so?'

'They carry out scientific investigations based on observations and share their knowledge for the benefit of humankind.'

'Yeah, yeah. All I'm askin' is for you to give us a heads-up about the way their research is goin', you know, what they've found so far. What mysteries they're lookin' into. It doesn't need to be verified or validated or whatever antics they get up to. Just a bit of foreknowledge, if you like.'

'Can't you ask officially?'

'I want you to tell me what's in their minds, not in their reports. But don't let on what you're doin'. Then I'll know you're one of us, and we needn't worry about the other business.'

'I'll tell you what I can,' Leona said with deliberately ambiguity.

'Good girl, I knew you'd be sensible. I'll have another chat with you in a few days' time.' Breckenridge smiled hideously and swaggered down the corridor, whistling out of tune.

Encounters

Kai finished his exercise routine and moved across to join Chen and Huang for lunch. Their ship, the *Xi'an*, had been travelling for eight months and they were within a hundred thousand kilometres of their destination. They were carrying supplies for the Empire's base on Mars, and they were on course to land in less than a day. The ship's instrumentation showed the pull of Mars's gravity was accelerating them towards their destination. However, as they were in free fall, they remained weightless. Lunch comprised a protein-rich soup which they sucked from their flasks. There were no rules regarding what constituted good table manners in space but, by tacit agreement, they ate together with their heads all pointing roughly in the same direction. Chen was enthusiastically telling Huang about Roborock. The bands could play their instruments five times faster than any human.

Huang was not impressed. 'I thought you still played the two-string *erhu* in that wasteland you come from, Chen. It was probably the only entertainment you had in your yurt.'

Chen was used to Huang's mocking banter, and he always gave as good as he got. 'Mine is very advanced people. Ghengis Khan, he invent yurt when your ancestors live in cave and go to bed with yak to keep warm. Which is why you look like . . .'

An alarm sounded and Chen left the sentence unfinished. He waited for Kai to nod and then floated over to his viz-box.

'*Shénme*? Missile launcher has locked on. Must be instrument error. No, there is message – from a Hesperian destroyer!' They gathered round the screen.

Navaho:

> We are on course to intercept you in 23 minutes. Prepare to be boarded. Do not attempt to resist or we shall attack.

Chen sent a reply:

Xi'an:

> What is your purpose, *Navaho*? We are unarmed transport vessel carrying non-military supplies.

The answer came back within seconds.

Navaho:

> All Khitan supplies are military. Your passage is act of aggression. You are in breach of Hesperian Decree 2930. Obey or you will be eliminated.

Xi'an:

> And you are son of drooling whore and monkey.

Kai was the pilot captain. He had a split second to order Chen not to click on 'transmit', but something held him back. Was this meant to happen? Chen sent the message.

The alarm sounded. '*Aiya!*' said Huang. 'Missile strike in three minutes fifteen seconds.' Kai read the next transmission:

Navaho:

> Surrender immediately to abort missile.

Kai knew he must save his crew and his ship. But his training was not going to help him. It hadn't covered this situation. He would have to rely on pure intuition. He'd rationalise it later.

'Say nothing. Strap yourselves into your launch harnesses,' he ordered. He kicked off from the bulkhead and dived to the control desk. He entered a stream of data. Thirty seconds later they were all pressed into their body moulds and the main thruster was firing at full burn. Kai watched the ship's velocity increase. After four minutes he was confident they'd escaped the missile. He tried to reach his com-pad to shut off the engines, but the g-force was too great. He lay still until the rocket motors finally drained the fuel tank. Both Chen and Huang looked rigid with tension.

'Okay, get a drink and we will review our status,' Kai commanded. He opened the biometric zapp on his com-phone and set it to monitor Huang's and Chen's blood pressure.

The three Khitans gathered around the conference table, gripping its handles. Chen looked pale and had curled his short body like a foetus. Huang, on the other hand, couldn't keep still. He swung back and forth restlessly and then pulled himself over the table until his face was centimetres away from Kai's.

'*Cào nǐ mā*! Why did you burn the fuel?' said Huang. 'It was supposed to get us home. What are we going to do now?'

'Watch and wait,' said Kai.

'We are heading for the stars at a hundred kps, out of control. We are on a one-way trip to nowhere.'

'Watch and wait,' said Kai.

'Wait for what?' Huang shouted. 'Wait to see what runs out first? The water or oxygen? Either way we are dead men.'

'Chen, run the astronavigation programme,' Kai ordered. 'See where this course will take us.' Realising Chen held himself responsible for the crisis, Kai wanted to give him a task. It would stop him dwelling on what had happened and show them Kai didn't blame him.

Chen slowly straightened his body and glanced at the instruments. 'We cannot land. We go too fast.'

'If we pass ahead of Jupiter, its gravity will slow us. It is the opposite of a slingshot,' Kai reminded him.

Chen ran the course prediction and the result came back instantly. There were no options because, without fuel, their speed and direction were unalterable. 'Simulator show we touch outer atmosphere of Jupiter. Its gravity catch us but we not pulled in. We swing through half orbit.' He paused to study the screen more closely. 'After that, computer say we collide with Europa!'

Huang looked flushed and his blood pressure alarm was flashing. He too needed a job to distract him from his fear. Kai summoned his attention. 'There is a supply for the turbogenerators. Look at the schematic and find a way of routing the fuel through to the retrorockets. Then work with Chen to reset the valves.'

Huang hesitated. He opened his mouth and shut it again. He nodded to Chen and opened up the system files. Within a few minutes they became absorbed in the engineering problem they'd been given. Their first three ideas proved to be dead ends, but eventually they worked out how the system could be reconfigured. Chen reported the new arrangement complied with safety regulations and Huang managed a wry smile.

Two hours later they'd reset the valves. Kai noted, with satisfaction, both his crew members' blood pressure had returned to mid-range. Huang asked what they should do next.

'Watch and wait,' said Kai.

⟨⁓⬤⟩

Maura met Geoff at the cage shaft. He was carrying the cylindrical message plaque and a small case. For once Maura had little to say during the descent to Port Authority dock, and Geoff was absorbed in his own thoughts about what might happen. They changed into their thermal suits and passed through the airlock to the quayside. Maura showed Geoff how to stow the cylinder in the vessel's sampling bay. Then they climbed down the bathyscaphe entrance tunnel and into the observation gondola. Maura ran through the predive checks, and Control gave them clearance to cast off.

Geoff brought out two pairs of headphones from the case he'd been carrying. He put on one headset himself and gesticulated for Maura to wear hers. 'What's this about?' she asked through the microphone.

'It's something I've been working on. They're standard headphones with some electronics of my own. It'll make our words unintelligible to sound recorders – and jam any spy camera. This way, no one else will know what we say.'

Maura shook her head. 'D'you honestly think the cabin's been bugged?'

'If you look carefully you can see where the paint's been scratched around the bolts in the middle panel on the control desk. Someone's removed it recently. It's my bet there are bugging devices hidden in there.'

'I'm not sure about this. A technician could have taken the panel off as part of normal maintenance.'

'I checked the job sheets. There's been nothing recent that's required work under the panel. I can't see any cameras but OPDEO's got some the size of a pinhead.'

'Okay, if you say so. Will your electronics affect any of the bath's equipment?'

'It'll be fine. The shell of the gondola's very thick, and the cameras outside won't be affected. But take the headset off when you're speaking to Port Authority Control, okay?'

They began the descent into the depths of the ice-bound ocean. It would take them several hours to reach their target location.

After a while, Maura broke the silence. 'We can talk in confidence through these headsets, right? So tell me why your marriage didn't last.'

'Well, I guess it was my fault,' said Geoff. He tried to laugh but then changed his mind and cleared his throat. 'My wife said I was living on another planet. That's pretty ironic, considering where we are.'

He half turned away on his swivel chair but Maura swung him back again. 'What did she mean?'

'Well, I never found out what she really needed from me. Perhaps I was too wrapped up in my work.'

'So you got divorced?'

'Yup.' Geoff bit his lip and wondered whether to continue. He met Maura's eyes. 'Since then I've tried various uni-net dating sites, but I'm hopeless at relationships,' he blurted.

'Why's that?'

He shrugged. 'I don't do emotional intelligence. Sooner or later I screw things up. I find it hard to know what women are really thinking.'

'Only women?'

'No, but the women I meet often say one thing and mean another.'

'That's a terrible thing to say, Geoff.'

'I know, but I think it's my fault, not theirs. I can't tell what they really want from me.'

Maura had been reporting periodically to Control but, as on the last dive, she lost the connection with the port when the bath drew close to the Cronus Rift. Once again their floodlights illuminated the volcanic chimneys, black sulphide 'smoke' pouring from the top of their vents. Geoff remembered a poem from his schooldays. *Among these dark satanic mills . . .*

He observed Maura closely and read tension in her face. At his request, she released the cylindrical plaque from the sampling bay. Geoff watched it float away with negative buoyancy, just as he'd predicted. Then he set all the cameras to record and kept careful watch through the observation windows.

'Who's that speaking?' asked Maura suddenly.

'What? I can't hear anything,' said Geoff.

Maura stayed perfectly still, her head on one side. 'Jaysis, I'm hearing a voice. I think it's them. Keep the bath steady, I've got to listen to this.' Then she laughed and leant back with her hands lightly clasped. Now and again she made eye contact with Geoff and gave him a thumbs up.

Geoff was bemused. *What's going on now? Is she hallucinating? Could she be ill? She hasn't shown any symptoms up to now. Has Europa affected her in some way? This moon's a place where abnormal is normal. Can she really be hearing an alien? Or am I losing my sanity?*

He tried to get Maura's attention, but she silenced him with a quick wave of her hand. He panned back and forth with the cameras and thought he saw some fleeting shadows. But he wasn't able to focus on the shifting darkness. There was nothing for him to do but wait.

'Okay, I've got her now,' Maura said at last, taking control of the bath. 'We're going up.' She set the course quickly and turned to Geoff. 'If you're sure those headphones of yours keep us private, I'll tell you what happened.'

'They work alright. Trust me, it's what I'm good at,' he said, more loudly than was necessary.

'Well, it was incredible. An alien spoke to me! It was kind of scary, but wonderful. He told me so much. I think it was a he.' She shrugged her shoulders. 'Sorry, I don't know where to begin.'

'Just tell me what he said, in the order he said it, if it helps.'

'Okay. Well, I heard a voice in my head. It sounded like my own voice. The speaker, he told me not to be afraid. He said I could call him by his name. It was something like Mecherbar – no – Mettravar, that was it. He was from a biological domain that's unknown on Earth. They call themselves Thiosh.'

'He was speaking to you in English?'

'You told me they wrote in English on your computers, when they hacked your systems. They've probably hacked other sites as well. He spoke like a character in an old book – kind of poetic.'

'How could he speak in your head? I don't understand.'

'I suppose it was telepathy. He said all the creatures like him are linked by their thoughts. He must be able to do it with other life forms. But don't keep interrupting me. I need to tell you while it's fresh in my mind.'

'Go on then,' said Geoff.

'He was sorry a face-to-face meeting wouldn't work too well. Their bodies are very different from ours – no arms or legs – more like fish. But they can make complicated things. They picture them in their brains and build robots that way, like the crab-bot that helped us last time.'

'You mean they use telekinesis.'

'Sure, that's the word.'

'So, we were right. There are robot-masters. Did he mention the crab-bot that's missing?'

'He knows military people have taken it. He understands we're different because we're scientists. He wants us to tell other Hesperians they have nothing to fear.'

'Ye gods, they must have been spying on us for ages!'

Maura reached across and gripped Geoff by the shoulders as if talking to a child. 'He's genuinely friendly. Thiosh have lived in peace for millennia. They want to live in harmony with all living beings.'

'But how do we know that?'

'He thanked us for the picture of the man and woman, and he wanted to give us something too. He said he would make our minds stronger. He could develop any potential we already had. It would be a gift to show his friendship. He said, in my case, I had intuition.

He'd let me link up with similar people so we could talk to each other in our heads.'

This is weird. Am I buying into this? 'Is it permanent? Could I do it too?'

Maura pursed her lips and frowned. 'Perhaps you're just a bit too rational. I expect he found it easier to talk to me. I was brought up believing in leprechauns and fairies. He said he'd give you something though – he promised. Perhaps he'll let you do even harder mental arithmetic.'

'Oh, hang on. I'm not sure I want anyone playing around with my head. Is he doing an experiment on us?'

'Not at all. It's more he wants to train us for something. It's some sort of mission.'

'Is that what you thought was scary?'

'Not that bit. That was good news. But the problem may be . . . he's friends with the Khitans.'

'Oh shit!'

Relocation

A party of Securopa officers stopped Geoff and Maura at the exit of the OPDEO complex. Geoff recognised the leader as the man who'd reprimanded them after Maura had set off the main alarm. 'Dr Geoffrey Kirby and Dr Maura O'Hara, come with me, please,' he said. 'You're under arrest!'

The officers led them back into the building. Then some of them took Maura from the group and ushered her away. Geoff turned and saw her looking back at him, but one of the guards stabbed him forward with the barrel of a tezla pistol.

They took Geoff down a level and led him along brightly lit corridors. This was part of the building he'd never seen before, and he tried to memorise the route they followed. Finally, he was pushed into a small room illuminated by a harsh, hanging light. In the middle were two chairs. The guards searched him, took away his com-phone and pressed him into a chair. Then they stood by the walls, holding their pistols in readiness. Geoff decided to act dumb.

A senior officer came in, whom Geoff recognised as Major Breckenridge. The major grabbed one of the spare chairs, straddled it the wrong way round and, addressing Geoff in a conversational manner, began to question him.

'Dr Kirby, d'you mind talkin' me through what happened durin' your first dive? You and Dr O'Hara seemed to be stuck on the seabed for a helluva time. What was goin' on?'

'It's all in our report to Professor Mitchell.'

'But I wanna hear it from you, Dr Kirby.'

'Well, a volcanic chimney fell across the bows and partially crushed the hull.'

'So whadya do then?'

'We dumped all the ballast and powered the bath in reverse. We were trying to drive out from under the chimney, as stated in our report.'

'That was how you escaped?'

'No, we were stuck fast for a long time, over an hour. But eventually we began to float up.'

'So how d'you explain the torch marks on the hull?'

'Sorry, I can't help you there. As I said in the report, the forward floodlamps were smashed and I couldn't see the bows.'

A shrill tone from a com-phone broke the ensuing silence. Breckenridge went outside to take the call. After a minute he returned, and he was laughing. 'We've got you now, Kirby. You've been interferin' with OPDEO's security equipment. That's a capital offence!'

'If you mean I took steps to stop you spying on us, then I admit it. But eavesdropping on private conversations is an infringement of human rights.'

'Listen carefully, Kirby. There are obviously some things you don't understand. When you're on Europa, you ain't got no rights. Soon you're goin' to tell me exactly what happened while you were stirrin' shit on the seabed. How do I know that? It's because . . .' Breckenridge was dragging out his words. 'When I inject some air into Dr O'Hara's pretty little veins she's gonna have a nasty case of decompression sickness. You know what that is? You've heard of the bends? First, she'll think tiny insects are crawlin' over her body . . . she'll become short of breath . . . the pain'll kick in . . . she'll lose control of her bladder . . . then her bowels. Her legs'll be paralysed and – unless she's put in a decompression chamber pretty damn quick – she'll die in agony. And you're gonna watch every second of it.'

Geoff leapt to his feet, his fists clenched, only to collapse as every muscle in his body spasmed in pain.

Still at high speed, the celestonauts passed rapidly through the asteroid belt. Huang and Chen settled to a routine of exercise and instrument checks. This included monitoring for a possible collision with a comet or a meteor. They laughed grimly about this, in view of the fact the astronavigation program had predicted they'd collide with Europa. Kai was confident their journey wouldn't end in disaster, but he only knew this by intuition. His meditation reinforced his certainty they would survive, but he had no definite information he could share. But it didn't matter in the short term; Huang and Chen had stopped asking questions.

Huang viewed the image of Jupiter with a mixture of fascination and horror. It filled his viz-box screen, its atmosphere in turmoil as clouds streaked around the equator, as if determined to put the sluggish polar regions to shame. The celestonauts strapped themselves in their flight seats as the ship looped behind the giant planet, its gravity slowing their progress like invisible treacle. As Chen had predicted, their trajectory left them on course to collide with Europa. Kai turned the ship round so it was travelling stern first, and fired the retrorockets in short bursts. They drifted down to the moon's icy surface and landed with the gentlest of bumps.

Huang peered through an observation window. '*Aiya*! Someone has built us a pagoda.'

'Prepare for extravehicular activity,' ordered Kai. 'But go slowly, and do not slip on the ice.'

They put on their life-support suits and left the ship to investigate the shimmering edifice that glowed with blue light.

'It is not real, only a hologram,' said Huang, his initial excitement turning to disappointment.

But the steps leading down below the surface were solid enough. They descended to a circular door that opened as they approached. After passing through an airlock they paused to carry out safety checks. Their helmet sensors registered breathable air at moderate temperature and pressure, negligible radiation, and no harmful bacteria, viruses, or chemicals. The immediate environment was benign, but they kept their portable biometers hanging round their necks to give early warning of hazards.

Another door opened automatically. Kai nodded to Huang, who unslung his plasma gun, took off the safety catch and peered in, looking left and right. Satisfied the way ahead was safe, Huang led them into a circular atrium, about ten metres in diameter. Bright sheets, like slices of ice, extended over the ceiling in a hexagonal pattern. Chen seemingly forgot about possible dangers and began to run from one archway to another, peering into the area that lay beyond. Huang looked at Kai, anticipating orders, but the pilot captain was sitting on the floor in a lotus position, his eyes closed. Huang shook his head sadly as Chen babbled about auto-moulding armchairs, underfloor heating and wall hangings like curtains.

'Be careful,' said Huang. 'I think this place is a trap.' But Chen kept searching the rooms, opening cupboards and drawers, testing the plumbing and bouncing on the mattresses. After he had disappeared for a full minute, Huang found him in a room that looked like a recording studio. Chen picked up some headphones, but Huang gripped his wrist. 'Do not touch,' he warned. 'We must not draw attention – at least – not yet.'

'What this place made of, you think?' asked Chen. 'Metal or plastic?'

'You should ask yourself first what it is for,' said Huang. 'We must find the exits, then check if anyone is here. When we have done that, we can talk.'

The two crewmen explored every centimetre of the complex. Chen commented on everything he saw and called Huang to show him things. Huang only nodded, while scanning the walls for possible joints or openings, and the floor for trapdoors. There was no sign of life and, indeed, no evidence the rooms had ever been lived in. Kai, meanwhile, continued to sit on the floor in an attitude of meditation. Huang and Chen took it in turns to keep watch.

After a couple of hours, Kai got up and summoned them to join him in what appeared to be a lounge. 'We are safe now,' he told them. 'Our journey has been arduous. You must rest for a while.'

'*Cào nǐ mā!*' said Huang. 'You tell us nothing. I think this place is a laboratory – to test us like rats.'

'Trust me. I will explain when I can,' said Kai. 'Meanwhile, use your time here wisely. The e-books in the library have been put there for our benefit. I advise you to study all you can about Europa, and particularly its ocean. Now I must leave you. Wait here until I return.'

Escape

Geoff didn't know the time or where he was. But he remembered the pain. He stretched his limbs and flexed his joints, pleased that the tezla gun had not caused him any lasting injury. He looked around. The focal point of the cell was the massively built steel door, equipped with a spyhole and an inundation point. It was a place for water from a fire hose to be injected, or possibly tear gas. Otherwise, the furniture comprised only a bunk, a sink and a bucket, all stained by previous use – use he could still smell.

There was some vulgar graffiti scratched on the wall above the board where he lay. But between an exhortation to 'Wank while you still can' and another to 'Go down frigging', he read 'M = E/c2'. It was a transposition of Einstein's famous energy equation. He wondered why anyone had bothered to write it. This was not a place of learning, only of fear and pain. What a damnable mess they'd got themselves into. He felt his stomach contract as he thought what could happen to Maura. She would have gone back to Earth if it hadn't been for him.

He noticed a tiny grille at the top of the wall, up by the ceiling. If only he could move his bed, he might be able to look outside, but bolts fixed it securely to the floor. Furious at his impotence, he picked up a tin cup and hurled it across his cell. It fell spinning and clanking around the floor. He looked back at the bed and, to his amazement, the bolts fractured with four loud cracks in quick succession. Then the bed itself heaved away from the wall and slid under the grille. Geoff felt momentarily drained of energy.

'Fuck.' It was the first time he'd ever said the word. He sat with his head in his hands. *Is this what insanity is like? Living in a world of hallucinations? The illusion you can move things just by wanting it to happen?* He went and touched the bed. It was definitely in a different place from where it'd been. He examined a broken bolt.

Maura said the Thiosh were telekinetic. They've made her telepathic. Have they expanded my brain too? And if so, why?

Geoff visualised the bed moving back to its original place. It scraped its way back to the wall, giving him more space to pace back and forth.

So I can transfer thought into a force, and it's stronger than my muscles. It must be a gift from the Thiosh – but also an obligation. They've equipped me for some purpose, but what? Could it be so I can reach Maura and escape?

The spyhole in the door was blanked off by a cover on the outside. He remembered it as a pear-shaped flap, pivoted at its top. He moved the cover in his mind and looked out. 'Yes!' he cried out loud. He could see a fish-eye image of the corridor.

Geoff considered his options. He assumed the Thiosh were aware they'd been arrested. Maura would have told them by projecting her thoughts. They could almost certainly access Securopa's computers to find out where he and Maura were being held. After all, they'd hacked into the UN network on Earth. They hadn't made him telepathic, but that didn't matter. If they wanted to tell him something they could use telekinesis to write on the wall.

Perhaps they already had. 'M = E/c2' was certainly Einstein's energy equation, but why was it written that way round, with a capital M? There had to be a reason. When the Securopa goons had frogmarched him into the detention building, he'd noted how the floor levels and corridors had been identified by upper and lower-case letters. Was Einstein's formula a code to tell him Maura's whereabouts? An exclamation mark had appeared after the equation; he was sure it wasn't there before. He took this as confirmation. She was in cell 2, corridor c, on level E.

They may not be able to escape the dome itself, but perhaps he could get a message to the UN. Then OPDEO might not be in such a hurry to torture them. He concentrated on how he could escape from the cell. He visualised the tumblers in the combination lock embedded in the door and controlled his thoughts to spin them round. He could move the discs and slide the toothed pin through them. *Sorted!* But there was a barred gate outside his door with a different sort of lock. It was electronic, operated by a remote controller. He telekinetically moved the armature in the relay against its spring. *Both doors open. Shall I make a break?*

There would certainly be surveillance equipment in the corridors. It was a shame Securopa had taken away the jamming device he and Maura had used in the bath. He could probably smash the cameras, but only if he could identify where they were, and that would be difficult. They would be small and well hidden. He had to find a way of disabling them; he already had an idea that might work. *No point in waiting.*

Thirty seconds later, he was outside in the corridor. He focused on the nearest fire alarm button and smashed it by thought alone. He gasped as he was hit by a monsoon of water, jetted from the sprinkler system. Once, on Earth, he'd walked on a ledge behind a waterfall. This was just as noisy, but a lot wetter. The sprays were so fierce he could hardly breathe. *But at least the cameras won't see me.*

He steeled himself to feel his way along the wall, his clothes hanging heavily on his body, clammy and cold. A door shut off the end of the corridor. He applied telekinetic force and ripped out the wiring from inside the electronic lock. *That'll keep Securopa busy for an hour or two.* He retraced his steps to the other end of the passage and opened the door there.

Two Securopa officers appeared in the fog. They pulled out their tezla pistols and ran towards him. He smashed the next glass-cased alarm to set off the sprinklers. He'd wanted to disorientate them, but they were on him in seconds. Electric arcs snaked over the body of one of his assailants. *Don't they know they shouldn't use pistols if they're wet?*

The other officer gripped Geoff in a bear hug. The guard kneed him in the groin, forcing him to the ground. He felt his wrists locked together. He calculated quickly. *About seventy-five grams, make it a hundred.* He applied pressure to his assailant's carotid sinuses, and the guard went limp.

'Have some of that, you fucker!' *Did I really say that? It must be the adrenalin.* Geoff ripped off his handcuffs. *So far, so good.*

He worked his way along corridors and up stairs, setting off the sprinklers ahead of him. Each time he encountered a locked door, he passed through, shut it again and disabled its wiring. He assumed there were enough linking corridors for him to find an exit from the building.

Up to Level E, corridor c. I'll be Maura's saviour. I'll have rescued her from imprisonment and torture. She'll be grateful!

He reached her cell, forced open the gate and then the door, went in, and . . . *shit*. There with someone else with Maura – a young man with a shaven head.

'Hiya, Geoff,' said Maura. 'We were expecting you. This is my friend Kai. We share our thoughts together.'

Geoff sagged onto the bunk and sat shivering. *Sod it!* he thought – and then, *I hope they can't read my mind.*

'Geoff, you are very wet,' said Kai. 'Dry yourself with Maura's blanket. I have a thermal suit in my backpack. Put it on and get warm again.'

'Forgive me, I was forgetting my manners,' said Geoff, rising to his feet and shaking Kai's hand. 'I had quite an exciting time out there. But if you're a friend of Maura's, I'm pleased to meet you.'

'I do not want to rush you,' said Kai, 'but we should not spend long here. I can lead you to an exit from the Unidome.'

Maura turned to face the door so Geoff could preserve his modesty as he changed. Kai busied himself typing instructions into his com-phone. 'I have disabled the cameras and turned off the sprinklers,' he announced. 'If you are ready now, please follow me.'

He continued to tap in commands, and gaps opened in the walls of corridors in places where previously no door could be seen. Geoff assumed the joints were so tight fitting they were virtually invisible. Kai led them down unmarked passageways, eventually arriving at the Topography Department's hangar. Waiting in one of the bays was a vehicle bearing some resemblance to a huge black bullet, with short stubby wings and mounted on skis.

'Wow, this isn't Hesperian. Is it yours, Kai?' Geoff asked.

'No, it is Thiosh technology. But it has been adapted for use by us humans. He made a sign like the parting of curtains and a hitherto invisible hatch opened in the side of the vehicle.

Kai waved Geoff forward. He climbed into the passenger compartment where he was met by a familiar figure: a tall, very upright woman with blue beads in her hair.

'I believe you know Leona?' said Kai, as he followed Geoff aboard. 'Without her, your escape would have been impossible.'

'Thank you,' said Geoff, and kissed her on both cheeks.

'You might need this,' she said, giving him a new com-phone. He was totally bewildered by the turn of events, but it clearly wasn't the right time to ask questions.

'Sit down quickly and strap yourselves in,' Kai told them. 'Geoff, come and sit by me in the cockpit.'

The hangar door opened and they blasted out, skimming just above the rough ice terrain. Geoff was fascinated by the craft's technology. He peered through the windscreen, the surface features of the ice blurring as the craft accelerated. He heard a sharp crack and glanced through a side window in time to see a cloud of ice crystals stream momentarily from the stabilisers as the rocket-sledge passed through the sound barrier. Geoff noted the phenomenon was evidence of a thin atmosphere.

With the vehicle on autopilot, Kai turned to Geoff and smiled. 'Okay, we can talk now. We are on our way to a base on Jupiter's side of the moon. As you will have guessed, I am Khitan and the Thiosh brought me here, together with my two crewmen. You and Maura have also been invited by the Thiosh. I hope you have no objection. I can assure you that Thiosh accommodation is more comfortable than an OPDEO cell.'

So much had happened in the space of a few hours; Geoff's head was spinning with questions. 'I've seen Maura telepathise with the Thiosh. Is that what you do too?'

'It was a skill I was given while I was still on Earth.'

'How did you get through Unidome security?'

'Leona has friends in the right places,' said Kai. 'She gave me the location of your cells and a zapp that opens security doors. It was a bonus you escaped from your cell yourself. It saved us a lot of time.'

'Is Leona one of your telepathic contacts?'

'Yes, she is an adept. But please accept my profound apology, Geoff. I regret I cannot share my thoughts with you directly, as I can with Maura and Leona. But I know you have been granted a different skill, which gives you great power, and I congratulate you on this distinction.'

Geoff paused to consider what Kai had said. He'd felt left out ever since Maura had made direct contact with the Thiosh, but Kai was clearly trying to make him feel included. Geoff reached out and shook his hand. 'Nominally you're my enemy but I'm beginning to think my own side is much more dangerous.'

'I agree with your analysis,' said Kai. 'When we reach our destination, I shall tell you all I know. But for now, if you want to swap seats with Leona, it will give you the opportunity to talk to your friend Maura in relative privacy. I know she has something she wants to say to you.'

Geoff returned to the passenger compartment and relayed Kai's invitation for Leona to join him in the cockpit. He settled back into the passenger seat next to Maura, and noted how the upholstery automatically contoured itself to fit his body. His companion reached out and put her hand on his arm.

'What a whirlwind! It's such a relief to get away from that place. But thank you, Geoff, for trying to help me. Ever since I arrived on Europa I've been in trouble, but it's always been you who's come to my rescue.'

'It's been my pleasure. But d'you know where we're heading? You could have gone back to Earth and avoided all this.'

'I know no more than you do but I haven't any regrets. Not so far, anyway. What's happening is too amazing for that. It's like you once said – we're pioneers on a new frontier.' Then, to his surprise, she leant over, kissed him on the lips and grinned.

The rocket-sledge slowed down almost to a halt and everyone peered through the observation windows. There was nothing to see except the Europan tundra until, suddenly, they found themselves alongside an illuminated pagoda. Geoff looked at Kai quizzically.

'The upper structure is a projected image,' said Kai. 'The real base is below the surface.'

'That figures,' said Geoff. 'I dare say we'll be lying low for a while now.

The Caves

The rocket-sledge came to rest inside a subterranean hangar at the pagoda hologram. The occupants disembarked and Kai led the group into the lounge. He told them to relax and make themselves comfortable. The new arrivals erupted in a storm of noisy chatter. Geoff appeared to add up the number of seats and spoke directly into Maura's ear. She replied behind a cupped hand, tilting her head towards Huang and Chen.

Kai summoned their attention. 'Ladies and gentlemen, it is my pleasure to extend a warm welcome to you all.' He looked around at his audience who gazed at him expectantly but, of all the members of the group, he knew his own crew members Huang and Chen were the most bewildered and confused. He'd overturned their world and left them with no explanation. In the present company, they understood the least about their current circumstances. He needed to reassure them.

'This place is our home for the time being and I can recommend it as a good hotel,' he said. 'But Huang and Chen, you have explored our surroundings in detail. I think it needs a name. What shall we call it?'

'Sorry to disappoint you, Kai,' said Huang, rising to his feet, 'but this is no hotel. It is self-catering. The accommodation is okay, but I am worried about what we must pay for it.' The others nodded in agreement.

'I do not know where we are. I do not know why we are here,' said Chen. 'But Kai save our ship from Hesperian missile. So, this better than before. But I think we hide now. This place is our "Khitan Caves".'

'Thank you, Chen,' said Kai. 'I have the privilege of telling you the caves have been constructed by beings known as Thiosh. Their robots continue to visit regularly to bring supplies and carry out maintenance. The service equipment is housed at low level, accessed by robots from under the ice. I think you will agree, the caves have been designed to make us comfortable. We owe our thanks to the Thiosh for their generosity and hospitality.' He paused as an acknowledgement from Saazat Mettravar flashed into his mind.

'It was also the Thiosh who enabled us to rescue our Hesperian friends Geoff, Maura and Leona,' Kai continued. The trio from the Unidome smiled at each other, nodding in agreement.

'Excuse me, Kai,' said Huang, standing up again. 'Can I ask a question please? Why have you brought our enemies here, people you call your friends? And another thing, Kai.' Huang's voice rose in pitch. 'To use some Hesperian English, who or what the fuck are these Thiosh?'

'Trust me, Huang. These Hesperians . . .' said Kai, raising his arm towards them. 'They truly are our friends. From now on we must work together. I will tell you all I know, and Geoff and Maura will fill in the gaps. Thiosh are an indigenous life form, which has inhabited this moon for hundreds of thousands of Earth years. I discovered their existence through an experience I had in a Buddhist monastery. You may be surprised that for centuries men and women have shared thoughts with other intelligent beings in the universe. Hesperians and Khitans from ancient times up to our present epoch have interacted with beings from other planets through mystical experiences, which all traditions on Earth have interpreted as "enlightenment". I do not pretend to know what Thiosh look like or how they live. But Geoff and Maura are scientists. They have had their own encounters with the Thiosh. Maura, tell us, please, what you have discovered.'

Maura stood up and, addressing the group in a loud, confident voice, she explained about the Thiosh, emphasising that they had saved her and Geoff's life and given them paranormal gifts – in her case the ability to telepathise and in Geoff's it was telekinetic power. 'You call it TK-force, don't you?' she asked him as she sat down.

Geoff stood up and cleared his throat. 'It's a skill humans can learn and is used, for example, by warship pilots. They wear sensors that pick up their brainwaves and send signals to transducers and relays to operate equipment. It gives them an almost instant response. But Thiosh telekinesis works without the need for sensors. I think they use their thoughts to manipulate gravity in some way, because the forces involved are greater than human strength. I haven't got the right skill-set to do telepathy, but I have acquired some of the Thiosh's remote handling ability. I used it to get out of a cell in the OPDEO detention centre. I think it's possibly a knack the Thiosh chose to give me because of studies I've carried out in the field of artificial intelligence.'

'I hear many stories like this,' said Chen. 'Men walk through walls or jump over houses. In my village, we have lot of magic but not much to eat. Here we have food, gym and swimming pool, all very nice. But we share this moon with clever fish and – sorry to say, Kai – thousands of Hesperian devils. This is dangerous place and we hide. Tell us please, why are we here?'

'It is a good question, Chen.' said Kai. 'I know you and Huang did not come here voluntarily, but the task ahead of us is greater than the needs of any individual. We must work together to accomplish a mission. For a long time, the Thiosh have been saddened by the conflicts that have afflicted the human race. They want to help us find a better way of living. This is more urgent now, because our hostilities directly threaten their own existence. The Hesperians have built a base on the other side of this moon, and their military arm, OPDEO, is constructing a fleet of warships that will roam the oceans below the ice cap. Sooner or later, conflict between Thiosh and humans will be unavoidable, unless a treaty of coexistence is negotiated.'

Huang put up his hand. 'The Empire is not afraid of conflict. What is this mission you speak of?'

'Peace is better than war, Huang,' said Kai. 'We have been selected to act as intermediaries, representatives of the two rival factions on Earth. Our task is to speak for the Thiosh, who are offering humans knowledge and expertise in return for guarantees of non-interference in their way of life. Our responsibility is great, but the opportunity for humankind is greater.'

The meals available from the omniprinter in the kitchen bore some resemblance to junk food on Earth, but served to satisfy their hunger. Geoff, Maura and the Khitans had chosen to sit together at the dining table and Leona said she'd join them later.

Chen was telling Maura how they'd been attacked by a Hesperian destroyer and had outrun a missile. 'We shot past Mars with no way back. But, by miracle, Kai brought us here.'

'Was it all prearranged, Kai?' Geoff asked.

'Not really. When I was a monk, I became aware my destiny was to come to Jupiter, and this is close enough, I think. But I did not know how it would happen. Our escape from the Hesperian destroyer was, in a sense, engineered by the Thiosh, just as they designed and constructed this accommodation.'

'So did the Thiosh make the Hesperians attack you?'

'That is a question that has troubled me. I have asked the Thiosh to explain, but they have not given me a clear answer. They said it was part of the bigger question of whether or not we have free will.'

'I've wondered about that myself,' said Maura. 'It feels like we're all being pushed along by an unknown force.'

Kai smiled in agreement. 'Regarding the attack, I am convinced the Hesperians were waiting to ambush the next Khitan transport that came along, and it happened to be us.'

'Are you saying the Thiosh used a chance event for their own purposes?' asked Geoff.

'Yes, I think you are right. But the consequent course of our escape must have been arranged by the Thiosh. I believe you could say it was orchestrated by them, using telekinesis and control of both the Hesperian and our computer software.'

'So, are they manipulating us?' asked Geoff, frowning. 'Are we their puppets?'

'If you take into account their motivation and their ultimate goal, I do not think they have behaved unethically, according to either Hesperian or Khitan traditions,' said Kai.

'These are some smart fish, to be sure,' said Maura. 'Have you seen the e-books in the library? They have advanced technology but they've been careful to minimise its impact on ecology. They've had an industrial revolution that hasn't harmed the moon. I'd like to know how they did that.'

Geoff had more questions for Kai. 'Did you know the Thiosh had built a refuge for you on Europa? What happened after you were attacked?'

'I had assurances from the Thiosh we would be safe. Perhaps you could call it intuition. I knew I had to come to Jupiter. Then after we landed here on Europa, I was contacted by the Thiosh leader, whom they call their Saazat.' Kai gave Huang and Chen an apologetic smile. 'I am sorry I could not explain this to you at the time.'

'I am glad you did not tell us,' said Huang. 'We would have sedated you and locked you up!'

'You needed time to adjust,' said Kai. 'I thought it best to leave you resting here in the caves while I took the rocket-sledge to the Unidome. You would not have understood the need to rescue our Hesperian friends.'

Huang nodded. 'I would have found a way to destroy their base. Their defences must be useless – you got in easily.'

'We took them by surprise,' said Kai. 'They did not detect our approach.'

'I thought the sledge looked like a stealth machine,' said Geoff. 'But how did you get into the dome?'

'After landing, I had what I call a visualisation,' said Kai. 'I saw Leona, and I asked her for help. When I reached the Unidome, a hangar door opened and she was there in person.'

'I like Leona, but I'm surprised she's been so . . .' Maura paused to think of the word. '. . . proactive, on our behalf?' she finished, making the statement a question.

'I do not know how she did it, but she told me where to go to find you two,' said Kai, looking at Maura and Geoff, 'and also how to get past the security barriers. Then she watched Securopa's cameras to see where their sentries were posted and relayed the information to me telepathically.'

'You knew Geoff would join us,' said Maura, giving Geoff a beaming smile.

'I think he enjoyed creating havoc, setting off the sprinklers and fighting the guards,' said Kai, laughing. 'It was a great diversion.'

Leona came in from the communications room. 'Sorry to interrupt, but OPDEO has put up another satellite,' she said. 'I think it's searching for our base. We mustn't use the pagoda hologram if their satellites are in the sky.'

An Invitation

Leona led them back to the room they'd thought was a recording studio, but they now understood to be a communications centre. They squeezed inside, filling the space. Leona had patched the OPDEO satellite positions through to the wall screen. In his time in the Unidome, Geoff had known her to be a competent office manager, but he had no idea that she had such technical expertise.

'Can we can send OPDEO a message?' Kai asked. 'We would have to do it without them knowing where it has come from.'

'If you time it exactly right, you can bounce a radio signal off combinations of the outer moons,' said Geoff. 'On to Io and back to Europa. I don't think they'll be able to trace it if you do that. I'll work out a signal route.'

'Thanks,' said Kai. 'I have written a draft. Please tell me what you think.'

'Can we send it in code?' asked Maura.

'I can transcribe it into OPDEO's high security cipher,' said Leona. 'I've got their encryption package on my com-pad.' Geoff looked up in surprise, but said nothing.

Geoff and Maura read through Kai's draft:

To General Flannery, Chief of Staff, OPDEO, The Hesperian Federation's base, Europa.

Dear Sir,

This communication comes to you from a delegation comprising representatives from the Hesperian and Khitan communities, under the auspices of the Unified

Nations Committee for Peaceful Uses of Outer Space (COPUOS). We send you our greetings. In order to avoid the unhelpful involvement of other terrestrial organisations, we would be grateful if you would treat this communication with the highest level of confidentiality.

Our objective is to promote peace and harmony between the geopolitical groupings on Earth, and to establish the arrangements necessary to benefit all living beings within our Solar System.

As we believe you are aware, this moon supports an indigenous life form, which lives under the sea. These beings, which we call 'Thiosh', possess a high degree of intelligence. Theirs is an ancient civilisation whose imperative is to avoid conflict with humankind. Indeed, their scientific knowledge is sufficiently advanced for them to be able to offer expertise to help us develop new technologies for the benefit of all. In return, they ask only to be allowed to live their lives in friendly cohabitation with people from Earth.

Because of the different nature of their bodies, it is difficult for the Thiosh to negotiate directly. They have granted our delegation the great honour of speaking on their behalf. Please indicate your willingness to meet with us, in order to explore the possibilities and necessary safeguards arising from cultural interaction.

We are sending you this message from a location which we regret we cannot, at the moment, disclose. Please reply via your recently launched satellite, in a transmission which can be received from anywhere on the hemisphere facing Jupiter.

Yours in peace,
Joint Hesperian/Khitan delegation.

'It seems very generous to me,' said Geoff, 'considering their interrogation techniques. But if we want a good outcome, I guess we should be forgiving?'

Maura pursed her lips. 'Breckenridge is a vile bollix, that's for sure, but we don't know about the others. Let's play along, but watch our backs.'

Kai and Leona went off to the communications room leaving Geoff and Maura browsing in the e-library. 'Chen was right. This is an amazing place,' said Maura. 'The network hyperlinks thousands of reference books and academic papers. I wonder how the Thiosh got hold of them all?'

'I've been wondering that too. And they're translatable from English into dozens of Khitan dialects.'

'The Khitans don't seem to be the aggressive tykes we hear about on the Hesperian news. D'you think there'll ever be an end to wars on Earth?'

'If we can offer Thiosh technology in exchange for peace, perhaps we can make the two sides see sense. They can either hate each other in their pig ignorant stupidity, or else they can cooperate and build a better future for all.'

Kai entered the library carrying a printout. 'Geoff, Maura, we have got an answer,' he announced. 'Tell me what you think.'

We send our greetings to the Joint Hesperian/Khitan delegation on Europa.

As you have realised, we have known for some time about the presence of intelligent life in the ocean of Europa, and it has always been our greatest priority to preserve and, indeed, nurture the extraterrestrial creatures that have developed here so far from the sun. We appreciate the extraordinary scientific importance of this discovery, and you have my word that our colony here at the frontiers of space exploration would never on any account do anything to the detriment of this fascinating life form.

We thank you for the initiative you have taken in offering to meet us to explore how we can further our common interests. We understand that you have established an amicable relationship with the Thiosh race and can speak for them. We look forward to learning from you how you have achieved this level of communication, which clearly has potential benefit for all humankind. Please be assured that, given your status as representatives of the Thiosh, we shall grant you all full diplomatic immunity.

Our only reservation with regard to your proposal is that, while you offer yourselves as intermediaries on behalf of the Thiosh, we require that their own representative is also present. You referred to their ancient civilisation and, by implication, we assume they have a leader who could be party to the discussions, notwithstanding the technical difficulties of ensuring a safe environment for him (or her, as appropriate) during the conference. Please confirm that the Thiosh leader is willing to attend. We are compelled to make our agreement to negotiate conditional on the Thiosh leader's presence, in order to minimise the risk of any future misunderstanding.

We surmise that your base on the Jovian hemisphere has been recently constructed, and we welcome the opportunity your presence on the moon offers for mutual cooperation. Please let us have the grid coordinates for your location so that we can set up a more permanent line of communication.

Assuring you of our very best intentions for the success of our future joint enterprise,

General Flannery, Chief of Staff, OPDEO.

Maura threw her arms in the air and inadvertently leapt off the floor. She sank slowly to the ground, shaking her head. 'Holy Mother, what a load of shite! Do they really think we'll believe all that baloney? This guy's as devious as a Ballysax bookie.'

'On no account should we tell him our location,' said Kai.

'What do you think, Geoff?' asked Maura. 'Shouldn't we be escalating this up to the Hesperian Government?'

'The Khitans are just as involved. We cannot approach one side and not the other,' said Geoff.

'The Empire and the Federation are intent on war. I do not think the powers on Earth will agree to help the Thiosh,' said Kai.

'You're right,' said Geoff. 'What do either of them know about Thiosh? Our best hope is to make some sort of pact with OPDEO, and then present it to Earth as a fait accompli.'

'As my great-granny might have said, I trust Flannery like I'd trust a tinker,' said Maura.

'I haven't heard that word for a long time,' said Geoff. 'But there is a chance we could reach an agreement. They'd do a deal if they could gain some benefit. But it would need to be shared with the Khitans or else it would upset the balance of power.'

Kai looked thoughtful. 'We do not have to decide ourselves. This base was built by Thiosh, and we are here because of them. As human beings, we delight in our own pride. But everything we have learnt about the Thiosh suggests they are cleverer than we are.'

'Of course, they must have a plan,' said Geoff. 'I think you telepathists should put your heads together and ask the Thiosh what to do. I can't help. I'm lacking in that department. I think I'll go down the gym and do some mental weight training.'

'Don't move Europa off course when you're flexing your brain,' said Maura.

At precisely 16.00 CHT, Kai taxied the rocket-sledge into OPDEO's service hangar. The Unidome's airlock inner door operated automatically to allow the delegates to pass through. Now they were inside, the seriousness of their situation weighed heavily on Geoff. From any rational point of view, to return voluntarily to OPDEO's base so soon after they'd only just escaped with their lives was the height of madness. But, whichever way Geoff looked at it, they had no choice but to go through with the conference, even though OPDEO had previously considered him and Maura to be dissident outlaws. Would they go back on their promise of diplomatic immunity?

A young woman in uniform met the arrivals and offered to act as their guide. She took their names and asked if they minded having their photo taken, for 'security reasons'. At the Saazat's request, Kai had instructed them not to bring weapons. They'd expected to be searched but, in the event, they were simply asked to sign a declaration that they weren't carrying any harmful substances or equipment. Geoff wondered whether Kai's crew had some ion guns hidden in their luggage. But there was probably no point; the OPDEO military staff and the Securopa guards outnumbered them – a thousand to one.

Geoff had forgotten how hot the environment was inside the dome. Then he wondered if the sticky feeling in his armpits was due to nervous tension. As their guide led them along a red carpeted corridor to the conference chamber, Geoff heard a piano playing ragtime jazz. It wasn't the synthesised version popular in the Hesperian Federation before he'd left Earth. This sounded like the original music of more than three hundred years ago. The melody grew steadily louder until they entered a circular hall where a group of OPDEO staff, both military and civilian, were chatting in groups. The pianist, dressed in white evening dress, sat at a gleaming Steinway. Coloured spotlights pulsed in time with the music, refracting and reflecting light through transparent streamers hanging from the ceiling. Most of the seating had been removed and tables were laid out for a buffet comprising both Hesperian and Khitan delicacies. At various points around the hall, an array of viz-box screens cycled a series of slides. There were sequences showing the construction of the dome, and how OPDEO had made the Europan colony self-sufficient. A video detailed the care the organisation had taken to protect extraterrestrial environments, and another showed how OPDEO used various resources from planets and asteroids to help Earth's underprivileged people.

They were joined by General Flannery who shook hands with each of them and welcomed them to the conference. He offered them refreshments, asked about their journey and apologised for not sending his own personal transport to collect them. He invited them to take a selection of canapés from the buffet and, as the general appeared to be eating the same food, they sampled the cuisine. Geoff sipped rare vintage wine from a crystal glass. Much of the tension he'd felt earlier left him, but he knew he had to remain alert. Flannery explained they would begin the conference proper in the morning and, until then, he hoped they would relax and enjoy the entertainment he'd arranged for them.

The general made a call on his com-phone and three couples entered, dressed like members of a burlesque dance troupe. Geoff now realised what the general had meant when he'd promised 'entertainment'. A smiling adjutant introduced Huang to a woman clad in a one-piece leather suit, laced across her prodigious breasts. Chen, however, seemed unable to take his eyes off a waif-like girl whose elfish face was half-tattooed with stars. The officer noticed Chen's interest and brought her over to meet him. Soon, both Khitans were laughing and joking with their new companions.

'This is terrible,' Maura whispered to Geoff. 'I never thought OPDEO would stoop this low.'

'I think they're trying to soften us up in some extraordinary way. Whatever the reason, I don't like it.'

The guide introduced Maura to a young man wearing his shirt open to the waist. Maura took him to one side and invited him close so she could whisper in his ear. Whatever it was she said, his neck and face flushed a rosy hue; he straightened quickly and strode away. Maura came back to where Geoff had been joined by a girl in a thin gauze evening dress. She removed the woman's arm from his waist and told her he was already spoken for.

'What was going on?' she asked Geoff.

'I was just being polite.'

'Well, from now on you can be polite to me.'

Geoff noticed Kai and Leona had also shaken off their escorts, but Chen was improvising an energetic dance routine with his partner, and Huang was engaged in an animated conversation with his Amazonian friend. The four redundant escorts began dancing in pairs.

'Let's get out of here,' said Maura. 'I'll ask our guide where we're sleeping tonight.'

'They've probably got our rooms wired,' said Geoff. 'I'll tell Kai to watch out for bedbugs.'

'Give him a while. Kai's sharing his thoughts with the Saazat at the moment. I think Mettravar is trying to deal with some opposition within the Thiosh community. I'll do the checking in for both of us.'

The Conference

Maura hadn't been in the high-speed elevator before. Geoff held up four fingers and the gesture control system responded instantly, causing Maura's knees to buckle as the lift accelerated. Geoff clamped his hands on her shoulders to hold her down as they stopped at the fourth and highest level.

'You might have warned me,' she said, smiling.

They stepped into a corridor and looked through a wall of glass at a panorama of sequin stars sprinkled over the blackness of the infinite void.

'I'll never get tired of this,' said Maura. 'It's like seeing the universe for the first time. I'm glad I came to Europa after all.'

'You never guessed you'd end up fighting for alien rights, though,' said Geoff. 'Do you regret anything?'

'Not at all. In fact, right now, I'm looking forward to a night in OPDEO's luxury accommodation.'

'Did they give you key cards for our rooms?'

'They didn't have to, there's iris recognition on the doors. They scanned us when we first arrived, apparently.'

'Oh, yeah – when they took photos "for security reasons". So, which are our rooms?'

'It's room singular, and it's this one.' Maura looked closely at Geoff's face.

'So, I do have to be polite then,' Geoff said lightly. He pretended to be unsurprised at sharing a room to give himself a few moments to think. He wasn't great at reading other people's emotions but he could hide his own when he needed to. Maura had fascinated him from the first moment he'd seen her. He loved her passion and natural rebelliousness. He'd also found her to be unpredictable – but now they would be together. It would be okay. He burst out laughing and kissed her.

～●

'I have to say I'm impressed by OPDEO's taste,' said Maura as she surveyed the flowing lines of the room's décor, imbued with the natural forms of flowers and plants.

'I expect OPDEO employed consultants. Is this Art Deco?' Geoff asked.

'More Antoni Gaudí. I love the arched screen through to the bedroom. It's like the entrance to the Sagrada Família.'

Geoff felt the need to change the subject. 'I must say they've given us a good bottle of champagne. Dom Pérignon, 2123,' he said, untying the carbon fibre cage to release the stopper.

'I hope this works out – the conference, I mean. It's a wonderful opportunity for Hesperians and Khitans to cooperate. The Thiosh are a unique form of life.'

'Flannery will only agree if he sees some advantage for OPDEO. And then only if it helps weaken the Khitan Empire.'

Geoff saw Maura's face drop. *Why do I always have to dash her hopes? But OPDEO cares for nothing and nobody except itself.*

Maura's eyes glistened in the room's gentle light, and he longed to make her happy again. He picked up the internal com-phone and ordered a selection of exotic dishes from the room service menu: citrus tomatillo gazpacho, butternut squash and pear ravioli with rosemary sauce, and grapefruit mint granita for dessert. He felt the need to show initiative, and he was confident she would like his choice.

'We'll eat soon,' he said. 'OPDEO will have electronically pasteurized the ingredients for preservation, but they'll taste okay. Shall I go in the shower first? I won't be long.' He planned to scan the food for drugs or poisons using the biometer he'd borrowed from Huang. He'd calculated their dinner would arrive while Maura was in the bathroom, giving him the chance to check it without causing her any alarm.

In the event Maura guessed what he'd done and simply accepted his reassurance the food was safe. They ate silently, both absorbed in their own thoughts, until suddenly Maura threw her knife and fork clattering and spinning onto her silver tray.

'We can't allow them to destroy the Thiosh,' she exclaimed. 'Humans have ruined the culture of every native life they've ever found. They've annihilated whole populations and devastated their homelands. We've got to stop it happening again. I mean it, Geoff!'

He was fascinated by her green eyes, now as bright as laser pointers. She took his hand and led him under the arch into the shadow of the bedchamber.

'Am I too emotional, d'you think?'

'No, I worry more about people who hide their emotions.'

'Why's that?'

'I tend to see things in black and white, figuratively I mean.'

'So you're good at maths?'

'Hm, apparently. I usually solve problems by the inspection method.'

'What's that?'

'I look at the problem and see the answer.'

'Aw, rapid! I wish I could do that.'

'Huh, I don't know. I always have trouble explaining how I get to the solution.'

'But you find it difficult to recognise people's emotions?'

'Very often, but I always know how you're feeling,' he lied.

'That's because I call a tusker a tusker,' said Maura, laughing.

'Pardon?'

'A tusker is a tool for cutting peat. I used to make slabs of the stuff for my grandad's stove. He was into a primitive lifestyle.'

'Oh, right, you say what you think. That's what I like about you.'

'So you do like me, do you?' she said, looking away.

'No, it's more than that. I love you, Maura.' She turned and they met each other's eyes. Geoff analysed what he'd just said. He had surprised himself, but he could find nothing wrong with his words.

Maura slipped off her silk dressing gown and stood silhouetted by the starlight. 'I've made it easy for you. You don't have to use telekinesis now.'

'Can you read my thoughts?'

'I think so, but I don't need telepathy.'

Geoff walked forward into the darkness. Gentle sensual hands removed his bathrobe. Unseen fingertips stroked his chest and he whimpered helplessly as they slipped down to his waist. Her body felt hot on his skin as she moved against him. Geoff cried out ecstatically, knowing full well he could be heard by OPDEO eavesdroppers.

The following day the delegation assembled in the lobby. Their guide led them into the conference chamber, now reordered with rows of seating in a conventional layout – except for one thing. They were astounded to find a thick glass tank lifted high on hydraulic jacks in the centre of a stage. Inside a dark streamlined shape circled slowly.

Maura gasped when she realised its significance. 'Mother of God, it's a feckin' goldfish bowl.'

'Did the Saazat know it would be like this?' Geoff asked. 'It's great to see a Thiosh close up, but I don't like the way he's been put on parade.'

'Neither do I. But he's agreed to be here to negotiate a non-aggression pact. He'll try to do that no matter what it takes.'

'How's he going to communicate? Is he going to write something on their computers?'

'I suppose he could, but he wants to negotiate through us. The telepathists have agreed Kai should act as the Saazat's spokesman.'

'You could do that, couldn't you?' Geoff would have liked Maura to have a leading role.

'Maybe, but it's better this way. It means I can speak freely in support of the Thiosh. I wouldn't be able to project to the Saazat without colouring my thoughts with my own feelings.'

General Flannery entered the conference chamber and all the delegates took their places on seats arranged in a horseshoe around the glass tank. The babble of excited voices died away, and the general began to speak.

'Good morning, Saazat Mettravar, ladies and gentlemen. I would like to express my great pleasure that today we are honoured to have with us the leader of the indigenous life form here on Europa, as well as two leading scientists from our Federation, and three Khitan celestonauts representing the Empire. I'm sure that their presence will lead to an unprecedented interchange of information that will greatly enhance our mutual understanding.

'The Unidome was constructed some ten years ago, initially by robots. Each had been meticulously sterilised to ensure that no biological organisms were brought from Earth. As you may know, Hesperian law prohibits contamination of the natural habitat or possible life forms at extraterrestrial locations. The Federation has an unparalleled record for undertaking research and exploration of celestial bodies, while minimising any conceivable side effects arising from our presence. Moreover, before any project to relocate resources from a planet or asteroid is authorised, it must first be demonstrated that there is a strong positive cost benefit for the Solar System as a whole.

'It is with this background that I sincerely apologise to the Saazat that a Thiosh machine was inadvertently damaged when it was involved in a collision with a Hesperian high-speed vessel. Please accept my assurance that this was a pure accident. We would be most honoured to carry out repairs to this machine if he were to forward the design details to us. We would regard this as a sign of trust and friendship, and an opportunity for us to demonstrate our goodwill. Could I ask the translator please, if the Saazat is able to agree to this symbolic gesture?'

Geoff felt uneasy. It was as if his skin had become shrink-wrapped. He watched Kai as he sat with his head in his hands. Minutes passed. The tension in the air was palpable.

At last Kai stood up to speak. 'The Saazat thanks you, General, for making your intentions so clear. But he would like to ask a question, please. Why did you deliberately torpedo a Thiosh maintenance machine?'

The assembly erupted in uproar. Flannery signalled to a commandant standing on the balcony and about a hundred Securopa paramilitary troops rushed into the conference chamber brandishing ion guns. They surrounded the Thiosh delegates and closed in. Huang crouched low and then charged. He released a volley of punches and kicks, and the leading Securopa troops were scattered like fragments from a grenade. *Whump! Whump!* The blasts resonated through the dome. A Securopa trooper holding Leona crumpled to the ground, shot by his own side.

Geoff saw a group of oversized soldiers come forward to seize Kai and Maura. *If they want a roughhouse they can have it. A hundred kilograms up the scrotum – that'll teach 'em.* 'Take that, you mother fuckers!'

Maura looked hard at Geoff as she stepped over the soldiers' bodies. Was she pleased or shocked by his actions and language? He couldn't tell, and had no time to think. He put his arm round her and hastened her to the side of the conference chamber. With their backs to the wall it would be easier to defend themselves.

Mettravar was swimming in circles at increasing speed. The lights flickered and switched to emergency LEDs. The air became very cold and wreathes of fog rolled over the floor of the dome. Then the hydraulic rams on one side of the tank collapsed. The structure toppled and disintegrated, creating a pressure wave of water filled with shards of glass.

'We're splitting up – we've got to get to the quay!' shouted Maura, pointing towards a fire door. A Securopa trooper was grappling with Chen. Geoff socked the soldier under the chin with an invisible punch and pulled the Khitan towards the exit.

'The Thiosh have cyberattacked,' Maura told Geoff. 'Come on, let's go. The others have gone another way.'

The door was locked at the entrance of the OPDEO Operations Building, but Geoff opened it in seconds. They stopped at the entrance of the cage down to the quay. 'Can you make the maglev work, Geoff?' Maura asked.

'No, not if there isn't any power. But we can take the stairs. It's only a kilometre down.'

They were breathing heavily by the time they reached the entrance to Port Authority quayside. The guards were sitting in the security lodge, staring at the interference pattern on their viz-box screens. They saw Geoff, leapt up from their desks and grabbed their ion guns, only to drop them immediately as if their hands had been burnt.

'See that – I've learnt a new skill,' said Geoff. Maura shook her head and smiled.

Geoff stared hard at the lock on the lodge door until smoke curled from the door jamb, locking the guards inside. 'Go through now,' he told Maura and Chen as he operated the turnstile leading to the water's edge.

They hurried along the quayside pier but all the berths were empty. Then, without warning, the waters swirled and a structure resembling an extinct biological order on Earth appeared from the depths.

'Jaysis, they've sent a mechanical whale,' said Maura.

'Get the uni-net back on line, for fuck's sake!' Flannery shouted to his IT chief as he struggled to reboot the system servers.

'They've split up, suh,' Breckenridge reported. 'Some of 'em got away in the *Aquila*. A Securopa sentry saw it take off. The rest got down to quayside. They overpowered the Port Authority staff and disappeared. They must have been picked up by a Thiosh vessel.'

'How the hell did they manage that? There was a complete power blackout. How did they operate the airlock? How did they power the cage? What was Securopa doing? Christ, they're armed, aren't they?'

'We're talkin' to Securopa now, suh. Quayside Security say they were attacked by a Khitan and two Hesperians, a man and a woman. The officers' guns became too hot to handle, and then they found themselves locked in. I think they were hypnotised in some way.'

'Check all the sound recordings from the underwater navigation beacons and launch the hunter-killer subs. And get after the *Aquila*. Launch the destroyers into sun orbit. They've probably gone prograde to get away as far as possible. I want these terrorists – all of them – preferably alive. And I want a full enquiry. What a balls-up!'

Part Two
On the Run

Attachment Disorder

Kai felt paralysed by depression. Now Mettravar was dead, he was no longer able to telepathise, either with humans or Thiosh. Conscious of his rank, he couldn't share his mental distress with Huang. It was only the presence of Leona that kept him going. She instinctively understood his disappointment and gave him encouragement. But she was not an engineer. She could not solve the technical problem which was threatening to bring their escape to an ignominious end. Soon they would be out of fuel, unable even to manoeuvre.

There had been no time for preflight checks when they'd stolen the *Aquila* from OPDEO's maintenance bay. Kai had ignited the thrusters for blast-off, burning chemical propellant mixed and vaporised in the combustion chamber. But the liquid oxygen and hydrogen tanks were small, only designed to accelerate the ship enough for the main propulsion unit to be brought into service. They'd exceeded the ignition velocity but still the main drive wouldn't start.

Huang had been studying the system diagrams. 'I have an idea. There is a heater to vaporise a carbon catalyst, but its supply tank is empty. I think we took the ship before OPDEO had completed its maintenance.'

Kai clasped his forehead. 'Leona, see if you can track down any comets in the vicinity. They are coated with hydrocarbons.'

She nodded and began to compare recent time-lapse images of stars to look for comets, but without success. After a while, she put that task on hold and began a routine instrument check. She moved around the cabin, gliding without effort with only a faint rattle of her jewellery. But she came to a sudden halt at the Skyscanner. 'Hey, that's interesting, there's a gap where there should be stars. I think something's blocking the light.'

Kai set the picosecond timer, fired a delaser pulse and watched for a reflection. 'It is still a long way off,' he said, checking the delay time. 'Let us take a closer look.'

Eight hours later they could make out a faint elongated shape on the viz-box screen. 'It looks like an asteroid,' said Kai. 'One of the Trojan family in the same orbit as Jupiter. It has very low albedo, so dark it hardly reflects any light. Perhaps that is why no one has identified it before. But it must be large – it already has a significant gravitational pull. It could be dark because of organic material. We may be in luck.'

Kai put the *Aquila* in orbit around the asteroid while they scanned the surface for a landing site. 'Huang, can you take the shuttle down and scoop up some of that surface tar?'

'It would be my pleasure,' Huang said, grinning, and he went to change into his flying suit.

Huang reported he'd landed safely. As instructed, he operated a probe to sample the surface material, and relayed the spectrograph to *Aquila*. The area where the shuttle had landed was coated with a layer of hydrocarbons of surprising complexity. Long polymers, complex cycloalkanes and even proteins were evident.

'Scoop a few kilograms into your storage bay,' instructed Kai over the intercom 'We only need a little as a catalyst. Then come and show us what treasure you have found.'

His task complete, Huang relayed each step of the launch procedure over the intercom. 'T five and counting; scoop stowed and locked; bay doors closed; launch configuration set . . .'

Leona ticked off each completed activity on her viz-box screen.

'. . . aux power go; main engine start; 10% power . . . 20 . . . 30 . . . 40 . . .'

Kai felt his pulse quicken.

'50 . . . 60 . . . 70 . . . 80 . . . 90 – engine shut down. Shuttle to *Aquila*, I am stuck. Please advise me how to get off this lump of shit!'

'Shut down as many systems as you can to conserve power,' said Kai, speaking calmly, in accord with his pilot captain training. 'We will review options and advise.'

He turned to Leona. 'The surface crust must have given way. The shuttle has either sunk into a gluey compound or something has combined chemically with its support legs. We dare not risk trying to land the *Aquila* down there. Help me. What are the options?'

'Could we attach a cable and haul him off?' she asked.

Kai checked the inventory. 'It is technically possible, but there is nothing on board with a breaking strain as great as the shuttle's thruster, and we know that was not strong enough. We have rope, but it is too weak to be of any use.'

'Is there a way of detaching the landing legs?'

'Yes, but Huang is not properly equipped for extravehicular activity. Perhaps he could risk it in his flying suit, but he would have to stand on the surface. He could get stuck like the shuttle itself.'

'Can he blast off with extra power?'

'He has already tried five times more thrust than he should have needed. If he tries any more he will use up all the fuel he has on board.'

He sat with his head in his hands. *I cannot do this anymore. I have lost Chen, and now I have sent Huang into danger. I thought I was infallible but my intuition is as dead as Saazat Mettravar.*

Danger in the Deep

Geoff stroked Maura's hair, his shirt wet where it had absorbed her silent tears. They sat huddled together on a hard bench towards the bows of the robot whale, in an area of living space that looked like a ship's wardroom. Even though they were travelling underwater, the Thiosh vessel rocked up and down as if it were passing over surface waves. Geoff wasn't sure if it was the craft's undulation or his reaction to OPDEO's attack that was making him feel sick. At least Maura seemed to be soothed by the motion; before long she was fast asleep. To keep his mind off his turbulent stomach, Geoff went to explore the rest of the 'whale-bot', as he'd chosen to call the vessel.

He found Chen in a small control room above the bows or, in nautical terms, a bridge. He was studying the instrument data on the viz-box screen in the centre of a console. Geoff looked at the desks and had a strange feeling of déjà vu. Their layout was exactly the same as those in OPDEO's baths. The screens showed they were currently on auto-control, but Geoff noted they would revert to manual after ten hours. That would give them plenty of time to inspect the whole craft. After that, he would consult Maura about setting a new course.

The whale-bot had evidently been designed as a transport vessel, either for equipment or small robots. As Chen pointed out, there appeared to be many recent modifications, presumably made for the sake of human occupants.

'Thiosh make whale-bot ready before conference,' said Chen. 'How they know we escape?'

'I wondered about that myself,' said Geoff. 'They must have done it as a contingency.'

Chen pointed to the illuminated wall panels. 'Why do Thiosh need lights? They are blind, I think. They live at bottom of ocean.'

'You're right,' said Geoff. 'But there may be benefits for their robots to be able to see. It would help them locate and manipulate equipment. Presumably they could have built-in light sensors and interpretation software.'

'I see small domes on front of boat when we board,' said Chen. 'They are like eyes maybe.'

They'd entered the vessel through an airlock at the top of the bot's head. Chen led Geoff down a ladder and showed him an entrance gate similar to the front of a car ferry, or possibly a mammalian lower jaw. It extended the full width of the whale-bot's head, providing access for large objects, machines, creatures – Geoff couldn't guess what the whale-bot's usual cargo might be.

'All entrances sealed by two doors, like airlocks,' said Chen. 'It is strange Thiosh make whale-bot full of air.'

'I doubt they did. I think the Thiosh could fill the hold with different gases, or perhaps water,' said Geoff. 'There are argon generation units in the service compartment. They're probably to keep equipment free from corrosion. But, if you look, there are air rebreathing units next to them. My guess is the Thiosh installed them just for us.'

Geoff and Chen continued their tour through a dozen or so other sections divided by bulkheads, set obliquely to the centre-line of the ship. Their accommodation was housed amidships. It replicated many of the facilities of the Khitan Caves. Geoff suspected some of it was the actual furniture, bathroom fittings and hard-copy books they'd used previously. The galley was equipped with a nanowave cooker and an omniprinter interface, similar to the food dispenser they'd had in the caves. But he was more interested in a cupboard in the storeroom. It was full of harpoons and a spear gun. Did it mean they'd be able to sail in open water?

Once again, there were six sets of everything. The Thiosh could not have known in advance how many delegates would find their way to the whale-bot, or if it would be needed at all. He was convinced Mettravar had attended the conference in good faith, hoping to negotiate a non-aggression pact. But then he'd given them the means to escape if everything went wrong. The fact the whale-bot could accommodate six people showed Thiosh couldn't see into the future. It was a relief to know their paranormal ability had limits. They were superhuman, but they weren't gods.

Chen pointed to a silver cylinder in a compartment near the stern. 'Fusion reactor. It generate electricity. Very advanced. My biometer register low-level background – like cosmic rays on Earth. But you see pistons? They are like old beam engine. Cranks and levers work tail up and down.'

'Actually, I think it's rather clever,' said Geoff. 'The mechanical linkage controls the stroke and speed of the fluke. It's not your usual digital system. It does make us seesaw up and down, though.'

―🐋

Geoff and Chen returned to the wardroom, where Maura was looking at pictures resembling lithographs fixed to the walls. Her cheeks were still stained with tears and Geoff didn't want to bombard her with questions. At least, not yet. He gave Chen a 'wait' signal with his hand and they both pretended to study the line drawings of ocean-going robots. There were portraits of former Saazats too, but they all looked the same.

'How are you feeling?' Geoff asked Maura eventually. He decided not to mention his own queasiness.

'I'm better now,' said Maura. 'But I know now OPDEO will never cohabit with Thiosh. We wanted to persuade them but they weren't having any of it. Another minute on the quayside and they would have arrested us again. It's the third time Thiosh have rescued us. First from the seabed, then the prison, and now we're on the run again.'

'What happened to Mettravar? Did you pick up anything, telepathically?'

'A rebel group hit OPDEO's computers and it caused his feckin' fish tank to collapse.'

'Oh, so other Thiosh killed Mettravar, did they?'

Maura stopped stretching and turned to face Geoff, one hand on her hip. 'Mettravar never wanted any aggression. He told them not to retaliate.'

'D'you think the rebels wanted Mettravar out of the way?'

'I don't know. Perhaps they didn't foresee the consequences of their cyberattack.'

'What happened to the rest of the group, after we split up?'

'All I know is they're safe and they're in space somewhere. They escaped in an OPDEO ship. Leona has shared her thoughts with me, but she doesn't know where they're going or what they'll do.'

'What about the loyal Thiosh?' Now Geoff had begun, he decided to blurt out all his worries. 'OPDEO has shown itself to be ruthless, right? We can assume it'll try to wipe out all possible opposition. Flannery and his crew know Thiosh are living in the Cronus Rift. They could nuke the whole area!'

'They'd be crazy to do that. The tectonic plates under the ice are unstable. A nuclear explosion would cause volcanic eruptions. They'd damage the ice cap and wreck the environment.'

'Well, alright. But they also have an arsenal of chemical and biological weapons. They'll find some other way to destroy the Thiosh.'

'Perhaps we find new home for them,' said Chen, entering the conversation. 'Somewhere under ice where they live safe.'

'It'd win them time if they found a hideout, but OPDEO would track them down eventually,' said Geoff.

'Maybe they build ships and travel to other planet? Kai can look for ocean somewhere, maybe on Saturn moon?'

'It's a feckin' shame OPDEO can't show some respect for a unique life form, the bastards!' said Maura.

'Ah, you're beginning to sound more like yourself,' said Geoff and, amused by his irony, he began to feel better too.

Geoff took Maura up to the bridge and she began studying the charts on the viz-box screen. She waited for the autopilot to switch off, and then set a new course. She aimed for the edge of a tectonic plate in the seabed where she expected to find more hydrothermal vents. The whale-bot was no speedboat, but its fluke drove it through the sea with natural grace. After a while, Geoff hardly noticed the craft's rocking motion. He felt he could relax and take stock for the first time since the trauma of the conference.

But his reverie was interrupted as the craft shuddered and tilted towards the bows.

'Why are we going down, Maura?' he asked.

'I don't know. I'd set the fins to keep us level. Has a crab-bot come again?'

Geoff flicked on the front floodlights and peered at his viz-box screen. 'I think we've rammed something. Hang on, I'm zooming out. Ah, there's a huge lump attached to the bows. I've got it now. Oh my God! Look, it's got tentacles.'

'Jaysis, it looks like a squid. It's feckin' enormous. We're sinking fast. I'm filling the buoyancy tanks with air.'

Chen must have heard the urgency in his companions' voices because he joined them on the bridge. 'Can we go backwards?' he asked. 'Pull up again?'

'Sorry, no reverse gear,' said Maura. She pressed the buttons on her viz-box screen and reconfigured the slide controls. 'I've shut off the power, filled the tanks with air . . . but it's not working.'

'You feel that pulse?' said Geoff. 'The squid's squirting us downwards. It wants us on the seabed.'

'What?' said Maura. 'It probably drags fish down deep so the pressure kills them. It's trying to do the same to us.' As if to underline Maura's analysis, the hull emitted a sound similar to a human groan as stress built up in its structure.

Geoff closed his eyes and thought intently. He managed to wrench off one the squid's tentacles using TK-force, but he had to let go to work on another. He couldn't pull them all off at the same time. He gave the squid's body a hard jab, but it absorbed the blow like a lump of jelly. He wondered about its vital organs, but he didn't know where they were. *Squids on Earth have three hearts. How many hearts has an alien squid?*

His train of thought was interrupted by a wailing alarm. 'There's a leak,' Maura cried. 'We'll break up if we go too deep!'

Geoff was at a loss. *The situation's out of control. Running away has solved nothing. But what choice did we have?*

Fugitives in Space

'Give me time, let me meditate,' said Leona, and Kai watched her as she crossed her long slim legs and floated weightlessly in the lotus position. She straightened her body. 'We're armed with a gigawatt laser, aren't we?' she said, her words jolting Kai back into the reality of Huang's predicament.

'Yes, why do you ask?'

'I have a strong feeling we should use it to drill into the asteroid's interior.'

Kai ran his fingers over the stubble on his head. 'It is not logical. Drilling into the crust is not going to lift Huang off the surface.'

She looked him full in the face. 'Trust me. I don't know how it'll work. Perhaps it'll be like surgery.'

They had failed to find a conventional solution. He knew her proposal was irrational, but he decided to try it anyway. 'Where do you want me to aim?'

'Into that crater,' she said, pointing to a circular ridge about five kilometres from the shuttle. 'A few seconds at half power should be enough, I think.'

Kai sequenced the weapons array and focused the laser onto the centre of the shallow depression. He ran up the generator, set the power level and hit the fire button. A brilliant shaft of electric blue light spiked into the crater. Plumes of incandescent matter erupted from the surface.

He shut down the laser, but fluid still jetted out from the penetration point, the colour visibly changing from dark brown to white in the weak sunlight. He ran a spectrograph on the spray and smiled. 'It is steam,' he said, and they watched a shining pool of water creep towards the rim of the crater as the vapour condensed.

Huang's excited voice broke through the static from the intercom. 'Hey, Kai, I felt a change – I tried the thruster and I lifted off!'

Within minutes the shuttle was locked onto *Aquila's* docking port. Once Huang had climbed out of his suit, Kai checked him with the medi-scan. 'You will be fine,' he told him. 'Drink a litre of rehydration solution over the next hour or two.'

'Physically I am okay, but I do not understand,' said Huang. 'You hit the ground with the laser and I became free. Please explain. Was that cause and effect?'

'Yes, I believe it was. The crater is now a bowl of soup made of water and protein molecules,' said Kai.

'It's what the asteroid wanted,' said Leona.

Huang choked as he gulped from his drinks bottle. 'How can a dead rock want anything?' he asked.

'You have to understand – the rock wasn't dead,' said Leona. 'All life wants to reproduce itself. We helped it, and it helped us.'

'There are more forms of life in the universe than we could ever imagine,' said Kai. 'Now, we must move on.'

***

To make their escape from Europa, Kai and his companions had been happy to steal any ship. But the *Aquila* had not been designed for stealth; its polished titanium skin shone brightly even in weak sunlight. Kai was certain that the Europan colony regularly scanned the dark sky for impending meteor strikes. The blink comparator they used to identify non-stellar objects gave OPDEO the means to locate the ship; once they were found, patrolling Hesperian destroyers would close quickly within distraydar range.

But the odds had improved for Kai and his companions. Thanks to the catalytic material they'd collected from the 'living asteroid', the *Aquila* now had a fully operational fusion ramjet. It could travel beyond the edge of the Solar System. Furthermore, the eruption from the asteroid's surface had coated much of the *Aquila's* casing with a thin layer of dark brown material, making it far less conspicuous.

Instead of OPDEO looking for a bright needle in a haystack, it would now be searching for a cowpat in a muddy field.

For the first time since they'd escaped from OPDEO's ambush in the Unidome, Kai felt he could relax. The *Aquila* was a large, well-equipped ship; while Huang worked out in the gym, practising his martial art skills against holographic opponents, Kai spent more time with Leona. Although her background was very different from Kai's, they had much in common. She had learnt the traditions of the Maasai at a young age and understood the sanctity of life, both present and past. Her family preserved their ancestors' artefacts as repositories of their spirit, in harmony with their environment: the sky, the lakes, the mountains. All creation, either animate or inanimate, was imbued with a life force, a component of the universal consciousness encountered by Kai through meditation. But his attraction to Leona was more than spiritual.

Although Kai no longer practised telepathy with Leona, they'd developed an instinctive understanding of each other's desires. Even on a large ship, the fact two men and a woman were living in close proximity was certain to cause emotional tension. For that reason, Kai and Leona had not yet consummated the intimacy they felt for each other. But Kai knew voluntary restraint would not last forever.

As their craft neared the main asteroid belt, Kai considered their options. He was sure they'd managed to escape detection so far, but he judged the best way to throw off their pursuers would be to hide for a while. 'How far away are we from another asteroid?' he asked Leona. She swung her braided hair over her shoulder and accessed the astronavigation program.

'On this course, we could rendezvous with 31 Euphrosyne in two days.'

'Euphrosyne. One of the five most massive asteroids. What else do we know about it?'

'Roughly two hundred and sixty kilometres in diameter with an irregular shape,' she said, reading data from her screen. 'It's another of the dark bodies that's never been properly surveyed.'

'What is its inclination?'

'It's not known exactly but it's been estimated at twenty-five degrees. Is it important?'

'That depends on its orbital position. But at a latitude of greater than sixty-five degrees, the polar regions would stay in darkness for nearly three years. It could be a good place for us to lie low for a while.'

⋊⋍

While they approached the planetoid, Kai carried out a distraydar scan and chose an area within a small, deep crater as a suitable landing site. To find them, an OPDEO destroyer would have to pass almost directly overhead. He was relieved to be able to rest knowing they were safe, and he needed time to decide what to do next.

They had enough supplies to last them for a long flight; they could travel to Mars, or even Earth, provided they weren't intercepted. Kai could return to Khitan territory and tell of OPDEO's intention to launch a pre-emptive attack on their Empire. But the Khitans already knew that was likely. He could break the news about the existence of Thiosh, and OPDEO's hostility towards them, but what could the Empire do to change anything? The way ahead was not clear. He decided to occupy himself with routine activities, at least for the time being.

'We had better set up a sentry post,' he said. 'I shall take the shuttle and install equipment on the rim of the crater. It will give us early warning if OPDEO come near. Huang, you are in charge until I get back.'

Kai circled the crater and chose a flattened peak where he could land. Once on the surface, he scanned for biochemical or electromagnetic hazards. There was a lot of background radio noise sounding like wind in a forest. But there was something else about it; he suspected there were patterns in the sound. He tried to get a fix on its source, but the signal was omnidirectional. It didn't seem like a natural phenomenon, but what did 'natural' mean on Euphrosyne? He contacted the *Aquila* to say he'd be carrying out tests, and they should ignore his radio transmissions until he gave the all clear.

⋊⋍

Huang locked onto Kai's frequency and prepared to wait. He turned to face Leona. 'What is he doing now? He never tells me anything.'

'Sorry, I don't know,' she said, looking up briefly as she carried out a routine instrument check.

'Why don't you know? You can read his thoughts, can you not?'

'No, not really. He's not clear in his thinking at the moment.'

'But you are very close to him. I know how he looks at you. What are his plans? How long have we got to spend in this hole?'

She stopped logging the instrument data and turned to face Huang. 'Actually, I don't think Kai knows himself. You should realise he's had two mentors in his life. One was an abbot in a monastery and the other was the leader of the Thiosh. Each gave him a sense of purpose, but now they're both dead.'

Huang gripped the support straps opposite her. 'We are hiding like bamboo rats. What will we do here? It is dark, it is barren, we can only see the sky above us. It is a prison.'

'If it's any consolation, I don't feel comfortable here either. But it was Kai's choice, and we must accept it,' she said.

Huang leant close. 'When I was stuck on the Trojan asteroid, you told him to fire the laser into a crater. How did you know that would free the shuttle?'

She let her com-pad stylus float gently towards the floor deck. 'When we left the Trojan asteroid, we'd made it possible for new life to evolve. Beyond that I can't tell you.'

'There are many things you are unwilling to explain. You know how to defeat the OPDEO security codes. You have their encryption programs in your com-pad. Breckenridge thought you were a spy. Was he right? Yes or no?'

Huang and Leona glared at each other, each determined not to break eye contact.

'You're wrong, Huang. Breckenridge didn't think I was a spy. He threatened me with interrogation to try to make me spy for him.'

'You have not answered my question!'

'If I was a spy for the Khitan Empire you should be glad.'

'I am not a thinker like you and Kai. I am a warrior. I fight for my friends.' Huang was shouting now. 'I would give my life for them, and they would die for me. Without loyalty, there is no honour!'

'There are loyalties that transcend frontiers, Huang. And if you're suggesting . . .'

Kai's voice cut in over the radio, his signal punctuated by crackling interference. 'I am Kai - - - - carbon biochemistry – what do you use? - - - - Have you always been this way? - - - - But where is your hardware? - - - - You exist in space, independent of material? - - - - Are there many like you?' - - - - You want me to help you? - - - - When the time is right.'

Out of the Frying Pan

Geoff had a sudden thought. 'Maura, Chen – go to the wardroom and sit on the table. Don't touch anything metallic.'

He went to the stores, grabbed one of the harpoons he'd seen earlier, and headed for the engine room. Much of the high voltage cabling had no insulation.

I don't suppose the maintenance robots worry about health and safety. Lucky for them – and maybe lucky for me.

He chose a position on an overhead gantry above the main generator. He needed to insulate himself from the metal walkway. He applied TK-force to the soles of his boots, slightly more than his own weight, and lifted himself off the surface. But trying to keep still in space was like walking on a tightrope. He was soon covered in bruises as he repeatedly floated up a few inches and lost his balance. He would keel over one way and then overcorrect in the opposite direction, swinging with ever-increasing amplitude until he crashed into the wall or the gantry handrail.

'Geoff, what the feckin' hell are you doing?' Maura called over his com-phone.

'Sorry, can't talk now. Don't touch any metal.' Geoff turned off his phone.

He tried a different approach. He jumped normally. Yes, he could hold himself in the air using vertical TK-force under his arms, each side equivalent to half his own weight. In the low gravity, he could easily jump up two metres. As long as he kept away from obstacles, he had enough space to stay upright. But it took all his concentration to keep himself stable.

The ship was creaking and groaning. Geoff felt drips falling on his head as the joints in the hull were strained. He steadied himself, threw the harpoon, but it overshot. He spun round, losing his balance. He TK-ed the harpoon back into his hand and tried again. This time it bounced harmlessly off the conductors. *Third time lucky? Yes, thank God!* The harpoon simultaneously struck the high voltage terminal and the hull. A brilliant electric arc welded the missile in place. The circuit breakers operated, the lighting reduced to emergency low level but, as he'd hoped, the generator kept running. The harpoon glowed like the sun as it conducted high voltage electricity into the hull. With a sudden lurch, the whale-bot rose upwards.

Geoff floated over to the electrical cubicles and opened the main breaker. Working under the emergency lighting, he found a saw, hacked off the harpoon and reclosed the breaker. *Nice job, he told himself as he limped back to the wardroom. And I've learnt how to levitate. I can fly even without wings.*

'What were you playing at, Geoff?' demanded Maura. 'You cut me off . . . Oh, you're bleeding. And you've hurt your leg. Sorry, are you okay?'

'I'm fine, just a few bruises. I couldn't think what to do. Then I remembered that old book by Jules Verne. The crew of the Nautilus fought a giant squid. But that was on the surface of the sea, and they used axes.'

'Of course, the Nautilus. It could electrify itself when it was attacked.'

'Yes, but only the handrails below the hatches – in the book, anyway. What we did was much better!'

'Thank you, Geoff,' said Chen. 'You do good job making squid go. We give it mighty shock. On Earth, men killed whales with harpoons, but your harpoon save our whale-bot.'

Geoff looked at the happy faces of his friends and envied them. He hadn't sought it, but he sensed he'd emerged as their leader. They would expect him to solve their problems from now on. He had a feeling he'd soon be tested again.

Europa rotated within the magnetic field of Jupiter and its saltwater ocean was electrically conductive. As a result, the moon had north and south magnetic poles. This was of academic interest for Geoff and Maura, who measured the intensity of the field as part of their daily instrument checks. However, the practical benefit was they could plot their course using magnetic compass bearings.

'You know, Maura, the ice cap's getting thinner the further east we go,' said Geoff.

'It could be because of volcanic activity on the seabed. If we can find some more hydrothermal vents, perhaps the Thiosh could hang out there for a while.'

'Well, at this rate we'll soon be able to surface under the stars.'

'That would be marvellous, altogether. Wouldn't it be grand just to take a stroll on deck?' she said.

Each day, Geoff noted a reduction in the ice cap's thickness. They maintained a course just below its bottom surface until, at last, they found themselves in open sea as Geoff had hoped. Maura switched on the distraydar and programmed the autopilot to steer clear of icebergs.

They all put on pressure suits from the escape compartment and climbed out of the top hatch. The sea was smooth and calm, gentle waves glinting in the starlight. Once again, they saw the mesmerising skyscape. Jupiter was in a crescent phase, twenty-three times bigger than the Moon seen from Earth. A dozen or more of Jupiter's other moons were visible, as were the outer planets, each easily identifiable by its colour; aquamarine Uranus, azure Neptune, and Saturn shining through its translucent rings, a golden sphere tinged blue-green like a ripening plum.

Chen waited until he had Geoff and Maura's attention. He was holding a coil of wire and smiling broadly. 'I make fishing line. Maybe I catch something.'

'You could give it a go,' said Geoff. 'But be careful how you swing your hook around. If you get a fish we'll scan it with the biometer and see if it's edible.'

Chen switched on the torch built into his hood and concentrated on impaling a protein cube on the end of the hook. But before he even cast his line, a large fish jumped clear of the waves. '*Aiya!* Light attract fish. I turn on floodlights and get more.'

'No, don't do that,' said Geoff. But it was too late. Just as Chen illuminated the whale-bot and all the sea around them, Geoff saw the OPDEO surveillance satellite tracking fast across the background of stars. 'Oh shit. Everyone inside. It's time to dive again.'

'I think maybe they see us,' said Chen. 'Sorry.'

'Yes, they may have done. The question is – have they got a sub nearby that can intercept us?' said Geoff. 'We'll go deep and try to make as little noise as possible. Meanwhile, keep scanning the external mikes.'

It wasn't long before Maura announced she'd picked up a new sound. 'A sort of pulsing throb. D'you think it's screw propellers?'

'I've put the sonar bearings on the screen,' said Geoff. 'There's something out there and it's moving fast. Make a ninety-degree turn, Maura.'

Geoff watched the fuzzy image on his screen change course to follow their manoeuvre. 'Okay, now turn the other way.'

'Is it still heading for us?'

Geoff performed some mental calculations. 'I'd say it's steering the shortest course to intercept us. I'm afraid it's a sub. Can we go any faster?'

'Sorry. We're the wrong shape for high speed.'

'It is my fault. I cause trouble again,' said Chen.

'Don't talk,' said Geoff. 'We'll shut everything down and stay dead quiet. If we don't make any noise, they won't know where we are.'

The screen image of the sub had become sharper and larger. It was close enough for them to hear the rushing sound of its propellers from inside the whale-bot. Geoff felt the turbulence as the vessel passed over them. But then, nothing. Chen clamped his hand over his mouth and suppressed a nervous laugh.

'That's funny,' said Geoff, frowning. 'I think it's lost us.'

But then the whale-bot lurched. Maura fell onto Geoff and they both toppled over.

'What the feckin' hell was that?' Maura asked, massaging her elbow. 'Did they hit us with something?'

Geoff levered himself upright and sequenced through the viz-box images from the cameras. 'Christ, they've caught us in a trawl net. The sub's got us in tow.' He focused on part of the net and tried to wrench it apart with all the telekinetic force he could muster, but it was not enough. He guessed the mesh was made from high tensile steel.

'They could have torpedoed us,' said Maura. 'But they obviously want us alive – and you know what that means.'

The following two days were some of the worst in Geoff's life. The submarine increased its speed and, as a result, the whale-bot swung to and fro as they were pulled through the sea. The fluctuation of their craft was matched by the disorder in his mind.

Geoff was suffering a crisis of confidence. It was only six months since he'd met Maura, although it seemed like six years. Because of the choices he'd made, they were now ensnared in a rolling and yawing net, dragging them towards an unknown horror. The memory of OPDEO's threat to torture Maura gnawed Geoff from within. She appeared calm but was saying little.

Chen somehow managed to take refuge in sleep. He'd revealed their position on the open sea, but Geoff didn't think it was entirely his fault. OPDEO's sub had arrived so quickly, he suspected it must have been tracking them already. Maura came and hugged him, but neither spoke.

Choices

At first, Geoff thought the explosion had happened inside his head, that the intensity of his thoughts had finally overloaded his brain. But from the shock registered on Maura's and Chen's faces, he realised they'd heard it too. He rushed to the control console, turned on the floodlights and flicked through the cameras' viewscreens. The whale-bot was still inside the net, but no longer caught against the mesh. Geoff panned around, looking for the sub. As it came into view, he had a flashback to a horror film he'd seen in his youth, when a man was eaten by piranhas. A swarm of shiny machines were snapping at the sub with serrated teeth.

'*Hǎo jíla!*' cried Chen. 'Gods be praised, Thiosh send shark-bots to rescue!'

They watched one of the robot fish bite a chunk out of a hydroplane. It was joined by the familiar outline of a crab-bot, flickering in the blue light of its cutting torch. Geoff noticed debris floating around. It must have been the explosion of a torpedo they'd heard. The sub had destroyed one of the machines.

Maura clasped her head and slumped into a seat. 'I'm hearing a voice again, Geoff. It's a Thiosh.' She became absorbed in her thoughts, but without the evident pleasure she'd shown during her first Thiosh encounter. Geoff watched her frown and gesticulate as she expressed herself telepathically, sometimes clenching her fists and banging the arm of her chair.

Turning back to his viz-box, Geoff saw the crab-bot abandon its attempt to cut through the sub's hull and begin work cutting through the blades of the screw propellers. Two shark-bots swam to the net and slashed through the mesh with their teeth until there was a hole wide enough for the whale-bot to escape. Geoff powered the craft through the gap and out into the ocean.

Maura roused herself from her trance. 'Voorogg spoke to me,' she told Geoff. 'He's the leader of the militant group who opposed Mettravar. I think they're able to conceal their thoughts from other Thiosh. They were about to rip the sub apart, but I persuaded him to hold off.'

'What? How d'you do that?'

'I told him about OPDEO's weapons of mass destruction. When I explained what OPDEO could do, he accepted he needed better weapons than just the cutting equipment he's got at the moment. Then, he'll either be able to fight OPDEO or negotiate peace from a position of strength.'

'Oh, great, so now we've started another arms race.'

'Hey, hang on,' said Maura, prodding Geoff with her forefinger. 'Don't I deserve some praise? I thought I handled it rather well.'

Geoff backed off, massaging his chest. 'The rebel Thiosh killed their own leader. How could you reason with them after that?'

'I stopped them killing the sub's crew. OPDEO would have gone berserk if they'd done that. And now we're free again, instead of being dragged along like a pike fishing lure. Come on, cheer up!'

'I don't like you letting an alien put thoughts in your head,' said Geoff, rubbing his beard.

Maura gave him a hug. 'It's okay, you needn't be jealous of a sulphur-eating fish. But all I want is to get away from here. Can they still follow us?'

'No, we're safe for the moment,' said Geoff, his voice muffled by Maura's hair. 'Now Thiosh bots have chewed lumps out of the sub, it won't be able to steer, and its propellers won't be a lot of use.'

'But OPDEO know we're here,' said Maura, breaking free. 'They could send something else. Quick, let's wag our fluke and get out of here.'

Kai pondered the significance of the encounter he'd had while he was away from the *Aquila*. He was aware the others must have picked up one side of his strange conversation with the Virtuon, as it had described itself, but they didn't question him. He was grateful they seemed prepared to wait until he shared his experience with them. They must have sensed he needed time to think.

Leona was blacking out the observation windows to prevent any passing Hesperian destroyer from seeing them. Kai was scanning radio frequencies for a signal with the patterns he'd detected before. Then a babble of Hesperian speech bombarded his ears. He sat rigidly in his flight chair. Leona put her hand on his shoulder and asked him what was wrong. He smiled grimly and gestured for her to sit down next to him. Then he took off his headphones and summoned Huang from the exercise room.

'There is terrible news from Earth,' he told them. 'The Empire launched a nuclear attack on New Amsterdam City, three hours ago. There was no warning. A source in the Septagon said the city was totally destroyed.' Leona gasped and put her head in her hands.

Kai continued. 'Once they were alerted, other cities in the Federation defended themselves with anti-missile lasers. They destroyed hundreds of Khitan warheads before they reached their targets.'

'What of the Empire?' asked Huang. 'Have the Hesperians hit back?'

'It is hard to tell. There is massive radio interference affecting all Khitan communications. I think the Empire is using electronic countermeasures to block the Hesperian missiles. There seems to be an impasse after the initial attack, but it will not stay that way.'

'The Khitans tried a pre-emptive strike,' said Leona. 'I was afraid the Hesperians would start a war. I never thought the Empire would attack first.'

Huang seemed unperturbed. 'I think this is good news. The Empire has acted strongly and with success. They have taught the Hesperians a lesson they will not forget, and now the fighting has stopped.'

'No, Huang,' said Kai. 'The deadlock will be only temporary. Each side will find new ways to attack the other, until either the Federation or the Empire is destroyed.'

'We should warn the Khitan government,' said Huang. 'They need to know there are Hesperians with paranormal powers. If Geoff and

Maura find a way of teaching others in their Federation how to use telepathy and telekinesis, that could change the strategic balance. It would be best if they perish in the Europan ocean – if they are still alive.'

'Shut up, Huang!' shouted Leona. 'That's an evil thing to say. Maura believes every form of life is precious and Geoff works for the UN, on a committee dedicated to peace.'

'Leona is right,' said Kai. 'New Amsterdam City has been destroyed. I fear millions have already perished. Saazat Mettravar wanted peace on Earth as well as on Europa. There may be other Thiosh who could help stop the war.'

'Why should Thiosh defend the Hesperians?' said Huang, his eyes blazing. 'They should be fighting for the Khitans. And what about you, Leona? You are Hesperian, but I know you have spied for the Empire. You are in a difficult position, I think.' The thought seemed to amuse him.

'I will follow Kai,' said Leona. 'He is our leader now. As you said yourself, Huang, without loyalty there is no honour.'

〜🐟

Kai was alone in his cabin. He was sitting perfectly still, cross-legged in the lotus position, the feeble gravity of the asteroid sufficient to hold him to the deck. He pictured Maura in his mind and she responded joyfully. She told him how pleased she was that he could telepathise again, and assured him that Geoff, Chen and herself were all well and in good spirits. But she quickly detected that Kai was carrying the burden of bad news. He told her about the outbreak of war, and they shared each other's anguish as they considered the tragedy unfolding on Earth.

Kai thought again about the conversation he'd had with the Virtuon. Intelligent beings with knowledge and resources beyond the imagining of mere humans. *Is it possible that aliens could end the enmity between Khitans and Hesperians?*

〜🐟

Maura flipped on the whale-bot's autopilot and turned to Geoff. 'It's terrible. New Amsterdam City has been destroyed. The Khitans knew about OPDEO's plans and decided to hit the Federation first.'

'Oh Christ!' said Geoff. 'My sister was in New Amsterdam. Why didn't the missile defence system work?'

'I guess they were caught by surprise.'

'The Hesperians will hit back. They will certainly knock out the Khitan base on Mars. That was the main purpose of their presence on Europa.'

'The Khitans are jamming the distraydar at the moment,' said Maura.

'I could help the Federation. I know about electronic countermeasures.'

'Don't try and join forces with Flannery and co. They're trying to kill us, remember?'

Geoff gripped the finger Maura was wagging in his face. 'Don't do that, please. I'm worried about my family.'

'I worry about mine too. But Voorogg will make the Thiosh strong. If they can neutralise OPDEO on Europa, the Federation will no longer have military superiority. It won't be able to destroy the Khitans on Earth, or Thiosh on Europa.'

'No, wait, we are Hesperians. What'll happen to us if the Khitans and the Thiosh destroy the Federation?'

'Sometimes you must choose between the least of two evils,' said Maura.

Kai opened the locker above his bed and took down the ancient paper book of Khitan scriptures. He sought comfort in a favourite text but, opening the book at random, an unfamiliar passage caught his eye.

> Space, time and matter are under my command. I am the tea master and the assassin. I change the essence of all things, material and immaterial. The knowledge of my existence is too much for Man. The heathen seek to destroy the Way of Truth. No one can see the path of the eagle in the air, or the snake on the ground. Likewise, the

path of the sage is invisible. You, *samanera*, shall rule the fish of the endless ocean. I shall be your mind and your shadow.

He was sure he'd never seen those words before. He sat down on his mat and contemplated their meaning. During the time he'd spent at the monastery, he had been a *samanera*, a novice. He had lived in accordance with the strict code of behaviour of the monastery, but he'd left before achieving the status of an ordained monk. Then the reference to fish – countless novice monks had struggled to solve illogical questions throughout the ages. Nevertheless, he was sure the riddle he'd been given had a significance for him alone. The Thiosh had summoned him to Europa; they were the fish that could never swim to the end of the ocean. They swam in a sea that had no shores.

Maura joined Geoff in the wardroom, where he was sitting hunched over his com-pad.

'You're doing a lot of calculations,' she said. 'What's the problem?'

'I'm checking on OPDEO satellite locations,' said Geoff. 'We need to release some helium and I don't want them to detect our location.'

Maura rolled her eyes.

'Okay, it's like this. The fusion reactor makes helium as a by-product. We can store it as a cryogenic liquid, but we haven't got infinite capacity. So we have to let it go. Satellites with spectroscopic detectors would see it and know where we are.'

'You're more of an engineer than ever I am,' said Maura. 'Do you think you could you summarise the status of Hesperian technology for me? You know, fusion reactors, robotics, space vehicle power units, materials, telecoms – that sort of thing. Perhaps write a report?'

This time it was Geoff who looked askance. Maura moved behind him and began to probe and squeeze his shoulder muscles.

'Why do you want me to do that?' he said. 'If you're thinking of telling Voorogg so he can design new weapons, then I won't do it. In any case, the Thiosh can hack Earth's computers and get all the information they need.'

'Sure, but you know where the weaknesses are. It'd help the Thiosh.'

'It would help the rebel Thiosh, you mean. If they destroy OPDEO, they could send robots and conquer the Hesperian Empire on Earth. They have no reason to love humankind. They'd probably carry on and crush the Khitans too.'

Maura twisted round to look Geoff in the eyes. 'I only want to help the Thiosh negotiate again, from a position of strength.'

'They could annihilate everything, make us all slaves, and rob Earth of its resources. How could you think of betraying . . . ?'

'Can't you see, we may have a chance to end the war?' said Maura, flicking back her hair from her face. 'It would be irresponsible not to take it.'

⌐●

The canoe is travelling at speed. Kai steers with a single paddle. He weaves between boulders barely visible through the spray. A Khitan monk stands upright in the bows. He leans forward into the gale-force wind. Kai cannot see his face. His carmine toga cracks like a whip. The wind tears golden feathers from his helmet. They are chasing a beluga fish. It is longer than their canoe. The monk hurls a spear but it hits a sacred rock. Fire falls from the sky. The water boils and the canoe capsizes. Kai feels his lungs fill with water. A crocodile swims through the fire. It holds Kai in its mouth and swims to the land.

Kai got up from his bunk, tore off his clothes and entered his shower. He set the temperature control to two degrees Celsius and stood for a long time under the stream of cold water. He would not flinch from his duty.

Opportunities and Threats

Kai called together his companions. 'Prepare for take-off,' he said. 'We are going home.'

'Yes!' cried Huang. He lifted himself from his flight chair and cracked his knuckles.

'You mean Earth?' asked Leona. 'I'm not sure we'd even recognise it.'

'Yes – we are returning to Earth,' said Kai. 'And I do not know yet what we will see. A lot may happen during our long journey, and we may find there is total destruction when we get there.'

'Where exactly on Earth are we going to?' Leona persisted. 'We all have different homes.'

'In time we may visit the places we truly call home,' said Kai. 'But there is something I must do first. It is a task I must carry out in the South Pacific Ocean.'

'Aiya!' said Huang. 'We can find a desert island. Perhaps the war will not have reached it.'

'The place I have in mind is deserted, it is true,' said Kai. 'But it is not a paradise.'

Huang and Leona busied themselves with preflight checks. Two hours later they strapped themselves into their harnesses and Kai counted down to lift-off. They accelerated at six G. It was as much as their bodies could stand for any length of time. They waited until the last of their chemical fuel was completely consumed and then ignited the fusion ramjet; it continued to increase their speed, but at a gentler rate. They would reach Earth in six months. Meanwhile, there was much to keep Kai occupied.

Breckenridge punched the air. 'Yeehah, at fuckin' last!' he yelled to no one in particular. The message on his com-phone told him the flare from the *Aquila's* main rocket exhaust had been picked up by the surveillance computers. The latest image was only ten minutes old. The ship was following a course towards the sun, and the general's staff officers were busy calculating its intended destination. The major ordered OPDEO's warships patrolling the Solar System interspace to remain vigilant and to intercept the stolen ship as soon as they detected it.

'Do we know where we're going?' asked Geoff.

'I think we should keep heading east,' said Maura. 'There's something making the sea temperature increase, and the current strength too. We need to get more data, if we can. Would you ever mind watching the auto-helm? I have to spend some time in my cabin. I have a real strong feeling a Thiosh wants to speak to me.'

Geoff felt frustrated he couldn't take part in Maura's telepathic conversations. Further negotiations with Voorogg would be risky. If he could hide his thoughts and Maura could not, then telepathy with him would be dangerous.

'Don't look so worried,' said Maura on her return. 'I've been sharing with Atherlonne. She's a lady Thiosh, and she knew Mettravar. Rather well, I suspect.'

'Did she say what she wanted?' Geoff asked.

'I think she'll tell us later. We've been invited for a close encounter.'

They were passing over hydrothermal vents again, but the seabed here was very different from the Cronus Rift. The black sulphide smoke was similar, but this time it puffed out of honeycomb orifices in the walls of a series of passages. The forward camera showed they were passing through a steep-sided canyon. Geoff noticed a small red fish swimming ahead of them. Something about it made him think it was a robot.

'That's our pilot,' said Maura, smiling. They soon reached forks in the passageways, and the need for a guide became more obvious.

A green light shone ahead of them and, as they drew nearer, they realised it was coming from inside a cavern. Geoff checked the biosensor signals measuring radiation, but he didn't detect any harmful rays. Easing the whale-bot gently through the entrance, Maura scanned the sides for a suitable bay and brought the vessel to rest. The illumination was surprisingly bright. The entire surface of the walls emitted a uniform yellow-green light. 'It's organic phosphorescence,' she explained. 'It's probably caused by extremophiles living off sulphur.'

Geoff couldn't decide if the brightness of Maura's eyes was an effect of the light from the observation windows, or the fact she was excited. 'You're beautiful even when your face is green,' he whispered to her. Maura laughed and dug her elbow into his stomach.

Several dark shapes were swimming nearby. A half dozen mini crab-bots surrounded their craft and began to attach hoses and cables to connection points on the hull. 'Looks like we're due for a full service,' said Geoff.

One of the bots was carrying a stack of rectangular boxes, some like suitcases and others like small chests. Geoff clicked on a viz-box button for the view from the tail-fin camera. The bot approached the side of their vessel's hull and opened a hatch they hadn't previously discovered. After about thirty seconds, a message announced there was a delivery for collection. They had no idea where to look for it but, entering the wardroom, they found a panel had opened to reveal a dumb waiter compartment containing one of the boxes.

Geoff hesitated, wondering why the surface of the box was now completely dry. But Chen, curious as ever, immediately fiddled with the inset catches until he could open the lid. Inside were three small packages.

'*Aiya*, presents!' he exclaimed. Picking one up, he tore off the protective wrappings and uncovered a small, grey disc. '*Go se*,' he said in disappointment. He tried the other packages and found they contained similar plasticised discs.

'They must be important,' said Geoff. 'But I've no idea what they are.'

Maura pointed to where Chen was already unpacking another box which had just arrived. 'Well, if the discs are spare buttons for those new clothes, we'll have to drill our own holes.'

Subsequent boxes contained food items. Chen tested the biscuits and chocolate. He smiled broadly.

The wardroom viz-box screen flickered into life, and short sentences appeared jerkily, like a message from an early twentieth-century ticker-tape machine. It was a welcome greeting from Atherlonne. Maura touched the screen to open the virtual keypad. She expressed their thanks for Atherlonne's hospitality, and for the presents they'd received, but then asked what the grey disks were for.

Atherlonne:

> There is therein some information which
> we give to you, to show our willingness
> to share our knowledge with your human race.
> They are computer memories of three kinds.
> One is of special interest for you, Maura.
> Genetic code controls our lives, as is
> the case for many hydrocarbon beings.
>
> The second disk is meant for Doctor Kirby.
> It holds the coding which our robots use.
> Although he is an expert in this field,
> he may not know within our universe
> powerful artificial brains exist
> without the need for electricity.
>
> The third disk is to help you to relax.
> There are some games for you to pass the time
> until we have to find another place
> where we can live in safety and in peace.

Maura (typing):

> You are very generous, and we thank you for your hospitality. I offer our condolences that you have lost your leader, the Saazat, because of OPDEO's duplicity. May we please ask a question about the future? There are matters of life and death that affect us all.

Atherlonne:

> A risk to life is never far away
> for people who have come from other worlds.
> Dying is part of living for us all.
> Every organic creature shares this fate,
> but please ask anything you want to know.

Maura:

> Okay – thank you for your understanding. It is a relief
> you have a refuge away from the Cronus Rift. We believe
> that OPDEO want to attack the Thiosh. They have
> weapons of mass destruction and are prepared to use
> them. Would this place, or somewhere like it, be suitable
> for all Thiosh?

Atherlonne:

> To live we need some sulphur-bearing springs.
> This hydrothermal vent is small in size,
> an offshoot of a fissure far away.
> No more than seven Thiosh can live here.
> The Saazat built this place to share with me.

Maura:

> I've telepathised with a Thiosh called Voorogg. He wants
> to make the Thiosh strong militarily, and then negotiate
> a peace treaty with OPDEO.

Atherlonne:

> Voorogg did not accept the Saazat's rule.
> The Thiosh do not have a single voice.

Maura:

> So how will you protect yourselves against OPDEO?

Atherlonne:

> We need another home where we can live.
> You could perhaps assist us in our search.
> At present time I cannot tell you more.

Mohawk was the largest battlecruiser in the Hesperian fleet. Even though it was highly automated, its crew numbered sixty-three navy personnel. It was armed with various directed energy and particle-beam weapons, as well as guided missiles with biological, radioactive, and fusion warheads. With its chemical, nuclear, and ion engine propulsion units, the entire Solar System was within its range.

'You're lookin' pleased with yourself,' said Clifton Tyrell to his co-pilot.

'I just gotta message from my wife,' said Ricky Carter. 'My little 'un had a birthday yesterday and blew out all the candles on his cake. Not bad for a three-year-old.' He pulled out a dog-eared photo of a toddler with fair hair and passed it to his commander.

Smiling, Tyrell returned the photo, steered the *Mohawk* into orbit around Vesta, and put the ship's engines on standby. He was pleased that, for once, he was circling one of the larger asteroids. His patrol required him to keep his craft between Jupiter and the Earth. A simple concept but, if he stayed in an uncorrected orbit around the sun, his angular position would rapidly advance ahead of Jupiter's. So, to maintain his station, he had to proceed backwards along his natural sun orbit, parking himself at one of fifty asteroids for three weeks at a time.

'This is gonna be borin',' said Carter. 'We'll be circlin' Vesta like we're on a piece of string. It might look like a grapefruit but it's got real gravity.'

'At least it'll be stable,' said Tyrell. 'Better than the last one, eh, Ricky? We nearly crashed into it twice.'

'Say, what about that? A guy on Europa just sent us a message. P'raps it won't be so borin'. The stolen ship's headin' our way!'

'Sir, I've lost the distraydar signal,' said Carter. 'The target was closin' fast and then a huge lump of space rock got in the way. The renegades are deliberately keepin' the rock between them and us. Shall I set a course to go round?'

'Negative,' said Tyrell. 'We can't risk them slippin' past on the other side. We've gotta keep ahead of them. Fire the retrorockets to reduce speed. They'll have to veer round the rock soon. As soon as we get a clear view we'll fire the fusion missiles in fan formation, two waves of eight.'

'Yessir – sixteen missiles primed and loaded.'

'It'll be a shame to lose the ship, but OPDEO command says it's too big a risk to try to board it. The renegades have some new psychological weaponry. We can't take any chances. We've just gotta take them out – period.'

Leona watched Kai aim the *Aquila's* gigawatt laser at the rock in their path. Its central area glowed white with an ever-expanding periphery until the whole rock exploded, splintering into a billion pieces. The shaft of blue laser-light momentarily illuminated a sphere of expanding debris.

Huang covered his face as if blocking a punch, but the *Aquila* sailed through the gap left as the debris dispersed. '*Hi-yah!*' he shouted triumphantly.

But the consequence continued to play out in Leona's mind. The impact of the debris caused the stern section of the *Mohawk* to break away, instantly emptying the ship's accommodation of its life-sustaining atmosphere. Those crew members, who had instinctively held their breath, vomited blood and passed out. The others who'd allowed air to leave their bodies, lost consciousness ten seconds later.

Debilitated by the unfolding horror of her vision, Leona allowed herself to drift under the acceleration of the fusion ram-jet, to the back of the command deck. She lay in shadow, appalled by the scene playing out in her mind. The unconscious bodies of the *Mohawk's* crew swelled to twice their normal volume, tearing open their flight suits and bursting their skin. A final image burnt into her memory: sixty-three ruptured corpses, doomed to circle the sun until the end of time.

Safe Havens

Geoff joined Maura on the bridge. He took her hand. Even in the green bioluminescent light, he saw she'd been chewing her nails. He asked her why she was worried.

'Leona's been in contact,' she said,

'Where are they? What are they doing?' he asked, anxious for news.

'They're actually heading for Earth.'

'I thought they might do that. Has Kai got a plan?'

'Leona doesn't know. He doesn't share his thoughts anymore. It's like he's built a wall around himself.'

'You told me before they were attracted to each other.'

'Leona's upset. Kai destroyed a Hesperian battlecruiser.'

'Did he, by God!'

'There were no survivors, and he didn't wait to find out if it was hostile.'

'It almost certainly would have been.'

'Maybe, but Leona thinks Kai has changed. She told me something odd happened to him when they landed on Euphrosyne. It's as if he's become fanatical, or on a crusade or something. She's very anxious about it.'

'Hm, has she talked to Huang?'

'She doesn't get on with Huang either. He just wants to fight Hesperians.'

'That fits,' said Geoff. 'Maybe the war has made our Khitan friends aggressive.'

'That may be part of it. But the old Kai was too noble, too spiritual to be violent. Leona knows a lot about Afrikan culture, and she thinks he's been possessed.'

'Oh, come on, no one believes in evil spirits anymore, do they?'

'Leona does.'

⊱━⊰

Leona longed to find out who Kai had spoken to on Euphrosyne, but he refused to discuss either the past or the future. Earth was now only half a million miles away. He'd already manoeuvred the ship to travel stern first so the ramjet would slow them down, and he'd changed course to use the Moon's gravitational pull for further deceleration.

The tension on the control deck was palpable. During a morning status meeting, Huang had demanded to know how they would land. 'The *Aquila* was not designed for re-entry. It will burn up.'

'That is correct,' said Kai. 'Now please attend to your duties and allow me to attend to mine.'

Huang met Leona's eyes and mouthed, '*Ta ma de*' – Khitan words she knew as a curse.

⊱━⊰

Reoriented to travel nose cone first, they approached the Earth's outer atmosphere. The *Aquila's* hull began to shake, and its surface temperature increased as a result of friction. Kai put the ship into a slow spin to minimise the buffeting caused by turbulence. Leona felt her inner suit sticking to her body as the ship's cooling system reached the limit of its capacity.

Kai ordered his crew to strap themselves into the shuttle and then he joined them at the controls. He sent an operating command via his com-pad to turn on the water sprays used to clean the shuttle's exterior, and immediately Leona felt the temperature drop. Then Kai opened the shuttle-bay doors. The roar of the air stream, already like a rocket exhaust, increased in intensity as the doors were torn away from the hull. They looked out through the gaping red-hot aperture at the night side of Earth, Khitan territories faintly illuminated by the

Moon. Huang appeared puzzled by its appearance, and then nodded grimly when Leona mouthed the words, 'No lights.'

Kai looked up from his com-pad and gestured it was time to abandon the ship. Leona momentarily lost consciousness, but recovered in time to see an incandescent streak marking the path of the *Aquila* above them. She stared at the sky for long seconds after it had disappeared.

Kai set a course south, keeping the shuttle at low altitude. There was ice floating all around, and still they travelled onwards. According to the distraydar, there was high ground rising to five hundred metres but, strangely, the area ahead looked flat. It was Huang who explained the phenomenon. 'There is an island there, covered in ice. It all looks the same. Wait – I see a shadow from a tower. *Aiya*, it is a lighthouse!'

They side-slipped down to low level and hovered above other man-made structures. They had been buildings once, but now they were ruins. Rusty steel chimneys lay collapsed across a roadway. What had been a factory was now half smashed, its innards spilling out through the walls. Tanks, pipes and cables were scattered over the ice. Some huge steel cylinders, ten metres high and ten across, lay bent and distorted, as if they had been crushed by a giant foot. Kai settled the shuttle on an area of clear ice, next to a complex of prefabricated buildings.

'What is this place?' asked Huang.

'It is where men used to heat the flesh of whales,' said Kai, but Huang still looked puzzled.

'I can explain,' said Leona. 'It was in the last century, when the underground reserves of oil had almost run out. Both the Empire and the Federation's governments tried to protect whales, but criminal organisations hunted them for the oil in their bodies, until there were no whales left.'

'In the end, only the strongest species survive,' said Kai. 'I do not expect the human race will continue for much longer.'

Leona looked away and stared at the sea.

The occupants of the whale-bot settled to a steady routine. Atherlonne contacted them each morning, CHT. Although she could telepathise directly with Maura, she chose to communicate via the wardroom viz-box screen, not to exclude Geoff and Chen. She told them that Mettravar had built the subsea cavern as a retreat from the Cronus Rift when the day-to-day running of the Thiosh community had become difficult. The Thiosh were split over what they should do after the Hesperians built the Unidome. It was then that Voorogg emerged as the leader of a dissident faction, in opposition to Mettravar and Atherlonne.

On one occasion, Geoff watched a question appear jerkily on the screen. Atherlonne asked Maura if she'd had news of Kai's party. 'Why doesn't she telepathise with Kai directly?' he asked Maura, in a confidential tone.

'Leona says Kai doesn't want to share his thoughts at the moment.'

'So why doesn't Atherlonne telepathise with Leona, then?'

'Leona's never shared with a Thiosh. It's really weird the first time you do it. You see the world from a totally different perspective. I have some idea of what it's like to live in an ocean because of my studies. But Thiosh society is complicated. When Atherlonne projects to me, she's careful just to tell me what I need to know and can understand. It's all a matter of trust.'

Geoff watched Maura type a reply confirming Kai, Leona and Huang were all well. Then she signed off.

Later, Geoff and Maura were alone in their cabin.

'You didn't tell Atherlonne anything about Kai developing a ruthless streak,' said Geoff.

'I'll project my feelings to her later.' She reached up to him with both hands, but Geoff broke away.

'You know, I feel a complete idiot,' he said. 'You can share the most intimate details with your telepathic friends. You have totally confidential conversations because you do it in your heads. I'm left completely out in the cold, even though you're the one person I want to be closest to. I might as well be a lapdog.'

'Oh, Geoff, I'm sorry. I haven't told you how glad I am that you're not telepathic. I can have a normal relationship with you, read your emotions from your face, give you little surprises, be really pleased to hear your news from your own lips. Let me tell you, telepathy is not all it's cracked up to be. I hear a lot of stuff I can't understand, and things I do understand that worry me sick.'

'What do you mean?'

Maura glanced at the door. 'Keep this to yourself,' she said quietly. 'You mustn't tell a soul, but, when Leona was Prof's office supervisor, she hacked into OPDEO top-secret files and copied them.'

'Good for her. OPDEO is a barbarous, immoral organisation.'

'Yes, but she was looking specifically for information useful to the Khitan Empire, in case of an all-out war with the Federation. Not only that, but knowing Prof was sweet on her, she used him to gain access to confidential documents. I don't know how I feel about all that.'

'Well, she's part of the crew with Kai and Huang now. It'll help her if she's a Khitan sympathiser.'

'But Kai doesn't want to talk to her anymore.'

'He's obviously on a mission. He's concentrating all his energy on that.'

'Yes, but she loves him.'

'Oh, okay, just tell me what I need to know,' said Geoff, bending to kiss her cheek.

During the following days, Geoff devised a way to interrogate the grey discs using his com-pad. Once he'd taught himself the simple but elegant Thiosh programming code, he provided a translation interface for Maura's disc. He also downloaded a number of games from the third disc. Atherlonne had explained they were supposed to amuse them all, but Chen made most use of them.

When Geoff studied his own disc, he was very excited by what he found. The code itself was extremely adaptable and could rewrite itself in light of its usage. But its real power came from its continuous connection with cyberspace.

'Can you believe this, Maura,' he said, 'we've got access to archived uni-net sites covering tens of millennia.'

'What, Thiosh, you mean? I'm happy for you,' said Maura, laughing.

'Not just Thiosh. It's linked to dozens of other uni-nets all over the galaxy.'

'Eh, you mean there are other intelligent beings out there?'

'It gets weirder, the more you go into it. There are even beings that aren't beings.'

'Sorry, you're not making a lot of sense.'

'There are beings that have no bodies and aren't alive. They're just intelligence – software without hardware, if you like.'

'Oh, that's terrifying,' said Maura. 'I've always been afraid of computers being cleverer than humans. They're bound to look after themselves at our expense.'

'It must depend on their programming,' said Geoff. 'Anyway, these beings aren't computers anymore. They're just minds.'

'That's beyond me. Let me tell you about my disc. Thiosh are totally different from any creature ever discovered before. They're perfectly suited to their environment.'

'How do they swim around so fast? They don't seem to waggle anything.'

'Their bodies are really just streamlined tubes. They suck in water and all the sulphur-rich stuff they live on, and shoot it out the back like a rocket.'

'Are they blind like we thought?'

'According to the data, they can detect depth, sulphur concentration, gravity waves and magnetism. They don't have any of our senses, not at all.'

'How do they reproduce? I haven't seen any protuberances.'

'Honestly, you men are all the same. Always thinking about sex.'

'I was only asking from a purely scientific point of view,' said Geoff, doing his best to look hurt.

'So, you'd be interested to know they use sulphur like we use oxygen. They expel carbon disulphide.'

'Wouldn't that make bubbles?'

'It's a liquid, heavier than water. They collect it and process it back to sulphur.'

'They have a chemical works?'

'They can make what they like with their TK-power. But their production hasn't affected the environment. The Saazats have always ensured that Thiosh technology doesn't harm life.'

'But what will happen now Mettravar's gone?' asked Geoff.

But, for once, Maura remained silent.

Going Home

Once again, Atherlonne communicated with the whale-bot trio via their wardroom viz-box screen.

Atherlonne:

> The time has almost come. There is a place
> which Mettravar forbade us to go near.
> You sailed eastward on the open sea;
> the current gained in strength as you progressed.
> Also, the sea grew warmer every day.
> If you continue further you will reach
> a place from which you cannot sail back.
> That is where the Thiosh must now go,
> and it's your destiny to lead the way.

Maura:

> Tell me, please, why must we do this?

Atherlonne:

> Now is the time to find another home.
> A new home for the Thiosh, but for you
> an old home which will welcome your return.

Maura:

> An old home? We come from Earth.

Atherlonne:

> Prepare yourselves for travel and return.

'Jaysis, can that really be true?' Maura said to Geoff. 'We'll soon go back to Earth, and the Thiosh too?'

Maura:

> You'll love it there. We have many hydrothermal vents
> rich in sulphur.

Atherlonne:

> We know it will support our form of life.
> However, some of us will stay behind,
> and for that reason, I will say goodbye.

Maura engaged the fluke drive and followed the pilot fish to the surface of the ocean, where, in the light of Jupiter, they could see dozens of Thiosh swimming through the choppy waves, all heading south-east.

Geoff was pacing around the wardroom. 'Look, Maura, I'm not happy about this. How are all these Thiosh going to get to Earth? Atherlonne must have the mother of all transport ships if we're all going to go.'

'Hm. I don't think we're travelling in a spacecraft. Atherlonne told me to head for the gateway.'

'A gateway in the sea? What are you talking about?' Geoff was absent-mindedly tugging at his beard.

'It's an entrance to a wormhole, like the Hesperian Space Agency created, when was it? Five years ago?'

'That only lasted a few microseconds. And it was an opening in space leading somewhere, but no one was sure where.'

'Well, I guess the technology must have moved on. Apparently it's fully functional now.'

'Hang on, what do we know about this?' Geoff began pacing more quickly, punching his right fist into the palm of his left hand as he thought of each question. 'Was it created artificially? Did the Thiosh make it? What are the risks? Who has been through it? Where does it come out? What happens if it drops you in the middle of a war zone? Can you get back again?'

Maura gripped his shoulders to hold him still. 'I don't know how it was made. I don't know how it works. But it's going to take us to Earth with the Thiosh. This will be our big chance to end the war.'

'I wish I had your optimism,' said Geoff.

'Come on, be positive. Mettravar always wanted to trade Thiosh technology for peaceful coexistence. The eejits on Europa didn't buy into it, but it'll be different on our own planet. I'm sure it will.'

The current had swung them around so they were now heading south. There was no point in fighting the ocean; it was soon propelling them at a greater speed than the whale-bot could manage on its own. The distraydar screen was speckled with images of individual Thiosh. They appeared to be content to go with the flow, even though the vortex would gradually suck them down. Geoff could not conceive what would happen after that. He had no choice but to trust their Thiosh friend, and hope for the best.

'Atherlonne's been sharing with me.' Maura paused to clear her throat. 'She thanked us for our time together. She was looking after us even before we knew of her existence. It was Atherlonne who redesigned the whale-bot to make it suitable for our use. Mettravar asked her to do it before the conference, and then she sent it to Port Authority quayside in case we needed it.'

'Mettravar must have known he was risking his life,' said Geoff.

'Sure he did. And there's something you don't know. Atherlonne's explained it to me. The whale-bot has a capability to change shape. It has a fat-bodied mode for carrying cargo. She left it that way to give us as much room as possible. But now it needs to be longer and narrower.'

'What! It's made of metal, not elastic.' Geoff started pacing again, this time back and forth across the bridge.

'Atherlonne says it's too wide to go through the gateway, but she can change its shape in transit. We're going to be more streamlined. It'll be an improvement, don't you think?'

Geoff faced Maura and shrugged his shoulders. 'I don't know what to think, I honestly don't. All I know is we're going faster and faster down an enormous plughole.'

'Well, it could be we're being sucked down a sewerage pipe to eternity, but there's no turning back. If you want something to do, just make sure we haven't left anything loose lying around. We'd better strap ourselves in. It could be a bumpy ride.'

The rushing sound outside the hull had increased in intensity. Geoff stared at the viz-boxes on the bridge console. They had begun to flash blank screens of different colours. He thought at first it was electronic interference but, when he peered out through the small observation windows, he could see with his own eyes flashes of light from different parts of the spectrum. Then he noticed something else. The circular windows had become elliptical.

The whale-bot began to barrel roll. Chen was quickest to react. Leaping to the control console, he flipped the bot out of auto-control and caught the rotation on the control surfaces. He manipulated the joystick controls with chopstick dexterity to keep the craft aligned with a graticule on the screen.

'Jaysis! That was a close one,' said Maura. 'I'd forgotten Chen's a celestonaut pilot.'

'His reflexes are razor sharp,' said Geoff. 'He wasn't wasting his time when he spent all those hours playing Atherlonne's computer games.'

'I liked her. I'm sorry she's not coming to Earth. I'm sure she would have helped end the war.'

Geoff put his arm round Maura and they watched Chen's mastery of the joysticks. The whirlpool was sweeping them around in an ever-decreasing circle. The instruments indicated the centrifugal force to be half their natural weight on Earth. Chen alleviated their discomfort by offsetting the hydroplanes so the g-force acted downwards, but it still felt very strange after they'd spent such a long period in low gravity.

Geoff was fascinated by Chen's skill. He'd shown himself to be better than the autopilot, although it had probably never been programmed for the conditions of the vortex. Geoff realised it was vital for Chen to keep the bot stable. If it once slewed sideways, the craft could pirouette and spin like a twig in white-water rapids. Perhaps the reason Atherlonne had streamlined the vessel wasn't only to get them through the entrance of the wormhole. It also made the craft more responsive. Previously, the experience of sailing the whale-bot had reminded Geoff of holidays on a canal narrowboat. Now it felt more like a racing toboggan.

After several hours, the forward lights began to illuminate clouds of bubbles and foam. The vortex was sucking them down a core of water and steam. It was too noisy for conversation. Maura had put her hands over her ears, but Geoff wanted to analyse the sound. It wasn't only caused by the turbulence outside; the hull itself was keening a lament. The vibration was causing Geoff's vision to blur and sometimes the whole structure shook with a resounding clang. He couldn't see any debris or rocks, but he sensed the force of the current was great enough to entrap huge chunks of coral reef, or lava rocks, or icebergs – anything was possible.

At last the violent shaking ceased and the external noise was replaced by the urgent ringing of an alarm. Geoff checked the readouts. 'Radiation levels are high,' he said. 'We're sailing through clouds of subatomic particles. I don't think we should hang around here too long. Chen, increase the propulsion to ninety-five per cent max speed.'

'Yes, Captain,' said Chen, in the formal tone of a celestonaut.

'We must be close to the middle of the vortex, like the eye of a storm,' said Maura. 'If we head for the point of lowest pressure, we should reach dead centre.'

'Captain, there is blue light on right side,' said Chen.

'It's probably where the radiation is coming from. It's causing Cherenkov emission,' said Geoff. 'You get it with nuclear reactors underwater.' He looked at Maura and she nodded. 'Okay, aim for it, Chen,' he ordered. 'Full speed ahead.'

The forward camera showed them approaching . . . something. Geoff struggled to comprehend the image before him. It was like looking down on a fountain with the water flowing in reverse, pouring into a volcanic crater of blue lava. It was unearthly, seething and rippling with unnatural motion. Geoff shut his eyes and covered his face with his hands. He was overwhelmed by the thought it was a vision humankind was never intended to see.

Seconds later, he found himself weightless and was aware both Maura and Chen had been screaming at the top of their voices. All signal levels were off scale, the screens were black, and there was no way of telling where they were. Was this the wormhole? How long would it take to reach Earth? He thought back to where Europa and Earth had been in their orbits, and calculated in his head. If they were really travelling to Earth down some sort of express highway at the speed of light, they should reach their destination in forty-three minutes. But his answer was purely academic. With all their control and instrumentation systems offline, they had no way of measuring time. Geoff was in a dream state, almost comatose. In spite of feeling a reluctance to speak or even look at the others, he glanced quickly at Maura. She was frowning with her eyes closed. They were in limbo, and all they could do was wait.

After what seemed like hours, Geoff made a conscious effort to raise his head and look around. Like him, Chen and Maura were slumped in their seats. He pulled his com-phone from his pocket and was surprised how heavy it felt. He checked Maura and Chen's biometrics and then his own. They had all retained a high adrenalin level but their pulse rates were almost normal. But what had happened to the whale-bot? It was eerily quiet and still. The screens were blank, and there was only profound darkness outside the observation windows.

He turned to Maura. 'We seem to have survived, but where are we?'

Part Three
Fight to the Death

Reunion

Maura booted up the navigation console. 'Ac-tu-all-y,' she said, and then paused, her face expressionless, 'we're back on Earth. You can unbuckle your harnesses now!'

Geoff and Chen cried 'Thank God' and '*Aiya*!' in one synchronised shout. They climbed out of their seats and swung each other like square-dance partners before collapsing in laughter.

'Hey, steady on,' said Maura. 'We're too weak for high jinks. We should have done more training.'

'Maura's right,' said Geoff. 'We must take it easy. And we don't know what we've come back to yet. Whereabouts on Earth are we, Maura?'

'The instruments show we're on the seabed at the bottom of the Pacific.'

'What's happened to Kai and the others. Where are they?'

'Give me a few minutes. I'll try and share with Leona.'

'Okay,' said Geoff. 'You do that and I'll run some status checks to make sure everything still works.'

Maura returned from her cabin and joined the others in the wardroom. 'They're all here: Kai, Leona and Huang. They're on Roosevelt Island. They want us to join them.'

'Roosevelt Island – in New Amsterdam?' asked Geoff in surprise.

'Sorry, I mean the one in the Ross Sea.'

'D'you mean Antarctica?'

'Very good, Geoff. Make sure you put on a thermal suit.'

'So we're not too far away from them. Have the Thiosh made it through okay?'

'To tell you the truth, I'm worried about that,' said Maura. 'Leona seems to think most of those who came are followers of Voorogg. He's in telepathic contact with Kai. I gave Leona access to some of my MIT files. Kai wanted to know the location of thermal vents at the boundary between the Pacific and Antarctic's tectonic plates.'

'Wonderful – the Thiosh'll be able to live there in peace.'

'But strangely Leona told me not to give them all the information. Why d'you think she said that?'

'Hm. She's a woman of mystery, all right,' said Geoff.

Geoff stood at the distraydar screen and watched the edge of the ice shelf draw closer. 'We've made good time. The bot seems to go about thirty per cent faster since it's been reshaped.'

'It's grand, don't you think?' said Maura, and Geoff smiled in agreement.

It wasn't easy to distinguish Roosevelt Island from the background landscape but, using the coordinates Leona had given Maura, they located the tumbledown shacks of the old whaling station.

'I hope this place doesn't make the whale-bot nervous,' joked Maura as they approached the quayside.

They scrambled down the rungs of the vessel's body and out onto the landing stage, where they stood awestruck by the scene before them – jagged mountains rising out of a sea of ice, brilliant white peaks casting indigo shadows, and ice sculptures backlit with sugared rims. A group of penguins began a wobbly march towards them as if in greeting. But soon the chill of the wind reminded them of their need for shelter.

'Here comes a rocket-sledge,' said Maura, the wind dispelling her misted breath as she spoke.

Leona climbed out and welcomed them, hugging and kissing them, while the trio from the whale-bot returned her greeting with equal enthusiasm. She led them aboard the sledge and handed them elastomeric thermal suits, gloves and reactive goggles. But, even after they were fully encased in thick layers of insulation, Leona continued to embrace and kiss them. Her body language was easy for Geoff to interpret – it was obvious she was mightily relieved to see them, and was in no hurry to transport them to the tumbledown shacks that comprised the whaling station. He was happy to be part of a celebration. After all, both groups had come through life-threatening trials since they were last together. But he suspected there was another reason. Did she now identify herself more with the whale-bot crew than with the *Aquila's*? If so, he would have to watch Kai and Huang very carefully.

Geoff mentally parked his misgivings and concentrated on the sensation of returning to Earth. After five years in space, the brightness of the sun, the cloudscape, and the sight of the jagged ice mountains filled him with joy. It was clear his companions were similarly excited, judging by the way they were giggling like school children. Leona was just as animated as she told them of the adventures she'd had with Kai and Huang in the *Aquila*. But when Maura asked about the fate of the *Mohawk*, she became more sombre.

At last Leona fired up the sledge and piloted the new arrivals to the whaling station complex, past the derelict shacks and broken equipment. Geoff was pleasantly surprised to discover the building they entered had been impressively restored. Once he'd taken off his outer garments, he felt very comfortable in the homely but well-appointed living space. The blazing log fire soon thawed the chill from his bones. Huang offered them shots of rum, evidently left by previous occupants, and the disquiet Geoff had felt as they'd journeyed through the wormhole became a faint memory. Kai came in and, in contrast to Leona, greeted them formally before asking Huang to show them to the prefabricated cabins he'd prepared as their sleeping quarters. Then Leona enquired if they all liked fish stew. Geoff had the impression it would make a frequent appearance on the menu.

After breakfast the next day, Kai called a meeting and related news of the war. He told them he'd been able to follow developments via

Hesperian and Khitan radio and TV transmissions. There'd been no nuclear exchanges for some time, but the Hesperians had recently won a series of battles fought conventionally. Their army had invaded Khitan territory and had marched westwards across Kathay. The forces of the Empire were in retreat, but this was deliberate. The Khitan strategy was to destroy everything in the path of the Hesperians, to ensure none of the resources of their land could be used by the invading army. The Khitan government had withdrawn to the high plateau region of Xizang, and had set up a command centre in Lhaza. The invading force had become snowbound in the mountains. But with spring coming, they would soon be on the move.

'The conflict has almost destroyed the Empire,' said Kai. 'The war is yet another illustration of humankind's base stupidity and ignorance. Once again, the homo sapiens species has been profligate in its expenditure of resources on a pointless venture, which is driving it to extinction.'

'I believe the Khitans launched an unprovoked attack,' said Geoff.

'Only because you Hesperian bastards planned to do the same,' responded Huang. For the first time, Geoff mentally sized up his muscular frame, and pondered how telekinesis could be used to defeat him in combat.

'Nothing has revealed the inferiority of human society more than the example of the Thiosh,' continued Kai. 'As a biological domain, they are clearly superior to us humans, in either the east or the west. They are welcome here on Earth. We must bow to their will and use our low-level intelligence to give them our full support.'

'Kai, this isn't like you,' said Geoff. 'What's happened? You are the wisest, most sensitive person I've ever met. Why are you talking like this?'

'The old ways have passed. There will be a new order, and the weak shall be swept aside.'

'Just a minute,' said Geoff urgently, but Maura gripped his hand hard and whispered to him to shut up.

He followed Maura outside to their cabin. They went in and Geoff slammed the door. 'You stopped me speaking. Are you on his side too?' he demanded.

'I am not. You'd better believe it. I just didn't want you to go head to head with him yet.'

'What the fuck is he talking about? Clearly superior? It's racist – or should I say domainist talk. You're the biologist.'

'I know, I didn't like what I was hearing, either,' said Maura. 'Kai's like a different person. Leona says something happened to him when they landed on Euphrosyne. Something that fundamentally changed him.'

'He didn't seem very surprised by our arrival via a wormhole. How did he know about it?'

'I don't think Leona told him we were coming. It must have been Voorogg. All the Thiosh knew about it.'

'You listen to their thought waves,' said Geoff. 'Why did Voorogg make the trip and not Atherlonne?'

'Not all Thiosh wanted to leave. Atherlonne thought it was her duty to protect those that remained.'

'Has the wormhole always been there?'

'Speaking as an oceanographer,' said Maura, 'if it'd been a feature on Earth for any length of time, I'm sure we would have known about it. Perhaps the Thiosh made it as an escape route from Europa.'

'You know, I can't believe that. I read about Thiosh history when we were in the cavern, but there was no hint they had lived anywhere else but on Europa, nothing about them using wormholes. If they'd had space-warping technology, they would have travelled before, wouldn't they?'

'I s'pose so. But if Thiosh didn't make the wormhole, who or what did?'

Lost at Sea

Over the next few weeks Leona and Chen organised the domestic arrangements of the settlement, and Huang occupied himself improving their accommodation. No one quite knew what Kai was working on. He disappeared for long periods and the others suspected he'd found a sort of hideout within the complex where he could meditate, or telepathise with someone or something.

Geoff busied himself monitoring the terrestrial uni-net so he could identify parts that were still active. He was disappointed to discover the Unified Nations seemed to be defunct. There'd been no activity on the UN network for over six months, and his encrypted messages of enquiry remained unanswered. As far as he could tell, the war had ground to a standstill. He was pleased neither side appeared capable of a knock-out blow, but frustrated there was no dominant power he could contact about the Thiosh.

He had hoped to win the support of the UN to reserve some areas of the seabed where Thiosh could live undisturbed. He'd known this would never be easy, but it was certainly impossible while the Federation and the Empire were at war. He discussed this with Maura, who agreed they had no choice but to wait to see what would happen. Meanwhile, she planned to carry out some scientific studies to assess how much the Earth, and its oceans, had been changed by the war.

Chen reported to Geoff that the top half of a satellite dish was sticking out of the snow on the west side of the settlement. They enlisted Huang's help and, after a day and a half spent cutting into the ice with a power saw and hacking out the blocks, they uncovered a brick building. Some of the windows had been smashed by what must originally have been a snowdrift. It had then compacted into solid ice, and this had sealed and protected the structure from further degradation. They sprayed de-icing fluid into the crevices around a heavy oak door. It was clearly the main entrance and, as it was not locked, it was relatively easy to open.

They had stumbled upon a laboratory. At some stage a group of research scientists must have based themselves in the complex, and much of the apparatus appeared still to be usable. Even the lights worked off the generator supply. Geoff and Maura busied themselves, restoring the lab to working order.

'The equipment here's pretty antiquated, but it's adequate for some basic research,' Maura told Geoff. 'Shall we use the whale-bot to carry out some surveys? I want to see how badly the sea's contaminated.'

'Good idea,' said Geoff. 'It's two years since the Khitan nuclear strike. Any fallout will have been carried around the Earth's oceans. It may have largely dissipated.'

'We can take the old Becquerel monitor to see if there are any hot spots.'

'Right, and if we dive down to the plate boundary, you could check out the extremophile microbes you love so much – and maybe we'll see how the Thiosh have settled in.'

'That's grand,' said Maura. 'Shall we take Chen? He can help us get ready to sail.'

———

In the event, Kai made Huang available to help them rather than Chen. After five days' intensive preparation, they were ready to leave. Geoff looked for Kai before they left, but he was nowhere to be found. Chen took them down to the quayside in the rocket-sledge. They called up the whale-bot and climbed aboard. Geoff was elated. Their strange vessel felt like a second home, and he'd come to realise he was happier at sea than on land.

Once the mountains of Antarctica had dipped below the horizon, Maura asked Huang to take the helm so she could spend time on deck with Geoff, standing in the bows while the wind frosted their faces with salt spray. They stayed like that for a long time before climbing down to the bridge.

The terrestrial GPS system was no longer functioning and they navigated by dead reckoning. After three days, Geoff's calculations showed they were above the Pacific–Antarctic Ridge, the divergent zone between two tectonic plates. He fastened the hatches and, returning to the bridge, he asked Huang to steer them slowly down to a depth of two kilometres. Maura sampled the water at one-minute intervals and detected alpha radiation at a level significantly greater than normal. Geoff periodically checked the profile of the seabed, and his attention was drawn to an area of activity.

'Maura, look at the sonar scanner,' he said. 'What are those objects shuffling back and forth?'

Soon they found themselves sailing though a group of Thiosh robots. Some were very familiar, and there were other types they'd not encountered previously. But the objects that fascinated Geoff most weren't moving at all. They were rectangular solids, spheres and cylinders. Such regular geometrical shapes were out of place in a marine environment. They had a metallic appearance, gleaming in the glow of the whale-bot's floodlights. Interspersed were irregular cones of non-reflective material. Geoff surmised they were heaps of spoil from excavations.

'You know, I think the Thiosh have joined the construction industry,' he said. 'It looks like they're building industrial plant.'

Maura checked the instrument readouts. 'The pH has gone up. I think there's sulphuric acid present. Perhaps the Thiosh are extracting sulphur from subterranean coal reserves. They're not bothering to crowd round the vents like they did on Europa.'

'What do you make of those rows of circular slabs?'

'A parking zone for mini-subs?'

As part of Geoff's duties at the Unified Nations, he'd had to review a great deal of secret information. Not for the first time, his experience weighed heavily upon him, and he wished he could be as innocent as Maura.

'They're the same as I've seen many times before,' he said, 'in secret reconnaissance photos. We're looking at missile silos under construction.'

Geoff realised the whale-bot had stopped moving. He looked up at where Huang had been standing at the helm, and found himself staring at the spiked electrode of a tezla gun. Geoff was momentarily bewildered. Then he laughed. 'Very funny, Huang. I like your joke.'

'Both of you, stand still with your hands on the chart table!' Huang ordered.

'What's the problem?' demanded Geoff. 'Have we spotted something we weren't meant to see?'

'It does not matter what you see. Soon Thiosh will govern the Earth. They will colonise the oceans, not just your plate boundaries. They will build great cities under the sea.'

Geoff made his voice sound confident. 'They'll have to talk to us humans first. We may agree to them staying, but they cannot take our resources without asking. The Southern Ocean is under Hesperian jurisdiction.'

'Your Federation will have no choice. The Thiosh will control the Earth from orbiting satellites. Any resistance will be vaporised with gamma rays. You are about to see a new world order!'

'And Kai, you and Chen will be honorary emperors, I suppose?' said Maura, her hands on her hips.

'Perhaps not Chen – he is too weak. But Kai and Voorogg understand each other.'

'I see,' said Geoff, putting his arm round Maura to keep her calm. 'So what is it you want from us, Huang?'

'I want you put away. You are Hesperian, and you know too much. But our friend Voorogg has a safe place for you. You will not be harmed, just kept where you cannot interfere.'

The tezla pistol glowed red hot. Huang yelped and it clattered on the deck. Geoff gave Huang a sharp poke in his solar plexus, hard enough to incapacitate any normal man for several minutes. But Huang wasn't a normal man. He stepped forward into a low stance and, with a shout, released a thrust-punch. Geoff was thrown sprawling over the main control desk. Huang bent over him with his fist clenched for a second punch. Maura leapt on his back and gripped him in a stranglehold. Huang slashed back with his elbow, knocking her across the bridge. Geoff rejoined the fight, but Huang sliced his legs from under him with a low spinning heel kick.

The Khitan grabbed the tezla from the deck. 'Now, do as you are told!' he ordered. 'Stand up and keep your hands on the table.'

Geoff got up slowly, helped Maura to her feet and looked into her eyes. She shook her head and sighed. Moving behind the table, Geoff defiantly planted his hands down on the open navigation chart, his fingers splayed to show he had no weapon. He looked around and his eyes alighted on the equipment on the bench behind Huang. The Becquerel radiation monitor was an old-fashioned piece of kit, about the size and weight of a nanowave cooker.

Huang neither heard Geoff raise the monitor in the air, nor the sound as it fell onto his unprotected head. The Khitan sank to the floor on top of the tezla, which discharged itself with the crack of a whip. A blue discharge corona snaked over his body for several seconds.

Geoff saw Maura's face, white as pack ice. 'Are you okay?' he asked her nasally.

'Better than you, by the look of you. You're pouring blood. I think your nose is broken.'

'I'll deal with it in a minute. We've got to do something with Huang. He's breathing okay – he could come round any moment.'

'Can we drag him to the storeroom and lock it from outside?'

'Okay, but I must take out the flares and the plasma gun first. We don't want him causing any more trouble. Then we'd better get the hell out of this place.'

Four hours later there was still no sound from the storeroom. 'I think I'll take him some water,' said Maura. 'You can cover me with the tezla gun in case he turns nasty again.'

'I'll go in first,' said Geoff. He unlocked the door and opened it slowly. Then, not seeing Huang, he kicked the door wide open and stepped inside with Maura following behind. There was a pool of blood seeping from under the storage racks. Moving as if in slow motion, Geoff peered behind – and saw Huang's body.

'Oh Christ!' said Geoff. 'I removed the harpoon gun, but I must have left a spear.'

'Jaysis, he's lying on his back! He didn't just fall on it. He must have pushed it right through . . .' Maura began to choke.

Geoff checked for signs of life, but after a few moments he stood up, staggering as he regained his feet. 'Sorry, he's gone. Did you know he was warrior caste? They can never stand being defeated. It means they've lost their honour.'

'I don't understand it. I can't believe Huang wanted to harm us. He wasn't evil. Perhaps we never got to know him well, but Chen looked up to him, and he was Kai's right-hand man. Now he's dead because of us.'

'We're not to blame. We only acted out of self-defence,' said Geoff. 'But I don't know if Kai and Chen will believe us.'

'Oh, sweet Jaysis, this is as bad as it gets,' said Maura, holding her head in her hands. 'It's like something or someone's corrupting our minds. Let's get back to the surface. I need some fresh air.'

Geoff sat down next to Maura in the wardroom. 'Did you get through to Atherlonne,' he asked, 'or whatever you call it when you're telepathising?

'I did,' said Maura. Geoff watched her carefully. Her eyes seemed unfocused. He decided to ask something scientific to get her talking.

'How does it work with the time lag?'

'What time lag?'

'Atherlonne's on Europa. That's at least six hundred million kilometres away. It'd take at least half an hour for a radio message to arrive.'

'I meant to tell you,' said Maura. 'All the Thiosh still alive are now on Earth. The group that wanted to stay on Europa hadn't reckoned on OPDEO's obsession to find and kill them. Atherlonne and a few others had to escape while they could.'

'So, they came through the wormhole as well? Where are they now?'

'They're in the North Pacific, but we don't want Kai or Voorogg to know. Leona and I have been keeping it secret.'

'It's great Atherlonne's on Earth,' said Geoff. 'Does she have any idea what Kai's up to?'

Maura met Geoff's eyes. 'It's not good,' she said softly. 'Atherlonne thinks Kai ordered Huang to hijack the whale-bot. Kai plans to use the rebel Thiosh to fight the Hesperians.'

'Oh Christ! Are we on the run again?'

'Atherlonne said we should get away from Roosevelt Island, but we'll have to go back there first to pick up stores and – more importantly – Leona. She's Hesperian and we can't leave her in enemy territory.'

Geoff closed his eyes to think.

'Geoff?'

'Okay, this is the plan. Do your sharing trick with Leona and get her to load the rocket-sledge with enough supplies for a long voyage. We'll meet up at the edge of the ice shelf north of the island.'

'How can we help Huang?' asked Maura.

Geoff looked hard at her. She was speaking as if he was still alive. He knew they must give his soul some peace, and theirs too.

'We'll take his body ashore in the inflatable. If Leona brings the rocket-sledge, we can send him back to the whaling station on autopilot. We'll attach a letter to Chen asking him to perform a ceremony appropriate for a deceased Khitan warrior.'

'Thank you,' said Maura. 'But you said a long voyage? Where are we going to go?'

'How about Oztralia?' said Geoff. 'And ask Leona to bring another radiation monitor from the lab. The Becquerel doesn't seem to work anymore.'

Walkabout

Maura kept the whale-bot underwater, carefully following the contours of the Parramatta riverbed as they entered Port Jackson. She raised the periscopic camera and scanned the skyline.

'I don't get this,' she said. 'Where's the Harbour Bridge?'

'Pan round,' said Geoff. 'Shit, that looks like part of the Opera House roof, on its side. There's a bit of a stump where the Sky Tower should be, but no sign of the Chifley or the MLC Centre. They're just heaps of rubble.'

Maura gasped. 'Jaysis, I've just done an external scan. The radiation's at more than two thousand millisieverts per hour. That's enough to kill you. Sydney must have been nuked. We can't dock here.'

Leona sat cross-legged in a lotus position. 'We must land somewhere else, a long way away,' she said in a monotone. She seemed to sense Geoff and Maura staring at her. She opened her eyes and spoke in her normal voice. 'There's a place on the western coast where the desert meets the sea. That's where we must go.'

'Are you sure?' asked Geoff. 'As far as I know, there's nothing there. I don't think we're likely to find any help in the desert.'

'I heard a calling from a very ancient place. But it's a very long way from the coast. We shall have to go walkabout to get there.'

'We'll do it like the old Aboriginal people,' said Maura.

'Perhaps more like their spirits,' said Leona.

The wind had reached hurricane force and the whale-bot was struggling to climb a mountain of water, only to plunge steeply down the other side of each wave. Maura took the craft down below the surface, where the sea was calmer.

'Can we take a look topside again,' said Geoff as they rounded South East Point. 'Perhaps we can stop at Melborn and find someone in authority to speak to.'

The sea was much calmer now but it was soon evident from the periscope's biometer that the wind from the city was carrying radioactive dust. They had no choice but to continue their course.

One thousand kilometres further west, Geoff asked Maura to enter the straits between Jangaroo Island and the Fleurien Peninsular. They extended the periscope and measured the atmospheric radiation.

'Shit,' said Geoff, 'it looks like Adelayd's been nuked as well.'

'Sorry, Geoff,' said Maura, 'but we've got to do what Leona says. You have to accept she can see into the future. She's had a vision. We should let her guide us.'

'It's really not a problem,' said Leona. 'We can't escape our destiny, no matter how hard we try.'

'Okay, I give in,' said Geoff. 'If everyone's happy to be irrational, that's fine by me. Carry on up the western coast and we'll see if we can land there.'

They did not surface again until they approached the North West Cape. They boarded the bot's inflatable, taking just the minimum of survival equipment. Maura programmed the whale-bot to dive to the seabed in five hundred metres of water. Geoff's biometer showed no significant levels of contamination, and they landed in a rocky cove. They knew they would need a cover story if they encountered any local residents. However, as they had become completely soaked sitting in the inflatable, they could readily claim their yacht had just sunk. They certainly looked the part.

In the event, there was no one to be seen on the beach or in the surrounding area. They buried their craft in the sand and climbed through an apple orchard to a single-storey farmhouse with a corrugated iron roof. Even while they were some way off, it was obvious the residents had abandoned the building. Geoff knew the population in the area had never been great, but he feared the war might have taken its toll even here.

The front porch was littered with pots, pans, clothes, and even a com-phone. The occupants had clearly left in a hurry, but there was no clue as to where they'd gone. There was a truck in the yard, and drums full of fuel in the barn. The solar panels on the roof were still working, providing power to a desalination plant. At least they would have plenty of water.

After they'd nanowaved food they found in a freezer and enjoyed a hearty meal, they took it in turns to keep watch while the others slept. The next morning Leona reported she'd had another vision during the night. The Earth had spoken to her. It was mourning the destruction of the Oztralian cities, and the millions of inhabitants who'd perished. It beckoned her from Aiers Rock, called Uluru by the ancient Anangu people long since exterminated by European and Asian settlers. It was a sacred site, inhabited by a spirit who would help them, the Earth had said. Geoff was sceptical. He'd hoped to find some remnant of the Unified Nations within a big Hesperian city. In his opinion, trekking over the outback to look for a spirit was, at best, a distraction. But Maura supported Leona in her conviction they must go to Aiers Rock, and Geoff acquiesced. He hoped the population of Aliss Springs may have escaped the devastation that had befallen the coastal cities.

Later that day, they loaded up the truck and set off, with Geoff at the wheel. They headed east, following a track into the outback. Initial progress was good but, after twenty miles, the track petered out. They continued, zigzagging around rocks and scrubby bushes. It was a relief to stop at night, mix up gruel from cereals and chew on strips of dried meat, provisions they'd taken from the farmhouse. They drank black tea to replace the fluids they'd lost during the heat of the day, but they had no way of washing. They slept under the constellation of the Southern Cross, surrounded by the bright eyes of dingoes, attracted by their unwashed bodies. They carried on the next day, and the next, jolting over the uneven ground, until they felt their internal organs would be pulverised to jelly. The truck suffered three punctures and, each time, Geoff changed the wheel, using one from the spare set they'd loaded in the back. *But what will we do when they're all gone?*

They were bumping down the bank of a flash-flood gulley when Geoff realised the vehicle was sliding out of control. 'Jesus Christ!' he swore as the truck's progress was arrested by an irregularly shaped boulder. They all got out and stared, open-mouthed, at the radiator spraying water like a burst artery.

'Can we repair it?' asked Leona.

Geoff shook his head. 'You'd need to braze it and we haven't got the equipment. I'm afraid this is serious.'

'Okay, we must keep calm,' said Maura. 'What are our options?'

'It's possible to walk in the bush,' said Leona.

'Ha!' said Maura. 'You told us we had to go walkabout.'

'The Aborigines spent their lives doing it. We can do it too. But we'd have to leave virtually everything behind – even the water. We can't carry jerry cans.'

'Leona's right,' said Geoff. 'My com-phone says it's over forty degrees. We'll have to travel as light as we can.'

'We could walk at night,' said Maura, 'but, without shade, we'd never sleep during the day. I guess we've just got to do it, somehow.'

They filled their canteens and set off in single file. Geoff was in the lead, followed by Maura and then Leona. There was no path; Geoff had switched his com-phone onto solar-power and he used its compass to keep them heading east. The soil was arid coarse sand, punctuated by clumps of hummock grass and isolated bushes. They bivouacked in the twilight, conscious of their empty stomachs. Leona poked around under a saltbush. 'That's lucky!' she cried, and she pulled out a white, tubular object. She wrapped it in a leaf and gave it to Maura to roast on their fire, while she set about finding two more. After their meal, Geoff asked Leona what kind of root it was they'd eaten. 'It was a grub worm, Geoff,' she told him, laughing.

They tried to make their water last, but soon their canteens were dry. Geoff became mesmerised by the shimmering mirror that appeared periodically before them. It galvanised his muscles and he had to will himself not to run. *It's only a mirage,* he told himself.

Eventually they reached Hopkins Lake, a baked salt plain devoid of any moisture. They collapsed by a rocky outcrop, their disappointment draining the last vestige of energy from their limbs.

Geoff reached out for Maura's hand. He had a flashback to the time they'd sat in the bathyscaphe, trapped on the seabed, expecting to die. It was then that Leona started listening to the ground. She crawled around the boulders, placing her ear to the soil. She broke off a reed and embedded it in the sandy earth. As she sucked, she inflated her cheeks and then spat liquid into her canteen. Soon there was enough to share. It was dark and gritty, but tasted delicious.

Geoff realised his boots were turning into flip-flops, as the tips of the soles became detached. Maura's and Leona's footwear was less damaged, presumably because they were lighter on their feet. Geoff led them on, his boots bound up with strips of cloth ripped from his shirt. When the sun went down, they foraged for food: roots, berries, even spiders. They were up at dawn to suck dew from crevices in the rocks, before trekking onwards. Their skin was peeling and blistered, and their tongues so swollen they could barely speak. It was sunset on the seventh day when they saw a streak of red on the horizon. 'Uluru,' Maura croaked, and in tacit agreement they continued walking through that night.

By dawn they reached the bottom of the sandstone monolith rising three hundred and fifty metres above the surrounding bushland. They skirted around the perimeter and, pouring from the mouth of a cave above them, they found flowing spring water. Moët & Chandon could not have tasted better. They laughed with relief. As they continued to climb up a steep gulley, a bush turkey ran clumsily past, flapping its wings. It rose a few feet in the air, only to fall to the ground again, its neck at an unnatural angle. 'What are you looking at me like that for, Maura?' Geoff asked, but he could not conceal his smile.

Later that evening, they sat by the mouth of the cave, taking it in turns to rotate the turkey on a makeshift spit. Drips of fat fell in their open fire, its bright yellow flame casting their shadows deep into the cave behind them, while the trickling spring water glinted in the starlight. They slept well that night.

Revelation

Geoff got up while the others were still sleeping and caught a rabbit. There were enough edible roots and wild herbs around to make a stew but, without a cooking pot, they could only roast it. After they'd eaten, they swept up the ashes and spread dust over the area where the fire had been. 'We mustn't do anything to damage the environment,' said Leona. 'This is a sacred place, and we mustn't despoil it.'

'Can you sense what it's trying to tell us?' asked Geoff.

Leona shook her head. 'No, but I think it's right we came here. The Anangu told a legend about two tribes who'd been invited to a feast, but were distracted by a group of "Sleepy Lizard Women". The hosts became very angry, and there was a terrible battle. The leaders of both tribes were killed, along with many of their followers. Those that survived ate the dead bodies of their foes. The Earth rose up in grief because of what had happened, and created Uluru.'

'That sounds familiar,' said Geoff. 'Two tribes at war – these days it's the Khitans and the Hesperians.'

'There must be something here we're supposed to find,' said Maura. 'Let's climb to the top and look around.'

'Hey, what's that up there?' said Geoff. 'It looks like a dish or an aerial.'

'It's probably military,' said Maura. 'Is it a distraydar scanner?'

'No, it's too big. Would you believe it? It's a radio telescope.'

'I haven't heard of any astronomers here. Let's take a look.'

As they drew closer, Geoff saw a building built into a gap in the sandstone ridge. At that moment, a man appeared, climbing down from the dish. They hurried to the foot of the ladder to meet him. He was old. Even with regenerative drugs he must have been at least eighty. But he was tall, his face seemingly carved out of red bloodwood.

'Hooly dooley!' said the man, pushing up the brim of his bush hat. 'What are you dropkicks doin' here?'

'We came from the city,' said Geoff. 'We escaped before the missiles hit, and thought we'd hide in the bush.'

'And I'm a boomer's auntie,' said the man. 'This place ain't no hideaway – it's too obvious.'

Geoff looked at his boots, still bound with cloth strips. 'Okay, you're right. But you'd think I was lying if I told you the truth.'

'Now you're talkin'. I'm Wally, by the way. You look as if you need a beer. Not to mention a shower an' a change of togs. You stink, mate!'

⊱━➤

In a flash of ruby light, the sun slipped below the horizon. Geoff and Wally were sitting under the great dish, surrounded by empty cans of 4X Gold.

'We should have waited for Maura and Leona,' said Geoff. 'They'd enjoy a beer too.'

'Nah, don't worry, mate. The sheilas'll still be doin' their hair for a while yet.' The Oztralian drained his glass and opened a bottle of Sullivan's Cove Single Malt. 'We've gotta make the most of this. They don't make it anymore. So, you're tellin' me you've come from another planet with a load of aliens, and now you're tryin' to find 'em a home. Is that right?'

'It was actually the moon of a planet.' Now Geoff had decided to tell Wally the truth, he wanted to be accurate.

'Struth! I preferred your war refugee story. By the state of your nose, you look as if you've been in a war.'

'Let's just say that was the result of an unexpected betrayal.' They tossed back their whisky and Wally poured another.

143

'Well, at least you smell better now.' Wally laughed. 'I'll show you round the rig tomorrow. It might interest you, you bein' scientists an' all.'

━━◆━━

Geoff was trying hard to understand why an Anangu warrior was using a skull as a drum. *It's my skull. He must have scooped out my brains. I must find them, but he keeps stabbing my eyes with cactus spines. Oh Lord, now I've fallen over the edge of a waterfall!*

'Geoff Kirby – you're as useless as a bucket of steam. We've been up for hours while you lie there, catatonic. You were well scuttered last night. If you've got a hangover, it feckin' well serves you right for drinking without us!'

It was Maura's voice. Geoff made an effort to focus and saw her standing over him with an upturned glass in her hand. Geoff thought about the glass. *It must have contained water. Possibly ice cubes too. The evidence is dripping down my shirt.*

'Sorry, Maura,' he croaked. 'It was Wally. He doesn't get many visitors. I couldn't refuse a drink.'

'Obviously,' said Maura over her shoulder, as she marched imperiously out of the room.

Wally's breakfast was amazing: emu eggs, roo sausages and toasted home-made bread. They enjoyed the feast, all except Geoff who wasn't feeling up to it. But he did drink half a gallon of coffee. When they'd cleared away, Wally announced he would take them on a tour of the site.

'Are you researching anything specific?' asked Geoff huskily. 'Quasars, super novae, black hole lensing?'

'Nah, mate,' said Wally. 'No one's interested in astronomy anymore. The war's killed all that.'

'So what do you do?' asked Maura.

'I listen to messages from outer space. Come on, I'll show you.'

Geoff and Maura exchanged glances and followed Wally, who led them to an air-conditioned room full of computer servers. They all wiped their feet on a sticky mat before entering. Geoff realised they were entering a clean conditions area.

Wally started up a com-pad and chose an audio file to play back. It sounded like white noise. He displayed the signal as a waveform on the screen, and zoomed in to show the separate peaks and troughs. 'You think it's random, but you get repeats in the pattern – you see here, and here, and here?'

'Well, I'll be damned!' said Geoff, excited. 'But the time interval between the repeats is different.'

'Too right, that's the key. I've studied this. The interval varies, but it's not random. I counted 8,105 variations. A hell of a lot, but not infinite.'

'So 8-1-0-5 is some sort of magic number?'

'You know, for a Pommie, you're a real bonzer bloke. Yeah, 8-1-0-5. I grappled with that for months, tryin' to figure it out. Then I found this official Khitan government rulin'. It was to try and get 'em all writin' the same. It had a list of characters, an' guess how many there were.'

'8,105?' suggested Maura.

'You ripper! Yeah, so I did the correlation. Each time the pattern repeated, I measured the time interval, one out of 8,105. I picked out the character from the list, stuck it in a translation program, and, great gallopin' goannas, I got a message.' Wally paused, clearly waiting for the next question.

'And?' said Leona.

'Well – it was pretty weird stuff. I'll show you the transcripts. They're kinda funny in a perverted way. Real creepy.'

'D'you know where it was coming from?'

'Think I do. First thought – it's from a Khitan on their Mars base. Second thought – nah, we did for them when we nuked 'em last year. Last thought – signal's comin' from the middle of the asteroid belt.'

'Like from Euphrosyne?' asked Leona.

Wally looked at her intently and then nodded. 'I gotta a computer programmed up. Used the dish to beam up a response an' had a fair old yabber with this thing. Once upon a time, he was a Khitan. He replicated his brain as software in a robot body. This robot got cleverer and cleverer. It taught itself the whole damn total of all existin' knowledge.'

'So it is possible,' said Geoff, unconsciously speaking his thoughts aloud.

'It learnt everythin' that's ever been discovered,' Wally continued. 'It could make slave robots, any damn thing. But it was its computin' power that really lifted off. It had a way it could control atoms, and, after that, it didn't need no robot body, or hardware, or nothin'. It became pure AI.'

Geoff gave Maura a knowing look, remembering what Atherlonne had taught them: there were beings in the universe that were just intelligence – software without hardware.

Leona seemed to be mesmerised by the waveforms on the computer screen. 'Does it have a name?' she asked.

'Yup. It, he, whatever – calls itself Shetani.'

Leona nodded, as if she'd expected Wally's answer. 'In my language, Shetani means Man-devil. It's definitely a he.'

>

Geoff was sitting under the dish with Maura and Leona. They were reading transcripts of Wally's conversation with the being called Shetani.

'This creature is evil,' said Maura. 'The first thing he did was kill off the human version of himself.'

'He's a nasty piece of work, all right,' said Geoff. 'He can artificially create disasters: earthquakes, volcanic eruptions, floods. Then he infiltrates victims' minds and enjoys their suffering, without being harmed himself.'

'Yes, but he's subtle, you know,' said Maura. 'The victims think he has good intentions and the end justifies the means. Slowly he gets people to corrupt themselves, stealing, grabbing power, even killing.'

'I understand now what happened to Kai,' said Leona. Geoff and Maura stared at her open-mouthed for several seconds until she continued.

'When we were on Euphrosyne, Kai went off in the shuttle to set up a sentry post. He radioed us to say we should ignore his short-range transmissions until we were given the all clear. Then he spoke to someone, or something. We only heard one side of his conversation, but it seemed he was talking to something that existed in space, independent of material.'

'We think there are many entities like that,' said Geoff. 'Atherlonne told us they were called Virtuons.'

'Well, all I know is, from that time onward, Kai's personality changed,' said Leona. 'He became introverted, and spent long hours scanning radio waves as if he was listening for something. But the big change was he seemed to be driven, totally focused on some mission, and it made him utterly ruthless. All his wisdom and compassion had been sucked out of him.'

'Okay, somehow you knew we had to come to this place,' said Geoff. 'I don't know what led us here, but let's assume we were meant to meet Wally and hear his story. You believe it helps us understand the past. The question is, what does it mean for the future?'

'Shetani is already amusing himself with us humans,' said Maura. 'He probably has an insatiable appetite for that sort of thing. He may have lots of experiments he wants to carry out on us.'

Geoff nodded. 'He wants us all as slaves. And he's not the only one. According to Huang, when he tried to hijack the whale-bot, the rebel Thiosh are planning world domination, and we saw what they were doing to achieve it. And Kai's in cahoots with Voorogg – Huang told us that.'

'I've had a thought,' said Leona. 'If Shetani has to communicate with radio interference, it means he can't do telepathy – at least, not at first. He gets close to people and then changes their brains somehow. That's what he did to Kai. But until he's got someone hooked, he has to communicate more physically. That could be why he's infiltrated Kai. He's using him as a go-between to incite Voorogg to take over the planet.'

'At least Shetani is putting a stop to humans persecuting Thiosh,' said Maura.

'That's not his motive,' said Leona. 'He wants the human race subjugated so it's easier to use us as playthings. He's a lazy bastard. He doesn't want to micromanage twelve billion people, or however many there'll be after the war.'

'Sweet Jesus, Mary and Joseph. This is my worst nightmare. An evil artificial intelligence using an alien race to build weapons to attack Earth, while the humans are trying to kill each other. Here we are, back on our home planet, but what on Earth can we do?'

'We must destroy Shetani,' said Leona.

Return to Antarctica

'Hi, Wally,' Geoff called. 'Have you got a boomerang, by any chance? I'd like to see one.'

'Sure, Pom, I've got an old one. But they were really only for the Abbo kids – God bless 'em! There aren't any anymore. Real throwin' sticks were for huntin' and flew straight. But I can give you a demo, if you like.'

Wally disappeared into his accommodation and came back with a beautiful boomerang made from polished tulip oak. They walked out to a high point on the ridge and, with a practised hand, Wally cast the boomerang high in the air. It circled and fell back at his feet.

'Thanks, I can see you're an expert,' said Geoff. 'But can I show you a trick the aliens taught me?'

The boomerang raised itself off the ground and hovered in the air before them. Then it shot off in an arcing trajectory, performed a figure of eight and returned to land before them.

'Hooly dooley!' Wally said, and pushed up the brim of his bush hat, unconsciously repeating his actions when he first met Geoff.

'I don't know how much you believed of our story, but I wanted you to know it was the truth,' said Geoff. 'You've helped us more than you know. We want to thank you. We can't give you anything. We came out of the bush with nothing. But perhaps one day we'll be able to return your hospitality.'

Wally grinned. 'Well, that's a pretty little speech, and I thank you for it. But I knew your story was dinky-di. You were so pissed, you could only tell the truth.'

'If I could ask you another favour, can we stock up with provisions? We've got the mother of all walkabouts ahead of us.'

'Nah, no worries, mate,' said Wally. 'I'll fly you back in my airplane.'

>——◆

Wally entered a command into his com-phone and the ground began to vibrate. For a moment, Geoff thought Wally had summoned an earthquake just by pressing a button. A huge, irregular hole appeared in the rock face. Geoff closed his eyes to accustom them to the shadowy interior. Then he opened them wide. A delicate flying machine, like a dragonfly, stood in a vast cavern, dug deep into the monolith that was Uluru. Geoff guessed the hangar was actually a tunnel, and the plane could be flown into one opening and out of the other. He turned to look outwards, and saw how the rock fell away in a steep but smooth incline. *Is that the launch ramp?* he wondered.

Geoff, Maura, and Leona climbed into the narrow fuselage and sat in line. Wally carried out the preflight checks, set each of the four propellers spinning in turn, and then powered the craft towards the cavern's mouth. The machine hummed loudly but without the roar of a jet or rocket engine. Checking the cockpit dials, Geoff realised the plane was powered electrically, the wings constructed entirely from photovoltaic cells.

'Hang onto your breakfast,' said Wally as he released the brakes. The plane crept to the brink of the launch ramp and tipped down. It accelerated virtually in free fall for a few seconds and then the wings lifted it clear. Wally banked into the prevailing wind and circled to gain height. They rose higher and higher, until Uluru was no more than an orange half-moon pinned to a damask backdrop.

>——◆

The journey passed like a dream. Wally landed close to the farmhouse they'd raided before their walkabout. They found it was still deserted, but they had no desire to linger on the coast. It was time to say goodbye. Maura and Leona kissed Wally, and he enthusiastically kissed them back. Geoff took his hand and held it for long seconds after shaking it. Then the trio walked to the beach and dug up the inflatable. There was still enough charge in its batteries to fill it with air. They powered the craft a few hundred metres from the shore and Geoff called the whale-bot via his com-phone. The glistening machine rose from the seabed and shot a fountain of water high in the air. Geoff felt it was pleased to see them, but then reprimanded himself for being crazy. As they climbed aboard they saw the solar-powered plane swoop over their heads, waggle its wings and turn to fly east, returning over the outback.

Maura plotted a course for Antarctica, and they set sail. Following the revelations at Uluru, they'd had intense discussions about whether they should go back. Geoff would have preferred to go anywhere else other than Roosevelt Island. He was worried how Kai and Chen would react to them now Huang was dead. He felt guilty even though Huang had taken his own life. But his conscience told him it was his duty to return.

Leona had admitted she'd had her own difficulties with Huang, but it was Kai she was most concerned about. She'd been very close to him, prior to their landing on Euphrosyne. She wanted to show him Wally's transcripts. They could reveal to him how Shetani was manipulating humans, using them for his own purpose. She hoped Kai would conclude he was also a victim.

Geoff pondered the significance of Wally's revelations. *How had Shetani managed to trick Kai, and why hadn't he realised he was being used?*

>---●

As they neared Roosevelt Island, they radioed the base and asked Chen to come out to meet them. He came alone, but stepped out of the rocket-sledge holding a plasma gun at the ready.

'He committed suicide, Chen,' said Maura hurriedly. 'We locked him up because he'd threatened us with a tezla pistol.'

Chen kept the gun pointing at Geoff, as if he expected a telekinetic attack. 'Why Huang do that?' he demanded.

'He told us we were going to be put out of harm's way,' said Geoff. 'We don't know why he attacked us, but I think he was following Kai's orders.'

Chen said nothing, and Geoff continued. 'There was a fight. We managed to overpower him and lock him in the storeroom. I tried to remove anything dangerous, but I forgot the harpoon spears. It was my fault. I'm sorry, Chen.'

'Geoff was hurt at the time,' added Maura. 'Have you seen his nose?'

They remained standing in silence for long seconds. Then Chen lowered his weapon. 'I think you tell truth,' he said.

'I not know Huang would try hijack,' said Chen. They were sitting around the log fire in the communal lounge. Chen had built up a huge stack of firewood after demolishing some of the disused wooden shacks.

'We wanted you in our crew, like the old days,' said Geoff, 'but Kai gave us Huang instead of you.'

'He is changed,' said Chen, sadly. 'You know what went wrong?' In answer to Chen's question, the Hesperians told him what they knew. Leona explained Kai had encountered an alien when they were on Euphrosyne, and Geoff gave an account of how they'd discovered the Virtuon Shetani was controlling humans for his own evil purposes.

At this point, Chen himself filled a gap in their collective knowledge. 'Maybe coincidence,' he said, 'but when Kai train as novice monk, there is Prior in monastery called Shetani. Kai goes back to the monastery when Abbot is dying, but Shetani no help. He not like Abbot. Maybe he poisons him.'

They'd expected Kai would soon join them but, when a man in a thermal suit came in from outside, Geoff thought at first it was someone else. He now had a full head of hair, as grey as a storm cloud. Geoff was ready in case Kai pulled a gun on them but, in the event, he only greeted them formally, without smiling, and waited for them to speak.

'We need to talk to you, Kai,' said Maura. She explained how they'd been surveying the ocean for radioactivity and had seen the undersea cities the Thiosh were constructing, including military installations. Their discovery had seemed to alarm Huang, and she gave a brief account of how he had died.

Geoff watched Kai carefully to note any response, but he remained impassive.

'To tell the truth,' said Maura, taking out a box file from a filing cabinet, 'we were afraid of what you might do to us if we returned. We went to Oztralia and met an old astronomer who gave us these transcripts of conversations with a being called Shetani.'

It was then Geoff saw it – a flicker of reaction in Kai's eyes.

'We've come back because we think it's vitally important that you read them – for your own well-being.'

Kai accepted a copy of the transcripts but made no attempt to look at them.

'I agree with Maura and Geoff,' said Chen. 'Please read papers.'

Kai put some more wood on the fire.

'It's possible for such a being to dominate humans,' said Leona, urgently. 'He can use them as slaves for his own purpose and gratification. Think, Kai, could that have happened to you?'

'Thank you for your concern for my mental health,' said Kai.

'This is me, Leona, remember? Look at the evidence, please!'

'If you will excuse me, I have urgent business,' said Kai. Then he put on his thermal suit and stepped out into the ice field, leaving the transcripts behind.

Virus

Maura was sitting with her arm round Leona, who was periodically keening as if she was in mourning.

'We just need to give him time to consider,' said Geoff, but he knew his voice sounded hollow. He was convinced Kai knew about Shetani, but was not aware the evil Virtuon was a threat to him and the whole of humankind.

Chen had gone out to chop up more firewood, even though they already had a huge stockpile. On his return, Geoff asked him if he'd carried out formal funeral rites for Huang, in keeping with his status as a Khitan warrior. 'Come and see,' said Chen. They dressed in their boots and suits. Chen led them outside where the sun was still shining. They followed the perimeter track and entered a cave in a glacier, excavated by spring water. Sunlight, filtered green-blue by the translucent ice, illuminated the first few metres of the tunnel. But, as they went deeper into the darkness, they turned on their flashlights, dazzlingly bright in the confined space. Once their eyes had adjusted to the reflective glare they saw him – Huang encased in a block of ice. His Khitan armour was a tomb within a tomb; only his eyelids were visible through slits in his armoured face mask.

'What will happen to him?' Maura asked.

'Ice cap is breaking,' said Chen. 'One day, tomb is part of iceberg. It melt and Huang sink to bottom. That is best.'

They took off their thermal hoods and stood bareheaded, until the cold forced them to return.

Next day, Leona visited the lab and found Maura setting up and testing equipment.

'There's some coffee left,' said Maura. 'Come and sit down with me.'

'I've been thinking,' said Leona. 'Thinking all night, actually. Yes, I'd love some coffee. I need it!'

'I didn't sleep too well, either. I don't think it's possible to force Kai to read the transcripts, is it?'

'No, he's rejected them without even looking at them. Now he's nowhere to be seen and the rocket-sledge is missing. He must have gone somewhere.'

'Where could he go?' asked Maura.

'Probably to Voorogg. He could have sent a robot vessel to pick him up. He could accommodate him, just as Mettravar did for us on Europa.'

'Before the fight, Huang told us Thiosh would take over the Earth. They'd destroy all opposition and make us slaves.' Maura waved her arms in agitation.' I feel so powerless, for Chrissakes!'

Leona put her arm round her. 'There's something you could do – if you're willing,' she said softly.

'Tell me. I'll do anything.'

'Well, I think we need to give Shetani a virus, something that will corrupt his software, big time – deliver a fatal error. I think Geoff might be able to design something like that.'

'Yeah, he probably could. I love Geoff, but he's a bit of a geek,' said Maura, glancing heavenwards. 'But how could we give Shetani a virus? How do we get to him?'

'You know, before Euphrosyne I thought Kai and I would become lovers. I think I know how to get close to him again. If Shetani is addicted to sensual pleasure, he may want to infiltrate me as well.'

Maura crinkled her nose. 'Leona, that's not a good idea. How would it help? Shetani's not going to let you corrupt his software.'

'We'll set a trap. You could put the virus in my brain. I know you can modify genetic code, and now you have a lab. Geoff will write the code, and you will embed it in my DNA.'

'No, no, no!' Maura shouted, slamming down her coffee cup. 'Even if it were possible, no one could predict what it'd do to you. It's far, far too dangerous.'

'And let Shetani turn the whole human race into puppets? Isn't that dangerous?'

'I don't want you to do it. Let me do it instead!'

Leona shook her head. 'Geoff needs you, and you need Geoff. I have no one – except Kai.'

'You would have made a great pair, I know, but Kai's so different now. A come-on might have worked in the past, but now he's obsessed by something. How are you going to make him amorous?'

'I may have to pretend a little, but leave that to me. You just work out with Geoff how to do the GM. I hate this Shetani with every cell of my body. I love Kai, but he's been perverted into a dehumanised slave. I'll do anything to get my revenge.'

When they were alone in their cabin, Maura told Geoff about her conversation with Leona. He agreed with Maura about the risk, but he couldn't help being excited by the challenge. 'Actually, the virus is the easy part. At its most fundamental level, Shetani's software comprises zeroes and ones. I could change all the ones to zeroes, or all the zeroes to ones. But we'd have to minimise the risk of him rebooting. The best chance would be to modify his code to random zeroes and ones.'

'So what's the hard part?'

'It's the brain–AI interface. Shetani is interpreting human brainwaves as expressions of feeling. We need to make Leona's brain emit the viral code as brainwave pulses.'

'Won't that interfere with her normal functions?'

'I think I could modulate her theta brainwaves to contain the virus information. They're frequencies our brains generate as we wake or drift off to sleep. Leona should only be affected for a few minutes each day. Otherwise she'll be completely normal. But the theta patterns also occur when we dream. I suspect Shetani will find them irresistible.'

'Be very careful, please,' said Maura.

Kai returned to the base but said nothing about where he'd been or what he was planning. He returned to his solitary style of living, eating and sleeping in a separate cabin, but Leona began to seek him out. She brought him special food and, while it was impossible for her to replicate Khitan specialities, she nevertheless managed to produce many appetising dishes. She commissioned Chen to catch fish, ducks and geese from the freshwater lakes and supplemented Kai's usual diet of shrimps, dried krill and edible sea-weed. Then she started bringing meals for herself as well as Kai, so they could eat together.

'I liked it when we could read each other's thoughts,' she said. 'Do you think we could do that again?'

Kai smiled and took her hand in his. 'I miss that time too, and it would be good to have someone to help me again. The Earth is entering a new era, and I have been focused on the changes we must make. I am sorry I have neglected you.'

'We met when you came to the Unidome on Europa to rescue Geoff and Maura,' said Leona, holding Kai's gaze. 'It was something I felt we had to do at the time, but do you think now it would have been better to let OPDEO keep them locked up? You must watch them carefully. They've killed Huang, and they want to stop you helping Voorogg. They may try to kill you too.'

'I know. That is why I wanted Huang to take them to Voorogg. He would not have harmed them, just kept them somewhere safely on the seabed. He might even have let them do scientific research. But I underestimated Geoff. It is a tragedy he misused the power the Thiosh gave him.'

'He overcame Huang with superhuman strength and killed him,' said Leona, as she massaged Kai's shoulders. 'You should take your revenge.'

'One day,' said Kai between grunts of pleasure.

'But what about these messages from Shetani? Was that who you were speaking to when we were on Euphrosyne?'

'I knew him in the past. In his new form he contacted me because he wanted to stop humans destroying themselves. He had acquired enormous power but he wished to use it wisely. He tunnelled through space–time and made a wormhole for the Thiosh to come to Earth. He asked me to help them create a new world order.'

'Geoff and Maura say Shetani is wicked, like an evil spirit,' said Leona. 'They claim he manipulates humans for his own pleasure. Let me take your shirt off, and I'll rub you with some perfumed ambergris.'

She opened the lid of the container and began kneading the waxy liquid into Kai's neck and shoulders. 'I found it when we first arrived and thought it might be useful.'

'Thank you. That is relaxing. It is very pleasant. Yes, you are right not to believe what Geoff and Maura tell you. They have been corrupted by the Thiosh leader, Atherlonne.'

'She blames us humans for the death of her partner Mettravar, and she is trying to vilify Shetani,' said Leona.

'Yes, these "transcripts" Geoff and Maura took from the Oztralian are, no doubt, stories invented by her.'

'But Chen said you knew Shetani when he was a human, and he poisoned the Abbot at your monastery. Is that true?'

'No, I was wrong,' said Kai. 'It was something I had suspected, and I challenged Shetani to explain why he had grown castor-bean plants when he was the Prior. But I felt ashamed when he explained he had done it out of consideration for the Abbot. He had only made castor oil to ease the Abbot's constipation. Hm, I love it when you do that.'

Geoff had created a nucleotide sequence to embody a fatal software virus. *If something is just an artificial brain, would destroying it be murder?* he wondered. But he knew, in any case, there was no way he could turn back. He joined Maura in the lab where she was working on the medication to target specific cells in Leona's brain. They would plant the new code in a part of her DNA that didn't serve as a pattern for protein sequences and should not interfere with the normal functioning of her body.

Yes, the word is 'should'. There's always an element of doubt. What's the next step? Maura will have to add the encapsulated DNA to a sample of Leona's cerebrospinal fluid, ready for re-injection.

'The serum to implant the virus – is it a medicine or a poison?' Geoff asked.

'Both, I suppose,' Maura replied. 'But then that's true for many substances. We have to hope it proves to be a remedy.'

The message Leona received from the sky wasn't jumbled into a radio signal or delivered to her com-phone. It could have been, but this was more beautiful, more intriguing. It was embedded in the aurora australis. Leona saw it in a swirling backwash of colours that had no names. It was a contract, a transaction, a three-way reciprocal promise. An offer based on humankind's most fundamental needs. If she gave her body to Kai, he would give his heart to her. They would seal their relationship by natural congress, and Shetani would endorse their union. She signalled her acceptance by holding a mirror to her window. The crystal ice flow crackled with spectral light as the incandescent heavens erupted.

Death Throes

Maura thought it was an earthquake. The bed she shared with Geoff had been lifted up and shoved violently against the cabin wall, the impact bringing down bookshelves and the wall-mounted viz-box screen. It was light outside, as it had been all night, but his com-phone indicated there was no power. She and Geoff extracted their thermal suits from an upturned locker and went outside, Geoff to the engine house and Maura to check if anyone was hurt.

Leona was lying on the floor of her cabin. Maura wondered if she'd been hit by debris, but she showed no sign of being injured. The lights flickered back on. She called Geoff. He came across to join her, and together they carried Leona back to their own hut. They made her as comfortable as possible, wrapped in synthetic furs. Maura stayed with her while Geoff went out to check the rest of the site.

Some of the structures on the ice flow at sea level had disappeared, including the whaling station jetty, boathouses, and the old processing plant. Other buildings had partially collapsed. There were even pools of seawater on top of the ice shelf. Evidently, Roosevelt Island had been hit by a tsunami. Fortunately the accommodation, the stores and the lab above the cliffs had survived. They had been constructed originally on the high plateau, presumably anticipating there would be a further rise in sea level due to global warming.

Geoff saw Chen outside and went over to check he was okay. He appeared shaken but otherwise alright. There was, however, no sign of Kai. The whale-bot had been secured in deep water but it was no longer sending any status signals. Geoff wondered if Kai had taken the craft to Voorogg.

Geoff entered the lab to check the equipment there. The seismograph was working and showed a sharp spike at the time the power had been lost. But the trace hadn't recorded any of the preceding tremors Geoff would have expected if there'd been an earthquake. He checked the lab's gravimeter. It was still functioning and showed a massive change in the gravitational field. The previous distortion around the wormhole's subterranean exit had disappeared. He printed out the new gravitron grid and returned to their cabin.

'You know, it looks to me as if the wormhole's collapsed,' he told Maura.

'Oh God, it can't be a coincidence. It must have been something to do with the virus. I think it's caused Leona to lose consciousness. Whatever we did to Shetani, the serum shouldn't have hurt her, but we need to see if anything's changed. Can you analyse a sample with her current DNA? Use a saliva swab.'

Geoff called Maura from the lab to tell her he'd begun the analysis, but they'd have to wait at least until midnight to get the results. Maura explained she'd been sharing with Atherlonne, who was currently local to the hydrothermal vents near the Aleutian Islands.

'What does she think happened?' asked Geoff.

'She said there was a major gravitational disturbance throughout the Solar System. Shetani was sucking gravity out of Jupiter when your virus got him. There was an uncontrollable power release, and it wrecked the wormhole. It looks as if your coding did its job.'

'Yeah, Wally has confirmed it too. Once I'd set up the computer to crunch the numbers, I got through to Oztralia using the 8105 code. Wally says he received Shetani's last ever transmission. His signal became more and more garbled, and then stopped altogether, right at the time the gravity spike passed through. Shetani is now officially dead, once and for all.'

'Thank Jaysis.'

'Right. But Voorogg has begun to attack anyway. Wally uses a telescope set up on the Moon to monitor what's happening on Earth. He said that rockets have been launched from the sea and they've put satellites in orbit. One of them fired a gamma burst that destroyed the Hesperian bunkers in the Mohave desert. Actually, Wally was pretty angry. He said we'd told him the aliens were our friends.'

It was the early hours of the morning, CHT, and Geoff and Maura were back in the lab.

'This doesn't look good,' said Geoff. 'Something's happened to Leona's DNA.'

Before Maura could answer, Kai staggered into the lab, caught hold of a bench to steady himself, but then slumped onto the floor. Maura rushed to him and, seeing his distorted expression, fetched him a glass of water.

Kai drank and swallowed. 'Forgive me,' he said.

'Oh, Kai, what's happened to you?' asked Maura.

'We must save Leona,' said Kai. 'Do you know how to do it?'

And so began another period of intense activity for Geoff and Maura, working to reverse the changes they'd made to Leona's DNA. 'I don't understand,' said Geoff. 'I thought we'd planted the code so it wouldn't affect her bodily functions.'

'We did,' said Maura, 'though we still don't know the purpose of all the nucleotide sequences that exist. But I think something happened when Shetani caught the virus. Perhaps he fought back in some way.'

Kai barely ate or drank. He stayed for hours by Leona's bedside, sometimes meditating, sometimes chanting Khitan prayers. Maura devised a new drug designed to cut out the code they'd added to her genetic instructions. But it became apparent that other changes had occurred. It looked as if Shetani's software had defended itself by reflecting the random programming back into Leona's DNA. Each of her chromosomes comprised hundreds of millions of the base pairs that formed the building blocks of the structure. It was taking too long to unravel all the changes and devise resequencing code to enable her to recover, even with Geoff's programming skills.

⤛⬤

The day she finally faded away, Maura asked Kai what arrangements they should make for Leona's funeral.

'You have seen Huang's ice tomb?' asked Kai. Geoff nodded.

'Leona was sympathetic to the Khitan cause, and a warrior too, in her own way,' said Kai. 'She should have the same funeral as Huang.'

With Chen's help, Kai prepared Leona's body. He dressed her in a white gown in keeping with Khitan tradition, and placed her on a canvas stretcher decorated with prayer flags. Using cooking pot lids as cymbals and drums they'd made from oil barrels, Kai invited the remaining company to make as much noise as possible. Chen lit a fire on the snow outside the cave where Huang was entombed, and then threw in a bag of powder. It flared up, sending bright green flames high in the sky. Kai chanted and scattered drops of fragrant oil on Leona's body from head to toe. He bent down, whispered inaudibly and gently kissed her lips. They carried the body inside the sepulchre and immersed her carefully in a tank of warm water. Chen removed the heating element and they stood, their palms pressed together in silent respect. Kai signalled Chen to cover the tank, and they filed slowly out of the cave, each deep in thought.

They congregated in the communal lounge. Geoff was puzzled. Kai was standing up but seemed reduced in height.

'I am broken,' Kai said quietly. 'I was once given an inestimable honour. I was privileged to be shown a path of wisdom and compassion. But I squandered that knowledge. I took a risk I knew was great. I thought there was a shortcut to bring peace to humankind.'

Geoff realised Kai was himself near to death. He was physically bowed down, his face grey, his eyes bloodshot.

'I acted impulsively,' he continued. 'As a result, I killed dozens of people who were nominally my enemy, but also my two closest friends. I am responsible for Huang's death, because I am the one who ordered him to capture the whale-bot. And it was I who killed Leona, whom I loved, because she died trying to save me.'

Chen put his arm round Kai's shoulder, but he shrugged it away.

'You must forgive yourself,' said Geoff. 'You were manipulated by a malevolent power. Once upon a time, they would have said you were possessed by an evil spirit. It wasn't your fault.'

'Shetani was not alive. He was no more than a computer programme,' said Kai. 'I allowed myself to be corrupted by machine code. That is my shame.'

'Evil spirits have always existed,' said Maura. 'Even if Shetani was not alive in the way we are, he could create wormholes, cause volcanoes to erupt, tap power from black holes. No human being could resist something that strong.'

'But I submitted to him voluntarily,' said Kai, raising his voice as the wind buffeted the hut, howling like a pack of wolves. 'I agreed to be Shetani's agent here on Earth. I thought I could use his power to stop humankind destroying itself. But I behaved like a criminal. I am a criminal. That is a burden I must carry alone.'

'You make choice for good reason,' said Chen. 'You have good motive.'

'You know, I saw Shetani in his death pangs,' continued Kai. 'He suffered all the pain of humankind. All the people he had forced to feel terror, agony, hopelessness – Shetani felt it all for himself.' The lights in the hut dimmed and then recovered as the emergency generator cut in.

'So Shetani got his just deserts,' said Maura. 'Don't beat yourself up anymore. Perhaps Voorogg will back off now Shetani has been destroyed.'

'Oh, Maura,' said Kai. 'I am sorry, but the Earth is in terrible danger. Shetani had been assisting the rebel Thiosh to conquer the world. I know, I relayed his messages to Voorogg, and may I be eternally damned for betraying the whole of humankind. But I am afraid that Voorogg no longer needs Shetani's help. He will be strong enough to conquer the Earth unaided.'

Maura watched the snow driving against the windowpanes for a moment. Then she turned and spoke. 'How can we can stop Voorogg? Atherlonne never wanted war. She knows him. Could she persuade him to back off?'

'I do not think so,' said Kai. 'Voorogg wants to capture her, and possibly kill her.'

'I'll contact her again,' said Maura. 'She must keep herself safe. She knows the locations of all Earth's hydrothermal vents, many more than you told Voorogg. I think Leona had a premonition we had to keep some of them secret.'

'I'll speak to Wally,' said Geoff. 'We need to know the location of all Voorogg's forces. He should be able to track them with his telescope. Chen, can you find out the status of the Khitan army, please? I'll try and get an update on the Hesperian military.'

'Is there anything I can do?' asked Kai.

'There is,' said Maura. 'You can be our leader.'

Kai took a deep breath. 'Thank you. You are good people, but I am not qualified to lead you. In my next life, I shall be condemned to eternal hell, but I will spend my remaining time on Earth as usefully as I can.'

It was late in the working day. General Flannery was startled by someone knocking rapidly on his office door. Before the general could respond, Major Breckenridge charged in clutching a piece of paper. Flannery slipped his glass of Bourbon into the bottom drawer of his desk and moved some papers to cover where he'd splashed some whiskey.

'Suh, suh,' said Breckenridge, his face twitching. 'I dunno how they did it, but the aliens are on Earth. They've launched their attack. They've got satellites with gamma lasers, and they knocked out half the Fed's missile silos and most of the navy's ships.'

Flannery glanced through the major's printout. It ended abruptly, midway through a sentence. 'The Septagon overreached itself,' he said. 'They put everything they had into the fight with Khitans. It was shit or bust. There's only a squaddie and his dog left to defend the Federation.' Shielding his right hand with his left, he entered the combination code for his safe and took out a red com-phone. Then, with a sigh, he put it down on his desk. 'Fuck. It'll take an hour to get through, and then an hour for a reply – if there's anyone left to answer. It looks like we're on our own, Major.'

'Suh?'

'But at least we'll be alright. Just make sure the subs have caught every last one of those fucking sulphur-eating fish. As long as we've cleaned up the sea here, we can manage okay on our own. Meanwhile, keep trying to find out where these alien bastards are lurking on Earth. We may be able to send them a little present from Europa.'

Return to the Empire

Geoff, Maura, Kai and Chen gathered by the fire in the communal lounge.

'I've been sharing with Atherlonne,' said Maura. 'She says Thiosh are very sensitive to gravity waves. When Geoff's virus wiped out the Virtuon, the gravity tsunami that washed through space–time would have been felt by all Thiosh. Voorogg will have realised something happened to Shetani, but Atherlonne doubts it will change his plans.'

'I am afraid she is right,' said Kai, sadly. 'Shetani used me to tell Voorogg what to do. His robots will invade both the Federation and the Empire. But he will use his main force to destroy the Khitan and Hesperian armies in Xizang.'

'Kai, you know what weapons Voorogg have?' asked Chen.

'Shetani gave me designs for robot infantry, which can move through terrestrial cities from building to building, clearing out any opposition with gas grenades and plasma guns. Other robots will be armed with sniper rifles. They lock a laser onto a target and guide a smart bullet. Voorogg will have built a cavalry division, using humanoid robots mounted on machine-mules. They will gallop over rough ground at high speed, or climb over mountains.'

'Could Atherlonne make machines to oppose him?' asked Geoff. He began to pace back and forth inside the hut.

'I don't think she'll want to do that,' said Maura, frowning at Geoff. 'As you know, she's a pacifist at heart. But I'm sure she'd support us behind the scenes. You know, with intelligence, that sort of thing.'

'She can make better our defending?' asked Chen. 'Make barrier to stop robots?'

'It may be too late,' said Geoff. He stopped pacing and sat down. 'I have information from the guy we met in Oztralia. Voorogg's sent a fleet of landing craft into the Indian Ocean. It's heading for Bangla Bay.'

'What's he up to, do you think?' said Maura.

'The rebel Thiosh want to defeat both armies,' said Kai. 'First they will destroy the Hesperian force approaching Lhaza, and then they will crush the remaining Khitan resistance.'

'It could all be over within a few weeks,' said Geoff. 'Voorogg's army could establish a beachhead in the mouth of the Ganjes and travel overland, through Bangla, and across the mountains to Xizang.'

'That's over the most mountainous regions on Earth,' said Maura.

'Yes, but they're robots,' said Geoff. 'They won't be affected by cold or lack of oxygen. They'll certainly find a way through.'

'What should we do, Kai?' asked Maura.

'If humankind is going to keep its liberty, then the Hesperian and Khitan armies must fight together for the freedom of us all.'

'I like your sentiment,' said Geoff, 'but how can they? The two armies are probably running out of ammo fighting each other.'

'I do not know the answer yet,' said Kai. 'But I am certain it will never be possible unless Khitans and Hesperians combine forces. Geoff, I must go to Lhaza. How can I fly the shuttle without it being shot down by Voorogg's satellites?'

Geoff was deep in concentration. He didn't notice Maura standing by him until she spoke.

'Wake up. What have you been doing? You missed your dinner.'

'Oh, sorry, I forgot.'

'It's half past one in the morning. Are you designing something?' She peered at the geometric shapes glowing on the screen.

He got up and stretched his cramped muscles. 'It's not easy refracting high energy gamma rays, but it's possible with silicon prisms. But you need an array of them to bend the beam through 180 degrees. See what I mean,' he said, zooming out to show the full picture.

'Leona had a necklace like that,' said Maura.

He saw sadness in her face. 'That's what gave me the idea. I think she's helping us even now.'

'I hope so, I really do. But how could you make it? It needs special glass.'

'Actually, I'm planning to use the lenses from the old lighthouse.'

'Are you serious? What's it for?'

Geoff gave Maura a lopsided smile. 'Just an idea I've had. I expect Voorogg will want to reflect on it.'

Geoff entered the hangar and sniffed the air. There was a peculiar odour he'd never noticed before. It seemed like a cross between rotting fish and toilet cleaner, but then his sense of smell hadn't been the same since the fight with Huang. He looked around for Chen and found him stirring a brown sludge in an open drum.

'Shuttle ready for take-off, but no more fuel for rocket-sledge,' said Chen.

'Have you checked all the buildings?'

'Special tank hold all rocket fuel.'

'So we're stuck here. Kai's taking the shuttle, we've lost the whale-bot and now we can't use the rocket-sledge.'

'It okay. I make more fuel.'

'What's your idea, Chen?'

'We have big stock nitrate, yes?'

'It's fertilizer for the horti-tunnel,' said Geoff.

'We mix ammonium nitrate with whale oil. AN plus WO. It make ANWO fuel.' Chen gestured at the contents of the drum.

'I'm not sure. It looks like a slurry of oily crystals to me.'

'I add water and it make emulsion,' said Chen, smiling broadly.

'So, you can pump it into the combustion chamber. Okay, I see what you're saying. You have my permission to do some experiments. But be very careful, okay? Your ANWO is likely to be very unstable.'

Kai circled Mount Gephel and, expertly spilling the air from the shuttle's stubby wings, he settled the craft down in the main courtyard of the huge monastery.

The rocket exhaust shut off abruptly and Kai climbed out of the cockpit. The Abbot hurried over to the craft and bowed low. 'What a surprise!' he said with a twinkle in his eye. 'Welcome to Drepung. Have you come far?'

'Yes, Father. From Antarctica.'

'Very well. Perhaps you would like to rest a while and then join us for evening prayers?'

'Forgive me, but my first priority must be to camouflage my craft. I do not want it to be seen by orbiting satellites.'

'Do you think white sheets will look like snow when seen from space?'

'Yes, Father. I am grateful.'

'Have you come to help us fight the Hesperian devils?'

'No, Father, I have come to persuade you to make friends with them.'

Kai entered a hall, the walls lined with statues of Khitan gods. Food was being prepared, and the smoke from the open fire stung his eyes. The Abbot got up and introduced him to Shan Chonglin and Yul T'an, leaders of the Khitan resistance army. Shan must have been in his fifties, a distinguished man with natural gravitas. His feathery moustaches were an inversion of his wispy eyebrows. Yul, however clearly kept herself ready for battle, in spite of her young, cherubic face. She wore her fur coat loosely over crossed bandoliers of ion gun cartridges.

A monk gave them each a bowl of rice, egg and vegetables. Kai suspected meat was in short supply, now the Hesperian army had cut off trade from the south. He scooped up the rice with his chopsticks, feeling all the time he was being watched by the statues, their exaggerated features made more grotesque by the flickering light of ghee lamps. He asked the Abbot about the history of the monastery and its teaching, partly from politeness, but also out of genuine interest in view of his own experience as a monk.

As soon as the rice bowls had been cleared away, they spread out maps on the plain wooden tables, and marked the mountain passes where the Khitans had halted the advance of the Hesperian army.

'Soon you will be attacked by another army,' said Kai. 'A legion of alien robots.'

Yul stared at the ceiling and clasped her shaven head. 'You speak the babble of a madman.'

'Wait,' said Shan. 'Let us hear what he has to say.'

'I was a pupil of Wu Jiu Li,' said Kai. 'I believe he was aware of the existence of intelligent alien life living on Jupiter's moon, Europa. Other Khitan adepts may also know of these beings, through psychic experience.' The Abbot and Shan exchanged glances.

'I myself have met the aliens,' said Kai. 'We know them as Thiosh. They were essentially a peace-loving race, but they were threatened by the Hesperians who built a base on Europa. A hostile group have found their way to Earth and have built a robot army to dominate all humankind. Their robo-troops are approaching in two columns, passing through Bangla. Soon they will be in the foothills of the mountains.'

'How do you know this?' queried Yul, leaning forward over the table. 'We have heard nothing. Do you have secret information? Where are your spies?'

'I will tell you all I know about the robo-troops. I trust you will be just as open with me.' Kai paused, looking from face to face. Shan and the Abbot nodded and Kai continued. 'I have surveillance information obtained from a high-resolution telescope sited on the Moon. It was relayed to me by an astronomer in Oztralia, who is sympathetic to our cause.'

'Oztralia? Is he Hesperian?' asked Yul, smiling unpleasantly.

'Yes.'

'Who else knows this?' asked Shan.

'I share the information with other Hesperian friends.'

'More Hesperians? How can you trust them?' Tiny flecks of Yul's spittle flickered momentarily in the lamplight.

'The Hesperian Government regards them as traitors,' said Kai. 'They escaped from a prison and have been hunted ever since.'

'All your friends seem to be double agents,' said Yul. 'You ought to be more careful who you associate with.' She stood up and began rolling her hips and stretching.

'No, you must be careful,' said Kai. 'Powers are at work beyond your imagining.'

Yul stopped exercising. 'Is it a power beyond our imagining that switched off the surveillance satellites? The Hesperians have maintained a no-fly zone for the last three months. Yet you landed your Hesperian shuttle in our courtyard. Could it be that you are a double agent yourself?'

'It was not the Hesperians who launched the satellites, but the rebel Thiosh. They are equipped with gamma lasers, which can destroy anything on land, in the air or on the sea. When the robo-troops are near enough to hold the ground, they may also destroy this monastery.'

'You are talking drivel!' cried Yul. 'You say hostile aliens control the sky, but you flew here, unharmed.'

'Ha! There is much that I cannot expect you to understand. What I can tell you is that a brilliant Hesperian computer engineer designed a gamma ray reflector. We shone a searchlight at a satellite. When it fired its laser, we reflected it back to disable it. The satellite was geostationary, monitoring the segment of Earth I needed to fly over. But I expect it will soon be replaced.'

'Tell us the truth. Who you are working for?' said Yul, resting her hand on the butt of her tezla pistol.

'Regarding my allegiance, it is true I was a puppet owned by something more powerful even than Thiosh, and yet my friends found a way to destroy it. But perhaps to you, I will always sound like a lunatic.'

'I sense you have suffered greatly,' said Shan, gently. 'Do you want to tell us your story?'

'In time, maybe. But my own experience is not relevant to our present circumstance. Let it suffice that my Hesperian friends, whom you distrust, saved my life and my honour. I have come to give you a message. You must act now to save yourselves.'

Robot Attack

Geoff and Maura spent most of the day in the lab, monitoring the Antarctic environment.

'The uni-net's been off for a while,' said Geoff. 'It's back now, but it's different.'

'How different?'

'It doesn't look good. The normal search engines no longer work. Instead there are pages and pages of stuff about reordering society: orders for food distribution, plans for sulphur mines, manufacture of workers' overalls, destruction of private houses, construction of tower blocks. It's a rebel Thiosh manifesto.'

'How's the war going? Are the Federation and the Empire still at each other's throats?'

'I asked Wally what he could see through his Moon telescope. The rebels don't know about the 8105 code yet, but they'll crack it in the end, I'm sure. As far as he can tell, the human armies are still fighting in the mountains. They're playing straight into Voorogg's hands. His robots will march in and pick up the pieces.'

'God between us and all harm,' whispered Maura.

'We've been in jams before . . .'

Geoff was interrupted as Chen burst into the lab. 'I disturb, sorry. But distraydar show ships come. What we do now?'

'Voorogg's robots!' said Geoff. 'The rebel Thiosh want to punish us for knocking out their satellite. What's their ETA, Chen?'

'Sea very rough. Maybe arrive tomorrow.'

'I don't think we can fight an army of robot soldiers. I wonder what Kai would do?'

'He know Sun Tzu teaching from long ago.'

'Which is?'

'If equally matched, offer battle. If unequal, run away.'

'Can we escape in the rocket-sledge?' asked Maura.

'I have not tested fuel,' said Chen. 'It still in storage tank.'

'Pump it in anyway,' ordered Geoff. 'Collect together tools, rations, water, batteries, tents, anything you can lay your hands on that looks useful. Maura, unlock the armoury. Pull out everything we've got: tezla pistols, plasma guns, ion guns. We needn't have qualms about killing a few robots.'

When they'd prepared themselves the best they could, they turned off the lights and peered intently at the distraydar screen. They watched five vessels land and each spew out a dozen bright dots like bursting seed pods. The quayside surveillance camera relayed images of humanoid creatures with muscular limbs articulated by exposed joints and heads with featureless faces except for two bright yellow eyes above a grilled slit. One of the figures pointed a gun at the camera and the screen went dark.

'I don't think this is a courtesy visit,' said Geoff.

'They not friends,' said Chen. 'They split in groups to surround us.'

'Maura, delete the files and shred any documents we don't want Voorogg to get hold of. Anything that shows where Atherlonne is hiding, or the work we did to assassinate Shetani.'

'Did it yesterday,' said Maura.

>──●

The group of three huddled around the computer screens sequencing images from the surveillance cameras. The robo-troops were breaking into the outlying buildings, smashing down doors and entering with their weapons ready to fire. But each viewing screen became blank after an insurgent pointed his weapon towards the camera.

'We're not going to be able to resist,' said Maura. 'Let's make a run for it.'

'Quick, get aboard the rocket-sledge and start the engine,' said Geoff. 'I'll try and hold them off for a while.'

Maura hesitated.

'Go on, just do it!'

'Okay, but don't be long. Please!'

As Maura ran out through the back, Geoff cracked open the front door.

I need to get the drop on these bastards, he thought.

Keeping low, he scuttled over to the heated water tower and levitated up to the tank platform. Three pairs of robo-troops marched into view, as if they were on a parade ground. Geoff focused on the plasma gun held by the robot on the right of the leading pair and swung it with maximum TK-force into its companion, knocking it down. The next two pairs gathered around their fallen comrade, whilst the unwitting aggressor repeatedly performed a gesture resembling a shrug of its shoulders. For a while, all the standing robots jerkily twisted and turned, taking short steps in random directions. Then one appeared to take command. It levelled its plasma gun at the guilty robot, which was now kneeling with its arms outstretched, but the lead robot was undeterred. Using an arc of green plasma like a scalpel, it sliced through the neck of the unlucky machine. The others pulled the fallen unit to its feet, and another of the group picked up the detached head and gripped it under its arm. The five continued their advance, leaving the headless body on the snow in a pool of purple hydraulic fluid.

Geoff had chosen his location for a fightback so that he would have a clear view of the controls of their snow-clearing tractor. He TK-flipped the ignition on, knocked the engine into gear and revved up, sending the vehicle speeding towards the approaching robo-troops. *Machines against machines.*

The leading robots aimed their plasma guns at the tractor, but its snow-clearing blade deflected the first salvo. Then they fired at the empty cabin. The discharge from plasma guns brought down the cabin roof, but still the snowplough ground onward, pushing back the robots. Then another group appeared at the side of the roadway. They fired into the vehicle's caterpillar track, making it slew to one side and roll over.

One of the new group spotted Geoff on the water tower and aimed its plasma gun. Its blast collapsed the tank and Geoff was washed off the platform into the snow. He shivered as the wind bit into his wet clothing, but he didn't think he'd broken any bones. He staggered to his feet, just as a huge explosion reduced the rocket-sledge hangar to a heap of splinters and shrapnel. 'Maura!' he wailed. He slumped to the ground again and offered no resistance as the approaching robots manacled him and frogmarched him away.

A disembodied arm poked out of a heap of snow only to disappear again. Then the whole mound erupted as thrashing arms hurled chunks of snow in all directions. Finally, a figure crawled from her icy grave. 'Holy Mother of God,' she muttered.

She unzipped her left boot and gently eased it off. Screwing up her face, she slowly moved her foot left and right, and then put the boot on again. Leaving it unzipped, she limped towards the debris of the destroyed rocket-sledge hangar. She stopped to check her time readout and then, shaking her head, she peered at the sun. She lurched towards the tangled wreckage: a twisted RSJ, a blackened rocket combustion chamber, a fractured skid rail, and pieces of wreckage distorted beyond recognition. She jerked back, and then bent forward again to lift a charred panel away from the severed leg of a robo-trooper.

Smoke was rising from all around, and air heated from fires was panicking the snow flurries into whirlwinds. She pulled down her hood, set the breathing filter to exclude smoke particles, and meandered erratically between the ruined buildings. Periodically she lifted her visor to call out, 'Geoff, Geoff,' but her cries were mocked by the howl of the wind. After an hour of picking over the debris, she oriented her com-phone compass and began to hobble across the Ross Ice Shelf towards the sea.

As the snowstorm blew itself out, she set her visor window to magnify. She scanned the horizon. A flotilla of icebergs was sailing slowly past the broken shoreline. A pair of Antarctic terns swooped low, inspecting her bent figure as she inched forward. The terrain became more treacherous as she limped closer to the sea. Slabs of ice had been raised up and then pushed together in a haphazard jumble. She slipped and fell, lay on her back for a minute, and then rolled over to stagger to her feet again. She fell again and this time she remained lying on her side, watching penguins sliding down an ice ramp into the icy water.

At frequent intervals, there was a sound like a muffled explosion, as chunks of ice as big as houses broke away from the cliffs and fell into the sea. Then, with a sharp crack, the surface she was lying on tipped upward. She cried out to her God and grabbed at her ice pick. It was tangled in her belt. Her legs slid into the water. She yanked the pick free and struck it into the ice with every ounce of her strength. She remained like that, hanging onto the pick as the ice platform drifted further from the shelf. Soon she was one hundred metres, five hundred metres, and then a full kilometre from the ice sheet that filled the bay.

She lay still, both arms clutching the ice-pick handle. A torrent of water poured onto her body and she looked up as a fountain of spray gushed from a dark shape just below the waves. Then it surfaced, water streaming down its gleaming, metallic hull. 'Thank Jaysis!' she gasped.

Geoff was ready to give up.

Nothing matters anymore. They'll keep me in prison a while and kill me too. I should be in a cell, not a half-collapsed multistorey car park. Why aren't I locked up? Oh, I know, this is underwater. There's no escape.

I can't think straight. This is a hallucination, or else I've had a breakdown. Nothing makes sense. The walls aren't straight. I'm in a structure made of interlocking pentagons and quadrilaterals, in three dimensions. Even the floor ramps up and down. Not steep, just a bit sloping here and there. I s'pose robots aren't bothered by a bit of gradient. But what's this place for? The furniture's like workstations. The tops are level but the legs are all different lengths. Perhaps odd legs don't matter if you're entirely digital.

Ah, I know – it's architecture to disorientate humans. They'll bring us here so they can tell us how to serve their new masters. Yeah, that must be it. It's for indoctrinating homo sapiens. A Thiosh underwater command centre. I'm fucked up in the TUCC. Maybe they'll brainwash me too. I'd rather be dead. Hang on, I've got a visitor.

'Please don't get up,' said the robo-trooper. 'May I introduce myself? I am Zakristan.' The robot pulled up a chair, sat down and crossed its legs.

Geoff noted the markings on the robot's armour, a designation that comprised just three characters. Geoff's logical brain inferred it must be a senior officer. He couldn't read anything from its face. Its features were fixed – except for its yellow eyes. They seemed almost curious.

'Excuse me, but have I got your attention?' asked Zakristan.

'No,' said Geoff defiantly. 'Only if I can find a way of giving you a hard reboot up your tin arse!'

'I understand that is what you call a play on words,' said Zakristan. 'Your name is Doctor Geoffrey Kirby?'

'Yes and no,' said Geoff.

'Your reply is a contradiction.'

'My name is Geoff Kirby. The "Doctor" bit is a title.'

'What is a title?'

'It's one way we organise ourselves. It shows a level of education.'

'You are very knowledgeable?'

'I know humans will never be your slaves.'

'Also, you have the power of telekinesis. Is that usual amongst humans?'

'I believe there are precedents. But they're rare.'

'Were you born with this attribute?'

'Lord, no! I was given it by Saazat Mettravar.'

'Why did he do that?'

'I don't suppose you understand generosity,' said Geoff.

Zakristan remained silent.

'He wanted us to represent him at a conference in the Europan Unidome. He'd hoped it would benefit both humans and Thiosh. He may have given me the skill as a sign of goodwill.'

'Was it not what you call a bribe?'

'No, that's a filthy slur. It was a free gift made out of friendship, with no strings attached.'

'Strings?'

'Obligations.'

'Did he give you other gifts?'

'I can make metal things get very hot. That's a sort of TK too.'

'TK?'

'Telekinesis.'

'Anything else?'

'Not that I'm aware of.'

'You have a Thiosh acquaintance known as Atherlonne, I believe?'

'She gave us hospitality when we were on Europa. She's another Thiosh who's always treated us with respect and kindness. She gave us her protection,' said Geoff.

'Protection from OPDEO or other Thiosh?'

'From OPDEO. We had no quarrel with any Thiosh until your metal maniacs attacked us.'

'Can you tell me where Atherlonne is now?'

'If I knew, I wouldn't tell you.'

'We believe you were responsible for destroying our ally, Shetani. How did you do it?'

'Shetani was conceited. He believed he was so perfect, there was no need to back himself up.'

Dissent in the Ranks

Maura slept deeply for several hours. When she woke up, the whale-bot had ceased its familiar rocking motion and was filled with a chorus of chirrups and percussive rattling sounds, rising and falling in pitch. The cameras showed the craft was surrounded by a pod of bottlenose dolphins. Maura limped to the storage lockers and donned her full hydroskin suit, buoyancy control and breathing set, before swimming slowly into the ocean via the top airlock.

The dolphins' animated bodies danced and postured as if in celebration. They began to whistle in unison, taking it in turns to rub their bodies against her before barrel rolling away and circling to rejoin the group. Maura stroked the calves of the dolphin cows and, when a large bull raised her up on its body, she hung onto its dorsal fin while it swam away like a torpedo. As it brought her back to the group, the other dolphins made bubble rings and spirals around her, a glistening cascade of geometric forms building to a crescendo of air, water and light. She was lifted and spun as the rushing bubbles massaged her body until, at last, the effervescence died away, and the dolphins were no longer to be seen.

Here we go, another interview with the metal man, thought Geoff as Zakristan beckoned him to an empty room. This time the robot officer wasted no time with pleasantries.

'Did you modify the DNA of your friend Leona?' it demanded.

'Why do want to know?' countered Geoff.

The robot appeared to soften. 'I ask because we need your help.'

Geoff waited for the humanoid to speak again, and suddenly he felt it was him who was interviewing it.

'Thiosh biochemistry is very different from that of humans,' said Zakristan, at last. 'Yet they have nucleic acids, which hold genetic instructions for every aspect of the correct functioning of their bodies. Something in the Earth's environment is seriously affecting their health. They are suffering a pandemic. I ask, do you have the ability to analyse the problem?'

'Oh, so now you want to be friends. Well, I'm sorry to disappoint you, but my field is artificial intelligence. I can design and run computer programs, but I'm not a microbiologist. It was Maura who had that skill and expertise. Maura, who died when you attacked the whaling station.'

'Actually, I can update your information. Dr O'Hara is alive and well, apart from a twisted ankle. She will be joining us here very soon.'

Maura greeted Geoff with a scream. He picked her up and was about to spin her round, but she told him to be careful. Then he kissed her mouth, her cheeks, her neck. He wiped away the tears from her eyes and then his own. Zakristan moved forward to intervene, then backed off and waited. Geoff told it severely that they needed to be alone for a while, and he led Maura carefully to his quarters.

At first in broken fragments, and then in torrents of rushing words, Maura explained what had happened during the robo-troop attack. After Geoff hadn't joined them in the rocket-sledge, she'd gone back to look for him. The explosion had knocked her unconscious and, when she came round, there was no one to be found. She was shaken up, but Atherlonne had projected and sent the whale-bot to rescue her. Sadly, the last time she'd seen Chen, he'd been sitting at the controls of the rocket-sledge.

Kai and the Khitan leaders were back in the main hall, surrounded by their maps.

'We have mined the passes,' said Yul. 'We will offer resistance, fall back to draw in the Hesperians, and then blow the charges. The avalanche should take out most of them.'

'Hm,' said Shan. 'We must not destroy the pass. It would separate us from the Holy Mount Kailash and Manasarovar, the Immortal Lake of Jade.'

'For thousands of years, our people have been blessed by bathing in the lake. It has been the quickest way to Nirvana,' said the Abbot.

'We are cut off anyway while the Hesperians are in the south,' said Yul. 'Killing Hesperians WILL be our Nirvana!' She ratcheted the handgrip of her ion gun back and forth defiantly. The Abbot looked at Shan and shook his head.

'According to my intelligence, there are robo-troops close to Manasarova now,' said Kai.

'So you're still babbling about aliens when we have a war to fight?' shouted Yul, slapping her forehead as if trying to waken herself from a bad dream.

'Send your scouts to the top of Kailash,' said Kai. 'Unless you see the robots yourselves, you will never believe me.'

'Kailash is a sacred mountain,' protested the Abbot. 'It must never be climbed.'

'But we must do it anyway,' Shan told Yul.

'I don't understand why Atherlonne brought you here,' Geoff said to Maura as they stood by an omniprinter, sipping tea. 'Wasn't Voorogg trying to kill her?'

'Atherlonne and Voorogg agreed a truce. All their lives are at risk, and that's changed everything.'

'Do you know what the problem is?'

'I do now,' said Maura. 'It's radiation sickness. Zakristan gave me specimens of Thiosh genetic code. I immersed them in water from Sydney Harbour. You know, where the concentration of waterborne radioactivity was highest. The samples were still in the whale-bot.'

'What happened?' asked Geoff.

'The nucleics didn't like it one bit. I think Thiosh are hypersensitive to fallout from the war.'

'Oh Lord, what will have happened to Atherlonne?'

'Actually, she seems okay,' said Maura. 'The prevailing current around the Aleutian Islands may have kept the radiation down.'

'But Voorogg's group is sick. Are they going to die?' Geoff asked, trying not to sound hopeful.

'Not if we use our knowledge to help them. There's a process called mitosis. We can use it to promote growth and repair. But first we must stop the damaged cells from reproducing.'

Geoff was pacing back and forth.

'Hey, stand still a minute,' said Maura.

'Sorry, I'm just trying to get used to the idea of helping the enemy.'

'That's it, we can help them. Together we can design proteins to knock out the degraded cells. But we'll need a lot of different types.'

Geoff gripped Maura on both shoulders and looked directly into her eyes. 'Can't you see, this sickness is working in our favour? They won't be able to take over the world if they become ill and die.'

Maura blew out her cheeks and shook her head. Not for the first time, Geoff knew she would crush his perfectly logical argument with some superior wisdom of her own. He could even guess what she would say next.

'You're being silly,' said Maura. 'We should always try and save life if we can.'

'I knew you'd say that. Okay, I know I can't win. If you can specify the parts of the Thiosh genetic code that get damaged, I'll design some proteins to take them out. We'll have to get Zakristan to make them into a serum. Can you explain to it what it needs to do?'

'Shall we start calling it "him"?'

Three horsemen dressed in peasant clothing leapt onto their saddles and galloped out of the eastern courtyard. Shan led Yul and Kai back into the East Sunshine Apartment.

'So, we owe you an apology,' said Shan. 'Our spies report a progression of strange beings, armed metal men and animal machines, approaching from the south.'

Kai gave Shan a tight-lipped smile, but said nothing.

'Your "robo-troops" are advancing on Lhaza,' Shan continued. 'Moreover, there has been fierce fighting in the mountains, but none involving our Khitan irregulars. The Federation's troops are in disarray. But they cannot flee south. The robots are driving them north towards the passes where we have set our explosives.'

'*Hi-yah!*' Yul shouted, triumphantly. 'Now we can crush the Hesperians once and for all.' For a moment, Kai thought he'd heard Huang speaking. He took a deep breath, preparing himself for what he knew he must say.

'No, you did not believe me about the robo-troops. You thought my words were gibberish.' Kai's eyes burned with passion. 'Now you must listen to what I say. Let the Hesperians into Lhaza. Make them welcome. Give them refuge and hospitality, as far as your resources will allow. Then you can blow your mines when the robo-troops come through.'

'Never,' shouted Yul. 'I knew you were a traitor!'

'Wait!' ordered Shan. 'We have underestimated Kai. Now we must hear him out. Let him explain what the alien creatures are, and why they make these terrible machines.'

'They are sea animals called Thiosh. They lived under the ice that covers Europa. They have advanced intelligence and telekinetic abilities, which they use to make and control robots. The aggressive military force called OPDEO set up a military base, and built submarines to roam the ocean under the ice. The aliens were the indigenous species, but they were willing to live in peaceful cohabitation with the humans.'

'So why do they attack us now? asked Shan.

'They have invaded Earth to save themselves from humankind. OPDEO wanted to exterminate the Thiosh. I know, I was there, together with my crew and my Hesperian friends, Dr Geoff Kirby and Dr Maura O'Hara.' Kai paused, making a conscious effort to control his emotions. There was also a Hesperian woman,' said Kai. 'Leona Adaeze, whom I loved.'

'Now I know who you are,' screamed Yul. 'You are one of the bastards who killed my brother!' She reached for her gun.

Losing Battle

'So, what are the options, Major?' asked General Flannery. He walked over to his drinks cabinet, half filled two glasses with ice, and poured in whiskey until the liquid was just short of the rim.

'Have some Bourbon,' said Flannery. 'It's synthetic, of course, but we do have unlimited supplies. All part of our self-sufficiency programme. Now tell me, what's the news from Earth?'

'I'm 'spectin' a report any hour now, suh,' said Breckenridge. 'The team have been workin' on it all week.'

'Come now, Major, you can quit stalling. The Thiosh robots are moving too fast for us to hit them at this distance. It takes too long for our missiles to reach them, and the bastards keep changing position. We have all this expensive armoury and we're stymied. We can't nuke anybody at the moment.'

'We stopped the Khitans usin' their Mars base for attacks. They were vaporised in seconds.'

Flannery smiled at the memory. 'Yep, we did that alright. But that's history now. We've got to think of the future.'

'Well, we're pretty sure the Thiosh'll come out top dogs on Earth. When the dust settles, we'll have some static targets we can obliterate. We'll have to be careful not to cause a nuclear winter though, suh.'

'Why's that, Major?'

'You know, if we throw up too much dust and vapour into the atmosphere, it'll start an ice age. It could decimate all life on Earth, or worse.'

'So, with our kith and kin slaves of Thiosh, wouldn't we be kind of putting them out of their misery?'

Breckenridge paused to think, and then smiled broadly. 'You mean Earth would get thrown back to the Dark Ages, and the only advanced civilisation would be ours, here on Europa?'

'Yep, you've got it,' said Flannery.

'And OPDEO would be ruler of the Solar System. Is that it, suh?'

'Earth is finished, Major. The fucking Thiosh have seen to that. We need to make sure we've rooted them all out from under the ice here, and then start civilisation all over again, with OPDEO calling the shots.'

'It's a beautiful idea, General.'

'I thought you'd like it. Some more Bourbon, Major?'

⤙⬤

Zakristan asked Geoff and Maura into his office. He now sat upright in his chair, not nearly as relaxed as he'd appeared during Geoff's first interview. It made the robot look more serious, even though his face was entirely blank.

'Voorogg wants to express his deep gratitude,' he said. 'Your serum is effective. Many Thiosh have already recovered. We have moved them into trenches in the seabed where the contamination is low. The main isotopes have a relatively short half-life. Soon, the level of radioactivity will drop to a tolerable level, even for Thiosh.'

'We are glad to have been of assistance,' said Maura. Geoff noted the formal tone in her voice.

'You have consistently tried to help Thiosh,' continued Zakristan. 'We do not have enough information to decide if you are typical of your human race. Even so, Voorogg has reconsidered his plans. He feels it is no longer appropriate to dominate the Earth by force.'

Maura met Geoff's eyes. *It's her 'told you so' look,* he thought.

'Voorogg sends you a message,' said Zakristan. 'You have been steadfast in your commitment to find ways in which humans and Thiosh can cohabit their environment. He wishes to work with you, to explore how this may be possible.'

'Janey Mack, that's grand! Does that mean you're calling off the robo-troops?'

Geoff wondered if the robot had failed to hear Maura's question. He was about to repeat it for her, when Zakristan replied.

'Voorogg believed that direct action was necessary to resist human persecution of Thiosh. As you know, he and his followers developed a method of screening their thoughts from Mettravar and his administration. Unfortunately, history has repeated itself.'

The robot seemed to be speaking more slowly than usual. *Be patient. Let him finish.*

'Voorogg issued a decree to call off the robot armies and make peace with the humans, but the Thiosh army commanders revolted. They are still intent on waging war against you humans. Voorogg is no longer in control of the armed forces.'

'Aren't you head of the robots?' asked Maura. 'You can order them to stop, can't you?'

'The protocols have been changed. They no longer accept my commands.'

'Oh, shit!' said Geoff.

Yul levelled her tezla at Kai and pulled the trigger. But it was the Abbot who took the blast as he leapt up to restrain her. Shan pinned Yul to the wall while Kai knelt to examine the stricken man. Realising his heart had stopped, Kai began cardiopulmonary resuscitation. Shan began chanting and, as Yul relaxed, he released her. She slumped to the floor, her head in her hands, groaning. Kai alternated chest compression with rescue breaths and, after a minute, His Holiness began to cough. Kai sat him up, brought him water and sighed with relief as the colour returned to the Abbot's face.

Shan surprised Kai by opening a bottle of *baijiu*. Within a few minutes the Abbot was explaining, in short phrases, the way they made their spirit, and Shan was elaborating on the difference between the versions made from sorghum and those from other cereals. Yul tossed back the drink and joined in the conversation. They all understood she'd not been defeated in battle. She'd only shot the wrong person. The Khitan warriors' code did not associate shame with such errors.

Speaking with simplicity and passion, Kai began an account of his life from the time he first ran away from his parents' home. He turned to address Yul directly to explain how a Virtuon had enslaved him. His role as Shetani's puppet had led to the death of Huang, whom he now knew to have been Yul's brother.

'Thank you for being so open,' said Shan. 'As I thought, you have suffered deeply. But you only did what you believed to be right and honourable. You must take comfort from that.'

'I no longer seek peace for myself,' said Kai. 'The whole of humankind is facing a crisis. The war between Hesperians and Khitans is only dissipating our strength. We must save the Hesperian army to save ourselves.'

＊

Shan stood between the open gates of Lhaza, his arms outstretched in greeting. General Courtney Watkins led in his battalion, their ion guns at the ready.

'Are you surrendering?' demanded the general.

'No, we are surviving,' said Shan. 'As you have found out at first hand, we have a common enemy. It poses a greater threat to our existence than we do to each other. Our only hope is to join together.'

'Tell your men to put down their weapons,' Watkins shouted to his Lieutenant Colonel, and soon Khitan and Hesperian soldiers were shaking hands and even hugging each other.

'General, you must come to the monastery and meet the Abbot,' said Shan. 'We have another guest, one who knows more than anyone else about our enemy. He is a celestonaut, you know.'

Shan led the general into the Chapter House, where the Abbot greeted him warmly. Then Shan introduced him to Yul as his second in command. They gathered around a large central table covered with maps and documents reporting the latest intelligence. The Abbot sent a messenger to fetch Kai from the monk's cell where he was meditating. He entered the Chapter House in a sombre mood.

'We were lucky to get away,' said Watkins. 'I think the robots had the wrong lubricants for extreme cold, and it halted them for a while. But that was after our initial contact. We lost twenty soldiers. I don't know how many of the metal bastards we killed. If you shoot them with an ion gun, it only knocks out the component you hit. They seem to be built with everything duplicated, and they repair themselves in seconds. But they didn't like our RPGs.'

'Actually, we should congratulate you,' said Kai. 'You forced them to change their route. I have information that they are now following the Yarlung-Tsangpo River. I assume this is so they can march in a wider column with more firepower. Now we have a little more time to prepare. Get your men inside the palace, and then we must build up our defences as fast as we can.'

The march of the robo-troops was relentless. The combined Khitan–Hesperian army offered stiff resistance at the entrance to the gorge at the river's Great Bend. They brought the robot column to a halt using their rifle grenades and portable anti-tank missiles. However, the robots sent drones to bomb their positions.

'We must retreat upriver,' Shan said to the general. 'We must do it fast.'

'What – you're giving up that easily?' said Watkins.

'Have you ever read *The Art of War*?' asked Shan.

'Huh, that book?' said Watkins. 'It was written in the sixth century, wasn't it? I hardly think it's applicable now.'

'In war, practice dissimulation, and you will succeed,' quoted Shan. 'We must look as disordered as possible and then regroup.'

'They'll keep pushing us back, if we retreat,' said Watkins. 'We have to stop them here, or we're done for!'

'The mighty Namcha Barwa will stop them,' said Shan. 'Our sacred mountain will save us.'

A handful of Khitan irregulars remained behind with Yul. She led her companions up the sheer face of the gorge. They stopped at a vantage point where they had a clear view of the valley below. She watched through binoculars as the mounted robot scouts came into view. They'd already passed through the narrowest point of the gorge, but she waited until the leading robot regiments were about to leave the hairpin bend. Now the gorge had become much broader, the robo-troops were advancing fast. Yul suspected they could see the fine snow rising from the main human force in flight. Then she triggered the explosives. Billions of tons of snow and rock erupted like a frozen volcano. Even from their location close to the peak, they could feel the mountain shake. The roar reached a crescendo, drowning the Khitans' cries of '*Hi-yah!*' as they celebrated.

The avalanche continued to rumble for many minutes. The eruption filled the valley with a fog of snow. Yul waited for the storm to subside to check if the tail end of the robo-troop army had escaped. Then some movements far below caught her eye. '*Ta ma de,*' she whispered, as scores of shiny figures broke out of the snowdrift.

In the palace, Shan took the call from Yul on his com-phone, and quickly found where the Abbot was sitting in prayer.

'Forgive me, Father,' said Shan. 'But we will have to blow the dam.'

'But the villages – they will be destroyed!' exclaimed the Abbot.

'They are evacuated – or almost. If we cannot halt the robots, then we will all be destroyed.'

'If these robo-troops survived the avalanche, how can we stop them? They are the creation of aliens we have never seen. They will invent more, build more, we will never defeat them.'

'Your holiness – you are my revered master,' said Shan. 'It would dishonour me to suggest that you must have faith. But there will be a worse catastrophe if we are defeatist. You have wisdom beyond normal comprehension. You and I have meditated for many years together. This threat can be no more than an illusion. The truth will triumph in the end.'

'My friend, I thank you for your reproof. Sometimes, even an Abbot must be corrected. It is possible I need more guidance than is appropriate for my position. But during the whole history of humankind we have never faced a peril such as this. These are extreme times, and I accept that extreme measures must be taken.'

'Father, you do me more honour than I deserve,' said Shan. 'But I admit, it pleases me that I have your agreement.'

Shan had persuaded the Abbot and yet, he hesitated. He pictured a tsunami sweeping down the river basin, crashing against rocks, carrying away village buildings, eroding the valley sides, scouring the very earth. He closed his eyes, said a prayer, and gave the order for a million cubic metres of water per second to pour down the Yarlung-Tsangpo valley.

Eight minutes later Yul him called him back on his com-phone. 'They knew it was coming. They must have seen it with their satellites.'

'What happened?'

'They worked ten times, maybe a hundred times faster than men. They threw up a wall of earth and rocks, and the water passed each side.'

'*Ta ma de!*'

'I am coming back to the palace,' said Yul. 'We must fight them to the death!'

Cerebral Dominance

Yul was lying with Shan behind a parapet on a flat roof, under the Potala Palace's finial spires clad with sheets of pure gold. They saw the robo-army's drones swoop low and fire missiles at the Eastern Bastion, smashing a gaping hole in the defences. The enemy's firepower cleared the defending troops from the walls and the robo-troops marched through the gap to the Red Palace. There they halted, apparently waiting for further orders.

'Did the Great Fifth Dalai Lama have the gift of prophesy?' asked Yul.

'I think you know that he did,' said Shan.

'Did he foresee this attack?'

'He built sloping stone walls three metres thick at the top and five at the base, with copper poured into its foundations to withstand earthquakes. But there were no drones carrying missiles in the seventeenth century. It is my prayer that he never knew there would be an enemy with such terrible weapons.'

Shan tried to identify whichever of the similar-looking robo-troops had the highest rank. Yul was ready with a rocket-propelled grenade. They could at least take out the robots' leader, even though they would certainly be killed in retaliation.

While they watched, the scene erupted in utter violent confusion. Robo-troops began running in zigzags, firing at each other. Their silver heads rolled like footballs down the roadways, shot off by their deranged comrades. Their drones circled, pulsing lasers at the rampaging machines, ripping open their armour plating and tearing off limbs.

As the ion gun *whumps* and the laser flashes gradually subsided, Kai slid down the curved roof from behind one of the spires and walked over to where Yul and Shan were lying. 'I think we are saved,' he said.

⊱⬛

Geoff had been correct. The rebel aliens had designed the Thiosh underwater command centre as an interface between humans, robots and themselves. Consequently, they'd incorporated a range of different environments to suit the possible inhabitants.

Atherlonne led a school of dolphins to part of the TUCC where the robots had carried out modifications to accommodate them. Fortunately, their needs were not very different from those of humans. It was only really necessary to half fill some rooms with seawater.

Maura called Geoff over to where she now had a desk in the TUCC office area. Geoff was glad Atherlonne had chosen to communicate via Maura's viz-box screen. Whatever the news, he wanted to get it first hand.

As courteous as ever, the Thiosh enquired after their health. Maura assured her that she'd fully recovered from the injury she'd suffered during the fight with the robo-troops in Antarctica.

Atherlonne went on to give Geoff and Maura her condolences that their friend Leona had passed away, and she expressed her admiration for the sacrifice Leona had made to rid the universe of the evil Shetani. Maura thanked Atherlonne and said how sad it was that so many of their friends had died: Leona, Huang, Chen and Mettravar.

Atherlonne:

> To pass away is not the end of being.
> Our inner selves swim to another place.
> It's happened many times to each of us.

Geoff noted the surprising similarity between the ways Thiosh and humans dealt with grief. His own emotions were confused. He welcomed the opportunity to understand how others felt, especially regarding Leona. But, at the same time, he felt impatient. 'Ask about the dolphins,' he said in Maura's ear.

'Wait a minute,' Maura told him, typing without a pause.

Maura:

> Kai shared with me what happened in Xizang. The robo-troops had defeated the human armies, but then they fought amongst themselves. Please tell me, what made it happen?

Atherlonne:

> I do not know in detail what occurred.
> The dolphins have a paranormal power,
> greater than any living species known
> within our Solar System or beyond.

Geoff read the amazement in Maura's green eyes.

Atherlonne:

> While they had no desire to interfere,
> they could no longer stand aside when Earth
> and all that live here were in deadly peril.

Maura:

> That's fantastic. Are you saying the dolphins saved humankind?

Atherlonne:

> I realise you're not aware that once
> the dolphins had advanced technology.
> The risk of war became so great that they
> resolved to fully deindustrialise,
> and live the life that nature had intended.
> Although their mental strength could boil the sea,
> they had not used their power ever since
> the age of ice twelve thousand years ago.
> They had no wish to intervene in wars
> caused by the greed and wickedness of humans.

Maura:

> But they changed their minds? Did you persuade them to get involved?

Atherlonne:

>I had to share with them for many tides
>before we reached a common point of view.
>I became convinced a natural life is not
>a hopeless dream but vital for us all.
>Provided that the dolphins stopped the war,
>I promised that the Thiosh would give up
>their technological society.
>This is a promise that we have to keep.
>It's our conviction you must do the same.

Maura:

>I don't know about this. The benefits of technology seem obvious to me: plentiful food, medicines, even weapons for self-defence. But then there are the weapons of mass destruction, and they've got totally out of hand.

Atherlonne:

>We'll try to show the path ahead for you
>and humankind to live another way.
>The dolphins carried out what they'd agreed.
>United, they made waves of energy
>to scramble rebel Thiosh minds' control
>of robo-troop battalions, east and west.
>They could not fully see the consequence:
>the self-destruction of the robot troops.
>No doubt this was fortuitous for us,
>for all the robo-troops have been destroyed
>in every place, on land and in the sea.

Maura:

>We thank you for what you did, and particularly for saving our friend Kai. I do not know how to react to the news about the dolphins, or what you are suggesting for the future of humankind. The implications are incalculable. But, for the first time in many years, there is peace between Hesperians and Khitans, and the Thiosh have eliminated the threat to their own society. The Virtuon Shetani was the most corrupt being ever, but

Leona destroyed him. At last, all sentient beings on Earth can look forward to a better future.

꜀ᴥ

'Progress, Major?' asked Flannery as he poured the Bourbon. He chose the largest glasses in his drinks cupboard and filled them leaving just enough room for the ice.

'The report's due any hour now, suh,' said Breckenridge. 'The team have been workin' on it all night.'

'Come now, Major'. There was a hell of a fire-fight, wasn't there?'

'Yessuh, that's right. There were skirmishes the whole world over, synchronised like, but they only lasted a matter of minutes. It looked like the robot armies were usin' some new super-weapon. The Thiosh didn't even have to use their satellite gamma lasers. It must've been a complete walkover for the aliens.'

'That's clear enough isn't it? What's your problem?'

'Well, suh, since then we've heard a lot of radio broadcasts about a new world order, and such like. No details about what really happened, just a lot of happy gibberish. I don't understand it.'

'Oh, Major, it's as clear as a cavalry bugle. Don't you see? Humankind has given in – at least, they have on Earth. It's a sure sign they're collaborating. I was fortunate to have a good education. I studied a lot of history. I don't suppose you've ever heard of Vitchy France?'

'No, suh.'

'Well, don't worry about it. Just realise what you're hearing is fake news.'

'So can we start the fight back, suh? Launch some nukes?'

'Nope, I don't want to start another ice age. It's too long-winded. I want to see results quicker than that, Major.'

'So do I, suh, so do I.'

'I've had some encouraging news from Research and Development. They've almost finished the gravity bomb. It'll be so powerful, it'll make our nukes look like fireworks.'

'Wowee – that'll be some baby!'

'It'll be awesome, and all the components can be made on Europa. The only snag is – it's too dangerous to test. At least, not this side of Mars's orbit.'

'Oh, that's a cryin' shame. Can we try it somewheres else – shoot it into Venus, d'you think, suh?'

'No, we don't have to do that. The first test's going to be on Earth!'

Part Four
Binary Star

Virtual Reality

Geoff and Maura were in their new 'lab' – the room where they'd researched a cure for the radiation sickness affecting the Thiosh. Maura pointed excitedly to a message which was appearing on her viz-box.

Atherlonne:

> I have good news for you. Chen is alive.
> I've sent a rescue team to bring him here.

'Thank Jaysis!' said Maura, meeting Geoff's eyes.

Maura:

> Can this be true? How did he live through that holocaust?

Atherlonne:

> He will explain when he arrives, although
> you need to know, his auditory sense
> was damaged when your rocket-sledge blew up.

'Does she mean he's deaf?' asked Geoff. 'That doesn't matter too much.' He felt elated Chen had survived. He hadn't realised, until now, how much he'd missed him.

Atherlonne:

> Kai's shuttle suffered damage in the war
> but now there's freedom in the air again.
> The Khitans have the means to bring him back,
> a winged machine that uses air to breathe.

'An aeroplane, yeehah!' said Geoff. 'This is wonderful news. We must celebrate.' He reached for the water jug and filled two glasses with water for a toast. But the Thiosh had more news, her words appearing spasmodically on the screen.

Atherlonne:

> OPDEO's voice transmissions . . . speak of new
> weapons . . . more terrible . . . than nuclear bombs . . .
>   in rockets . . . they intend to . . . fire . . . at Earth.
> Their type . . . is one I do not . . . recognise . . .
> But I have heard . . . the name . . . gravity bomb.

Geoff dropped his glass and it smashed on the floor.

Geoff and Maura waited in the transport bay for the new arrivals and the two Khitans passed through the airlock at the same time. The reunion should have been a joyous affair. Indeed, they greeted each other with much hugging, kissing and excited chatter. However, Geoff couldn't shake off his sense of foreboding. Kai had already received the news from Atherlonne. Only Chen was unaware of the latest development, and he was preoccupied with his own problem. He was clearly worried by his deafness. They all made an effort to put him at his ease and, as long as he could see their lips, he understood what they were saying.

Geoff led them to their messroom and programmed the omniprinter to make coffee. They congratulated Chen for surviving the robo-troop attack. He explained he'd been detaching the stern restraining ties from the rocket-sledge when it blew up. He'd set the rocket engine working at low power in reverse thrust, because of the strong tailwind. The explosion had been very close, but he'd been shielded from most of the blast by the hydraulic bucket doors, used to reverse the hot gas stream.

Chen didn't know how long he'd lain unconscious. When he'd come round, the site had been deserted. All the other survivors of the explosion had departed. Much of the accommodation block had been demolished, but he'd been able to uncover some food and light a fire. During the following days, he'd searched the site for items to help him survive. These included a radio which he converted into a transmitter to send simple pulse signals. These were picked up by Wally, who'd been monitoring the site via the unmanned astronomical station on the Moon. Wally transmitted the news via a message in 8105 code, and it was picked up by Kai who informed Atherlonne by telepathy. They realised the signals had almost certainly come from Chen. Consequently, Atherlonne sent the whale-bot, equipped with a robot search-dog, to find him. Chen finished his story and they lapsed into thoughtful silence.

'Does anyone know anything about gravity bombs?' asked Maura, abruptly.

'Ha! I know some of the theory,' said Geoff, 'and I thought it was only theory. It's been postulated that if you make a perfect void, it will act like a lens to focus dark energy.'

'I don't know any of this stuff,' said Maura. 'Where does the dark energy come from?'

'It is everywhere,' said Kai. 'It is sixty-eight per cent of the total energy of the universe. A gravity explosion could change the Earth's orbit, shift its rotational axis or even rupture the whole planet.'

'Oh, my Jaysis!' said Maura.

'Kai's right,' said Geoff. 'Military scientists have been researching how to make space–time singularities trigger black holes. The lunatic fringe in the Hesperian High Command suggested the principle could be used in a bomb. But it's an extrapolation of human madness. I can't imagine why OPDEO would want to fire one at Earth – it's utter insanity.'

'We must stop them,' said Kai. 'According to General Watkins, a remnant of the Septagon High Command is in hiding. It includes a couple of Hesperian Army Five-Star Generals. In theory, they have authority over OPDEO. Can we get a message to them?'

'I can contact Wally in Oztralia,' said Geoff. 'He's the expert in communications. He may be able to get a message through.'

'Have the Hesperians still got any long-distance missiles?' asked Maura. 'Could they intercept the bomb, perhaps nuke it?'

'I'm afraid that would be difficult,' said Geoff. 'OPDEO's nuclear warheads are designed to separate into dozens of individual units, each on a different course. If OPDEO has done the same with its gravity warheads, it won't be easy to intercept them all.'

'Could we negotiate with OPDEO?' suggested Maura. 'Maybe they just want to scare us into giving them something.'

'They've never conceded anything to anyone in the past,' said Geoff. 'Remember our last attempt at negotiation?'

'Let's get Atherlonne on screen to see what she thinks,' said Maura. 'She could give us advice.' She began to type with two fingers onto her com-pad.

Maura:

> Can I ask, please? OPDEO's gravity bomb. Have you any idea how we could stop it?

Atherlonne:

> I do not have to tell you what to do.
> You know already what is necessary.

'That's strange,' said Maura. 'She's not usually so abrupt.'

Geoff racked his brains. He knew there was a solution, but something seemed to be blocking his line of thought. Could he break through to the answer? He closed his eyes and bowed his head while the others waited for him to speak.

'Sorry,' he said, after a few minutes. 'My mind's blank. We can try Atherlonne again, or she could talk to her friends the dolphins, but I think it would take a Virtuon to stop the gravity bombs.'

'What did you say – a Virtuon?' said Maura. 'That's it. I must become a Virtuon!'

'Hang on,' said Geoff, gripping Maura's arm. 'I don't know if it's possible. In any case, it would mean you'd leave your body. You haven't thought this through.'

'I must do this,' said Maura, shaking off Geoff's hand. 'It's been my life's work to find an alien species. Since we found one, it's been my absolute priority to protect it. If OPDEO are bombing the Earth because the Thiosh are there, then I must save them, and the human population. With respect to you all, I claim the right to finish the job I began.'

Geoff was appalled. Was Maura, his passionate partner and lover, prepared to break up their relationship to become pure artificial intelligence? But it was her passion that motivated her, he told himself. He knew he wouldn't want her any other way. And yet . . .

'Maura, on behalf of us all, I thank you for your offer,' said Kai. 'But, with respect, I feel I have a greater claim to be transformed into Virtuon state. But not one with unrestricted power. I believe it may be possible to be a Virtuon with safeguards to prevent abuse.'

Geoff suspected Kai had known all along Virtuonisation was the answer.

'As you know,' continued Kai, 'I have been party to ignoble actions, which have threatened the Earth with disaster. Actions which led to the death of my friends.'

'But it wasn't your fault,' said Maura.

Kai shook his head. 'Man is shaped by circumstances and it is he who causes them. If I were to become a Virtuon and were able to save the Earth, it would compensate for the terrible wrongs I have done. The fact the Earth is in such danger is largely my fault. It is my duty to save it.'

Then Chen spoke up. 'Excuse me, I understand problem. I do not know if we save Earth. But if gravity bomb do not destroy us, there needs big change. Humans, Thiosh, dolphins and all other creatures must live together. You three know this best.'

Geoff was amazed. He'd never heard Chen make a speech before.

'You three must tell world,' Chen continued. 'For me, I am only bus driver in space. Where I come from, we do not speak proper Khitan even. Now I cannot hear too well either. But I can be Virtuon. Choose me, my weakness is my strength.'

Everyone stared at Chen in surprise, all except Maura. She frowned and stood up, her hands on her hips.

'I'm not going to let you men take this away from me! I will do this thing, whether you like it or not. But actually, if you think about it, it's the only logical solution, as Geoff would say. We will need Kai to deal with the Khitans, and likewise Geoff to sort out the Hesperians.' She thrust her hand out towards Geoff as if to cover his mouth.

'And, though we love Chen, with the best will in the world, I can't see him as a Virtuon. In any case, he has to stay human so he can help Geoff look after the baby.'

All that could be heard was the air-conditioning system. Then Geoff spoke. 'What baby?'

'Yes, Geoff, I was going to tell you soon. You're going to be a father.'

'So you would desert our baby and me to become a Virtuon? Are you crazy, Maura?'

'Maybe. We don't have to discuss it anymore. I'm determined to do this.'

There was silence. Everyone was looking at Geoff.

Maura's going to have our baby and she's upset. She's speaking in a high voice; her face is flushed and she's drilling me with her green eyes.

His memory flashed back to a time long ago, when he'd been with her in the Unidome sky gallery. She'd been angry because she'd thought he'd only befriended her so he could look for aliens. Her emotions had made no sense to him then, and they didn't now. He stood and reached towards her, but she didn't react.

Geoff sat down again and shook his head sadly. 'I once told you I always understood you, but it wasn't true. I must have said it more in hope than reality. But, before you finally commit yourself, there are several things you should consider.'

He got up, standing head and shoulders above her, and counted off the issues on his fingers.

'One, this is new, untested technology. Any attempt to defuse the bombs would be dangerous. Two, Earth and Jupiter will soon be aligned. Assuming OPDEO has a delivery system with a fusion ramjet, they could hit the Earth in no more than twelve months. Three, taking into account all our combined knowledge, we still have no idea how to make you a Virtuon.'

'So we've got a year to find out,' said Maura.

Geoff met her eyes and she fell into his arms, burying her face and sobbing against his chest.

New Life

Maura was lying on the makeshift bed Geoff had set up in their lab. Her stomach was bare and rather shiny. Geoff had coated it with clear gel. 'Zakristan is turning into a real star,' he said. 'This ultrasonic scanner has superb resolution.'

'I know, the robot porters unloaded tons of stuff,' said Maura. 'Where did they get it all from?'

'Zak just told me it was spare. It looks new, so it may have come from a supplier's warehouse. He said he'd left plenty, so we shouldn't be depriving anyone. Anyway, just look at this, he's sucking his thumb.'

'She's sucking her thumb,' corrected Maura.

'Oh, you can't see from this view. I'll try and look from another angle. He should have all his bits now at twelve weeks.'

'You mean all her bits.'

'Well, maybe. Can you feel her move?'

'I didn't realise she'd be moving already. I can't say I've felt her yet. It's still too early. But isn't she just beautiful?'

'Yes, she's a part of your body,' said Geoff, emphasising the last word.

'Don't, please.' She raised her hand to cut him off and change the subject. When will you have the neuromorphic circuits ready?'

'They're finished now as plugboards. We haven't got time to make proper chips from them.'

'Just as long as they work. Okay? And get that mag-res scanner up and running. You've got a million layers to neuro-image.'

'It's a lot more, actually.' Geoff could tell her the exact number, but there was no point.

'And then the calibration with the electrical current maps – what you call megging.'

'Only because it's too hard to say magnetoencephalo . . . whatever it is.' Geoff placed his hand on Maura's stomach. 'D'you really want me to make you a Virtuon?'

'I do – so don't waste time trying to argue me out of it.' She got up and put her top back on.

'You realise you don't have to die physically. There are ways we could map your brain into a computer and make a clone of you, to live in parallel.'

'Holy Mother of God! D'you think I haven't considered that?' she said, her eyes flashing. He put his hand on her shoulder.

'I'm sorry, I know you mean well.' She wrapped her arms around his waist. 'Why do you think the Virtuon Shetani killed his human body?' she said, her cheek pressed against his chest.

'I've been trying to work that out myself. I can't decide whether there's a practical reason why an organic brain can't live alongside its digital counterpart, or if Shetani did it because his mind was simply evil through and through.'

'You mean he killed his body because he hated himself?'

'Maybe, or perhaps as a Virtuon he was afraid the original Prior Shetani could clone a rival artificial brain.'

'I think I'm more worried about being able to telepathise with the AI version of me,' said Maura.

'Why's that? Telepathy is a wonderful gift, surely?'

'You're wrong, Geoff, it's a burden. It's not easy sharing someone else's ideas, opinions, memories. A lot of their thoughts clash with your own. Leona was a wonderful person, but she'd had a terrible struggle trying to decide where her loyalty lay. It was painful to know all that.'

'But the organic you and the digital you will have the same motivation.'

'If you created a duplicate brain, I'm afraid I'd be able to share its thoughts. I'd never be able to cope with all the extra knowledge and power it needs to fend off OPDEO. I don't want to live in parallel with it. I'd have a nervous breakdown. Do you understand?'

'Oh God, it's so difficult. I don't want to lose you, Maura.' He hugged her as if he was trying to weld her body to his.

'Hey, careful, remember I'm pregnant. And you won't be losing me. I'll just be, well, different.'

><

General Flannery hastened to intercept Breckenridge as he passed through the concourse.

'Major, I heard you'd tracked down another Thiosh.'

'Yessuh. We caught the varmint in a trawl net. It was tryin' to get back to the Cronus Rift.'

'Good work. Where is it now?'

'We've got it in the interrogation centre. We're just about to add a little phosphorus to its sulphur ration. I know it could talk to our computers if it wanted to. I just wanna know if there're any others hidin' down there.'

'Does it realise it's being questioned?'

'Oh, sure it does. We've been teachin' it Morse Code with some electrodes – long and short pulses.'

'Okay, keep me informed. Where are the G-bombs now?'

'Just headin' for Mars.'

'Isn't that some way off course?'

'It's to save time, suh. We can slingshot around Mars and increase speed. Then we'll separate the warheads and let the Earth pull 'em in.'

'Okay, Major. You've done well. I'll see you in the bar at lunch. I think you deserve a drink!'

><

It was late. Geoff and Maura had spread out their nightclothes on the bed. 'It's a shame we didn't save any of Shetani's code when we corrupted its software,' said Maura. 'I guess it would be really useful to us now.'

'I know what you're saying,' said Geoff, 'but our focus was to kill it, not reproduce it. Anyway, it would have been incredibly dangerous to have any part of it still functioning after we gave it the virus.'

'I was just thinking, if its programming was so advanced, you could have learnt its language.'

'Nice idea, but I don't think it would have helped. What we must do is design a self-teaching program. It'll learn all there is to know and how to optimise itself.'

'But it'll just start with all I know, won't it?'

Geoff froze for a moment. *I can't do this – not if she has to kill her body to make it work. I can keep her safe, but I can't tell her. I have to carry on as normal.*

'Are you okay?' asked Maura.

'Sorry, I was distracted for a moment.' *Keep focussed,* he told himself, zipping up his pyjama top. 'Yeah, all you know is an enormous quantity of data. We'll have to use a huge amount of computing power to replicate your brain.'

Maura laughed. 'Are you flattering me?'

'Not really. Brains are fantastic organs. We can't engineer anything nearly as compact and efficient, but we've made a lot of progress in AI recently.'

'I s'pose it won't matter how big and complicated the program is if it runs without hardware. But how can that be possible?'

'You'll have to develop the ability to move individual atoms, telekinesis on a very small scale, working at a level of picometers. That's very tiny. I need to search my own brain to find which part does TK and build that into the model with an auto-teaching capability. Then it'll be able to apply forces to smaller and smaller objects.'

'That'll be a fantastic help doing the housework,' said Maura. 'Geoff?'

'Sorry, my mind drifted off.'

'You're thinking about absolute power corrupting absolutely, aren't you?'

'Yes, that was it,' he lied. 'I'm doing everything I can to protect you – and us. But it's not possible to give you all the power you need and limit you at the same time. That would be a fundamental contradiction.'

'Then you'll just have to trust me not to get corrupted,' said Maura. She flipped off the bedside light and snuggled up close, embracing him with her arms and legs. 'The best thing is, if you give me TK-power, then I'll have a part of you in me. Perhaps that will keep me under control.'

Geoff busied himself checking the alarm setting on his com-phone. *I trust you but can you trust me?*

General Flannery pressed a button on his office com-phone. 'Breckenridge – would you believe it? A message has come in on the hotline!'

'From the Septagon, suh? We thought it'd been wiped out by the aliens.'

'Well, it was. Those stooges are trying to trick us into thinking the High Command is still operational. But, somehow, they've got wind of the G-bomb. They're kind of agitated about it.'

Breckenridge's laugh was cut short by his nervous tic.

'They want me to abort the bombs,' Flannery continued.

'I s'pose they would, suh.'

'I told them to take their buoyancy aids next time they go swimming with the aliens. The sea may get kind of rough.'

Breckenridge alternated his laughter with more hiccups.

'But this is important,' said Flannery. 'Somehow the Septagon got a warning. I made sure R and D wiped everything off the server and I put all the files in the strongroom. But someone's been speaking out of turn about the G-bombs. I'm relying on you, Major. Find the bastard who leaked the info and erase their memory – permanently.'

Janey Mack, this is incredible! Zakristan has sent a robot midwife. It's written on her uniform. And she's got two assistants. How do they know what to do? Their knowledge can only be theoretical. At least their hands look soft – synthetic rubber, probably. The room's okay. It smells of antiseptic. I guess that's a good sign. The floor's a bit wonky but the bed is level. I'll have a look round before I settle down on the mattress. It's probably self-profiling, but I'm not expecting the last word in comfort today. These paintings are nice. They've got brush marks like originals – how do they do that? I think they're scenes from County Kerry. That one looks like Macgillycuddy's Reeks. The wall screen's just like a real window, except the view keeps changing.

'How are you feeling now?' says Geoff.

'Not too bad so far, thanks. How are you?' *I bet he's still upset. He's given up trying to understand me. Whoa! Here comes another contraction. They're getting sharper . . . P'raps I should have had the drugs after all.*

'Can you get these robots to help me, Geoff. I'm soaking wet.'

'You can talk to me directly, dear. My name's Millie.'

Millie the mid-bot, how perfect. But why have they given her a high voice? A lower one would have been more soothing.

'There, is that better?' says Millie.

'Thank you.' *It isn't really, but I'll be even stickier soon.*

'Ten minutes between contractions,' says Geoff. 'It won't be long now.'

Are these robots programmed for emergencies? So much can go wrong during childbirth. I could die today, and that's ironic. I'm planning to die anyway. But am I really going to end my bodily life when I love Geoff and I'm about to have a baby? P'raps I should never have gone to Europa, but then I wouldn't have met Geoff, or found out the truth about OPDEO. Or have a chance to destroy it. Is that what this is about? My mission? Who d'you think you are, Maura? Joan of Arc? There's plenty of evidence she was seriously unhinged. P'raps that applies to me too. Oh shit, the pain's building up again.

'Aargh!'

'Just relax,' says Geoff.

He's mopping my brow with something damp. I'll give him a smile. Ah, Millie has a pair of callipers. She must want an accurate measurement. I think she's measuring the dilation of my cervix on different axes. No doubt she'll take an average.

'Don't poke me with those things. I'll rip open!'

'Four centimetres,' says Millie. 'You're doing fine. Keep doing your breathing.'

I wasn't planning to stop breathing, you stupid mid-bot. Oh, this is hell. I can't move. I think my back's seized up. My insides are twisting harder and harder. I must breathe steadily, in through the nose and out through the . . .

'Oh shit, God save us!'

'Eight minutes, that time,' says Geoff.

What's he thinking now? It's a shame I can't read his mind. I'm sure he still doesn't understand my decision. Choosing to leave my body, do I understand that myself? I'm so confused. But when I talk to the others, I'm categorical and dominant. I do it to hide my uncertainty. What'll it be like to become a Virtuon? Pure artificial intelligence. Geoff will build in self-learning programmes. I'll be incredibly knowledgeable and powerful. 'Omniscient and omnipotent', as our village priest used to say, but he wasn't talking about Virtuons.

'Oh, bleedin' hell, I wish this was over.'

'Seven minutes.'

Five months, that's all we've got before the G-bombs hit Earth. Mary, Mother of God, I'm so frightened! Brain emulation is so difficult. We don't know if what we're doing is right. We're only halfway through the neuro-imaging and we've still got to map the electrical currents. Even when I'm a Virtuon, it'll be a while before I can take on OPDEO. What the hell have I done? My insides are being ripped out. Let me die now!

'Six minutes.'

I haven't told anyone the baby's name yet. What presence will I have in her life? I'll never be able to touch her. Jaysis! It'll be like watching her through a window. And Geoff too. And what will it do to us? He'll never look at me the same again. In fact, he'll never look at me. There'll be nothing to see. Clodagh, oh, my Clodagh! I've been so stupid, and now I'm being punished.

'Six and a half that time. Don't worry, it's going well,' says Geoff.

I need to talk to him, but now's not the time. He said my artificial brain will be the same as me only for a millisecond. After that it'll go off grabbing more and more knowledge and suck energy from here and there. I won't be me anymore. Will I really have consciousness, or just be a bunch of numbers? I'll be like a bulldozer without a driver. But OPDEO are evil. They want to destroy the Earth, every living thing in the sea, on land and in the air. I must stop them, whatever the cost. Just thinking about them makes me sick.

'Oh, Sweet Mother of God, the pain!'

'Well done, Maura. We're back to six.'

This is our one chance to stop those bloody fascists. One of us must do it. I'm closest to nature. I've studied it all my life. Geoff's much more academic than me. Kai's more spiritual. I'm not sure Chen's up to it. Atherlonne could do it, but she's a pacifist and the job ahead will be violent. I didn't know about the dolphins. They gave up technology tens of thousands of years ago – how fantastic is that?

'Jaysis Christmas!'

'Five minutes. Keep doing the breathing.'

'Whose having this feckin' baby, you or me?'

It's me having the baby, and they expect me to make the jump. Giving up my Clodagh. What the fuck have I done? I'm already using her for my own ends. I convinced the others it's my brain that must be uploaded into a feckin' computer. I made myself sound adamant. I said I was prepared to sacrifice my body and my motherhood. I used Clodagh as my trump card so I could get my way. But what a way.

'Shit, shit, shit!'

'Four minutes. You're doing fine.'

'Aaaaaargh!'

My arse is going to split in two. I might as well become AI. My body won't be any use after this. Not with my arse in two bits. As long as Clodagh survives. Please God, save her. Let Clodagh live, that's all that's important.

'Three minutes. This baby wants out.'

Something's happened. Clodagh's digging her nails into my vagina. She's ripping it apart. The mid-bot is fiddling with her feckin' callipers again. God, I'm not going to be able to hold back much longer.

'Maura, dear, you can push now,' says Millie.

Living Wake

Perhaps the designers had never intended the occupants to spend long periods in the TUCC. But for humans trained as space travellers, their accommodation was not unpleasant. True, the floor sloped all over the place, but that made walking the corridors more interesting; the building had no windows, but the varying landscapes shown on randomly spaced wall screens effectively eradicated feelings of claustrophobia and imprisonment. Geoff preferred the freedom of the ocean but he was surprised how well he'd adjusted to this artificial environment. The different areas enabled the inhabitants to work at their respective projects, interact, rest and enjoy entertainment, without an excessive yearning for the outside world. The days passed only too quickly.

Geoff was at his desk in the open-plan office working on his com-pad. He looked up and was surprised to see someone waiting to gain his attention.

'Oh, sorry Kai. What's on your mind?'

'The uni-net is working properly again. Can you help me, please? I want to set up a webinar.'

'I think I can fix that for you. What's it about?'

'Basically, I am proposing a conference about the future of our planet, and I would like you to chair it.'

'Why me?'

'Because you are a representative of the former Unified Nations. I believe we have to start again, but with an expanded membership. I want to propose the foundation of a new institution, dedicated to achieving peace and harmony on Earth. We could call it the League of Sentient Beings.'

'Well, it's worth a try. I like your positive thinking. I'm still wondering if we'll even have a future. Who do you want to attend?'

'Could we link together General Courtney Watkins, Shan Chonglin, Atherlonne and Voorogg? I do not think the Abbot of Drepung would want to get involved, but I can ask him. Also, perhaps, Yul T'an. Why not? She is good at offering a different point of view – at least, she did to me.'

'She argued with you?'

'She tried to tezla me.'

'Right, well, we'd better also include the leader of the dolphins. Atherlonne calls her Cetania, but I don't know how she'll communicate. Her whistles and clicks are a form of language, so we need to set up a translation program. Actually, I think Wally could help us there, let's count him in. And, of course, there's my partner, the would-be Virtuon.'

It was lunchtime. Clodagh was fast asleep, monitored by Geoff's home-made baby alarm linked to Maura's com-phone. The four adult humans were in the kitchen, along the corridor from their bedrooms. Chen was busy selecting recipes, checking the nutrient content and programming the omniprinter. Maura, Geoff and Kai were sitting at a table where a robot auxiliary had set places for a meal.

'Well, I don't think we should be too unhappy about this,' said Maura, brightly. 'Just think of it as a wake, while I'm still alive. I went to quite a few of those before I left Earth to go to Europa. Most of my elderly relations opted for assisted suicide. It's better than wasting away and losing your marbles.'

'But you're still young,' said Geoff. 'You told me your aunties were in their two hundreds and all their bones had been replaced with plastic.'

'Well, if I'm going to have a funeral, I don't see why I should miss out on all the cucumber sandwiches and the sherry. I insist we have a party, while I'm still alive.'

'You are very brave,' said Kai. 'But you do not have to put on an act for us. We have the deepest respect for you. It would be right to celebrate your life and achievements, and we should do that seriously.'

'Oh, don't do those sickening speeches, I couldn't stand that. I think Chen should make us a Black Forest cherry cake. You could do that, couldn't you?' she called across to Chen, who nodded happily.

'It's my favourite,' she said. 'Death by chocolate, can't be so bad.'

'I do not understand your Irish jokes,' said Kai.

<hr>

It was late afternoon, CHT. Geoff was sitting at his desk in the lab. He was writing up his day's work in his technical journal.

'Monday 12 September 2140: I've now tested all the software relating to Maura's brain, plus essential additions. The self-learning subroutines are well proven and I've copied them across. The energy extraction procedure works well on a small scale, and there should be no difficulty with more powerful sources. But I have yet to build TK ability into the program. It's going to need it at molecular level. I've tried to map areas of my own brain while doing TK exercises but, so far, I haven't found the parts that activate. I can now rule out the frontal lobe, the parietal, and all other areas of higher brain function. The next step will be to try the more primitive structures, the first parts to develop as we evolved as homo sapiens.'

Maura entered. 'Hiya, what's new?' she said, twisting round a lop-sided chair to level it on the sloping floor.

'Ah, you're just in time. If I put on the mag-res headset and practice moving this pen around without touching it, see if you can pick up any discharges in my cerebellum.'

'Oh right, I think there is something. Like tiny tracer bullets shooting down your axons.'

'Great,' said Geoff. 'I knew it had to be somewhere.'

'But I thought that part was a sort of ancient brain for low life forms. I mean, a lot of reptiles have developed cerebellums,' said Maura.

'Interesting, isn't it? Perhaps the early humans and their cousins had TK skills, but lost them later on. Can you start up the megging

recorder? I want to correlate the flashes with specific movements.'
And what Maura doesn't know is soon I'll have the rest of my brain mapped as well.

⤙⬛

Next morning, Kai called Geoff to ask him to help prepare a tribute to Maura. They met in the TUCC library. It was a room with a few cabinets containing a limited number of hard-copy atlases, charts, 3-D pictorial records and original paper documents. But its main use was to display data from the library servers as quantum dot images on wall screens.

Kai had been collecting information from the uni-net. 'I see Maura got a first at the Marine Science National University of Ireland,' said Kai, 'and was commended for her PhD thesis at MIT. The papers she has written have been published in all the best academic e-journals.'

'She's a bright girl, alright,' said Geoff. 'She plays the Irish harp, sings beautifully, and she was on a national viz-box programme about traditional dancing.'

'So there is a lot we can say about her at the party. Tell, me how did you meet her?'

'Ha, that was typical of her. She'd set off all the sirens and strobes in the Unidome. She was so excited about being able to fly, with the gravity being so low. She'd gone right up to the top and landed in a prohibited area. The goons in Securopa spotted her and they pressed the main alarm button. They were such prats. She was obviously harmless, just a young girl.' Geoff's voice was breaking up.

'Did they fine her?'

Geoff cleared his throat noisily. 'No, she just got a lecture. I got the same because I'd landed next to her to talk her down. She was more worried about the black mark on my record than on her own.'

Kai smiled broadly. 'She was wonderful to me, after Leona killed Shetani. I was about to jump into the Ross Sea after what had happened. But Maura wanted me to be your leader again, and you all forgave me. Her kindness gave me hope.'

'She has empathy, alright. She's amazingly intuitive. Maura and Leona together were incredible. When I wanted to dock at a big Oztralian port, they both told me we had to walk across the desert to

Uluru. And that's what we did. Walk, mind you, even though we'd set off in a truck. Sorry, Kai. I know it hurts you to talk about Leona.'

'No, it is okay. And you are correct. They both had a telepathic gift that was very strong. In Maura's case, it has given her a natural affinity with Thiosh. She understands them and, I think, loves them. That is why she has been so determined to save them.'

'She's got quite a temper on her too, you know. I remember when I got drunk on Wally's whiskey when we were in Oztralia. She gave me a hard time, but it was mainly because we'd been drinking without her.'

Geoff began to laugh, but then had a flashback to another time when Maura was angry. He was lying on the deck of the whale-bot, his nose broken. *Best not to mention that.*

'It is clear she loves life,' said Kai, 'and that must make this "jump" as she calls it, exceptionally hard for her, and also for you, Geoff. But she is utterly determined.'

'Yup. I wonder what she'll do when I jump before her.'

'Sorry, Geoff. I do not understand.'

'Please don't tell her but, all the neuroimaging and megging I've done on her brain to reproduce it artificially, I've also done on mine. I can Virtuonise myself. Maura mustn't do it, not now she's got Clodagh. It would be too great a sacrifice for her, and a disaster for our child. Maura doesn't know, but I'm going to jump instead of her.'

'You would do this in Maura's place?'

'Yes, after the party, I'll run the start-up programme, and drink the Pentobarbital myself. I need you, Kai, to calm her down when she finds out what's happened. Also, I'd be grateful if you'd run the command file on the network to make me a Virtuon. It's called Zaijian.'

Kai smiled grimly. 'You love her deeply, I know. But she is determined to save the Thiosh single-handed.'

'Yes, but originally she wanted to settle down and have a family. She was very open with me the first time we went down in the bathyscaphe to look at the Europan seabed. She needs to bring up Clodagh herself. In time, she may meet someone else instead of me.'

'You do not have to kill your own natural body,' said Kai. 'You are not telepathic. You could lead a separate life.'

'If Maura is prepared to live only as AI, then I must do the same as her. My jump needs to be in place of hers.'

'I admire the fact you are prepared to end your natural life for the sake of Maura. I do not think I should try to influence either of you, but I do not relish the prospect of having to tell her what you have done.'

'She'll get over it,' said Geoff. 'You've seen her with Clodagh. She's totally infatuated with our daughter. Remember, she took her decision to jump before Clodagh was born. I'm sure she was too hasty. I reckon she regrets volunteering to jump. She probably feels she can't back down.'

'I will talk to her. Like I said before, I am willing to become a Virtuon if it makes up for the harm I have done in the past.'

'I know that's how you feel, but there's no time. I'm sorry, but it would take too long to replicate you. My artificial brain is almost ready to fire up.'

Computer Error

It was the early hours of the morning. The baby's plaintive crying had woken Geoff. He'd tried to get up quietly, but soon Maura was wide awake too.

'I knew you'd make a great dad, to be sure,' she said. 'You're forever leaping out of bed to see to Clodagh.'

'It's okay, really. She really likes the milk from the omniprinter.'

'I'm sorry I'm not feeding her the natural way. I would have preferred it, but I didn't want her to get used to something I couldn't finish.'

'Yeah, I guessed that was it.'

'I thought you'd be a lot more antsy than this,' said Maura. 'But you seem to be rather distant. What's the matter?'

'Well, perhaps it's because our relationship is fucked. OPDEO wants to take over the Solar System by fucking up the Earth. And if ever we thought we'd be a normal couple one day, there's fuck all chance now. We could've let Kai Virtuonise.'

Maura took a deep breath. 'Did you think of volunteering for the jump?' she asked. 'I don't remember you offering yourself.'

Geoff looked away. 'Maybe that was because I haven't mastered being human yet.'

Kai had finished decorating the lounge for the party. Geoff's stomach knotted when he saw the bunting, the streamers, and the balloons. He forced himself to smile as Chen came in carrying a cake.

'Wow!' said Geoff, simulating surprise. 'Black Forest cherry cake. Maura's favourite.'

'Schwarzwälder Kirschtorte,' said Chen. 'German is more easy than English.'

'The room looks great. Thanks for all your work. I don't know how you found all these photos of Maura.'

'It okay now uni-net is back. Many pictures from school time.'

'On a farm, riding horses, mucking out pigs. She seemed to be enjoying that,' said Geoff.

'And she play sport in team with helmets and shovels,' said Chen.

'Oh, I think that's camogie. Like hurling.'

Seeing Chen's blank expression, Geoff tried to explain how the game was played. 'You have to knock the ball between the posts, either above or below the crossbar. Below is better. It's very fierce and violent.'

Chen smiled and nodded. 'Back home, we play *Beikou tarkbei* with wood sticks. It is ancient game. Ball is knob from apricot root. Sometimes we play at night-time. We put cloth on ball and make it catch fire.'

Geoff forced himself to concentrate. 'Really? What are the rules?'

'No rules,' said Chen.

Geoff decided to leave that subject. 'Okay,' he said, 'it's time now. Can you fetch Kai, and I'll go and get the Virtuon-girl.'

Geoff walked down the corridor but, feeling dizzy, he stopped to lean against the wall. *This is a celebration of Maura's life. It's supposed to be happy. I've got to keep up appearances. But how the hell can I? I must be positive about Maura's decision but, to become a Virtuon, she needs to end her natural life. How will she react when she finds I've beaten her to it? I can't think any more. It's time to go and fetch her. She'll have put on her party dress – and the shamrock leaves I made for her with the omniprinter. She'll wear them in her hair. Oh God, the green will match her eyes!*

He entered the bedroom. Clodagh was crying in her cot. *Why hasn't Maura seen to her? Is she so deeply asleep, she hasn't heard the baby? Oh, please God, No, no, no!* He lifted Maura's wrist to feel her pulse, but her skin was already cold. He picked up the flask from the bedside table and lifted it to his nose. *Pentobarbital!*

He sagged to the ground, sobbing. No, this wasn't supposed to happen. He saw the note propped up on the dressing table. It said

'Geoff' on the envelope, handwritten. He held the letter for a while, his hand shaking. He didn't want to rip it open. It was her last gift to him. He knew he would keep it for the rest of his life. He hunted through drawers, pulling them out and emptying the contents on the floor, rummaging until he found what he was looking for – a steel nail file. He opened the envelope carefully and pulled out the letter.

> *Hiya, Geoff. Surprise, surprise - I've left early! I'm really sorry to miss the party. You must have gone to so much trouble to make it really special for me. And I bet you were going to say lots of nice things. It could have got quite maudlin, of course. It's been hard to get people to laugh at my jokes, lately.*

Clodagh began to wail and Geoff picked her up to rock her in his arms. He continued reading.

> *But, you know how you called me intuitive? You often wondered why things were obvious to me and not to yourself. I could never do telepathy with you, but I didn't have to. I guessed you were not going to let me jump. I had a look on the network at all your mind-uploading files. Some have a prefix 'M' and some start with 'G'. I wasn't surprised to see there were just as many G files as Ms. And they were just as big. I know you neuro-imaged your cerebellum to capture your telekinetic ability, but I could see you hadn't stopped there. You had a complete replica of everything in your skull.*

Clodagh had fallen asleep but Geoff continued to rock her, afraid she'd wake up if he stopped.

> *I found a launch file called 'Zaijian'. It's a Khitan word, isn't it? I asked Chen what it meant, and he told me it's the word for 'Goodbye'. I'm not great at reading computer code, but I could see you were set up to launch*

your files, not mine. My guess was you were going to hit your jump button in the middle of the night, and drink the Pentobarbital as a nightcap. You might of course, have tried to keep your organic brain living in parallel, but that's a good recipe for a nervous breakdown. This way, you don't have to take the risk.

Clodagh was making sniffling sounds. *Probably dreaming,* thought Geoff. He laid her in her crib and turned back to the letter.

I must admit, after I had our baby, I very nearly changed my mind about becoming a Virtuon. She's a wonderful child, and she doesn't deserve to have the weirdest mum in the universe. I nearly let you carry out your plan. After all, you would have loved to have had all that computing power at your ~~fingertips~~ neurons. But in the end, I realised my first decision was the right one.

Give little Clodagh a kiss for me, please. You may have to do a lot of that in the future. At last I've found a man who's a perfect dad.

Take care, it's time to say Zaijian.

All my love, Maura.

Geoff made his way back to the party room, but couldn't speak. He beckoned to the others. They all shuffled into the bedroom. Kai and Chen knelt beside the bed and chanted Khitan prayers. Then they wrapped Maura in a saffron cloth and lifted her onto a stretcher.

'Zakristan will look after her body until her funeral,' said Kai. 'I will arrange for her to be cremated. She wanted her ashes to be scattered over the sea. It is contrary to her Catholic tradition, but she was insistent.'

Geoff turned abruptly and left the room. Sitting at his work desk, he accessed the master server from his com-pad. At least I can recreate her artificially, he thought. Opening the Zaijian code, he made the global edits to execute Maura's files instead of his own. He clicked on Run, and . . . nothing happened.

Geoff scavenged his brain, trying to find ways to start the virtual mirror of Maura's intellect. But, after two hours, he had to admit he'd run out of ideas. He fought to control his trembling body. *It's no good, she's dead. Her body's dead and her mind's dead. I've failed her and I can't even beg forgiveness.*

Spy Wars

Geoff couldn't account for the last two hours. He wondered if he'd been sleepwalking. But now he was in the lab, looking at words on the screen of his com-pad – words from an alien creature, expressing her sympathy:

Atherlonne:
> I'm sorry that you suffer so much pain.

The message had been sent twenty minutes ago. He typed his reply:

Geoff:
> Thank you. I appreciate your sympathy. But Maura's mind must live on, in a different form. Can you look at my coding, please? There's a huge amount of data, and I've made a mistake, somewhere.

Atherlonne:
> I will, of course, assist if I am able.

Geoff returned to the party room where Chen was taking down the decorations. He asked him to look after Clodagh, and then went back to his desk to wait for Atherlonne's reply. He knew he ought to get some sleep, but he was too worried.

Perhaps I've been too ambitious, thinking I can upload a human brain. There is no way of telling how Shetani did it, but there's a huge amount of computer expertise in the monasteries. The monks in the Middle Ages researched the natural world, astronomy, languages, and even martial arts in some cultures. Their libraries were repositories of knowledge, recorded conscientiously and artistically. Nowadays, the Khitan monasteries are cutting-edge software houses. I should have asked them for help. Why did I think I could do it all myself?

⊱⬤

Geoff looked at his time read-out and realised it was sunrise over the surface of the sea three miles above him. A new message appeared on his screen.

Atherlonne:

> You have the scans until this week but then
> there is a memory gap which should be filled.

Geoff:

> I never intended to let her jump. I was going to do it instead. She will have lost a few days' memory, as if she'd been unconscious. But she should be able to carry on thinking from the present time.

Atherlonne:

> Her program needs another data file,
> maybe a special memory of some kind.
> I checked her com-pad and her com-phone but
> I fear there was not anything that helped.
> Nobody knows her better than yourself.
> What is it that she needs to be complete?

Geoff went back to the bedroom. *Damn it, I could never telepathise with her. She knew I was planning to jump, and she kept that knowledge secret. What other secrets did she have?*

The contents of the drawers were still strewn over the floor. There must be a clue somewhere. Where do I look? He went through the pockets of her thermal suits, flipped through her hard-copy photo albums, and opened a small box of personal items. A gold crucifix, a cameo brooch, the natural pearl necklace he'd given her, emerald earrings the colour of her eyes, her old-fashioned fountain pen.

How strange! Maura must have used it to write me her letter in traditional handwriting.

He was about to close the box when lightning flashed in his brain. The inside of the box was too shallow. He emptied the contents, carefully this time, levered up the padded base and took out a slim notebook.

Poems! Why didn't I know Maura wrote poetry? Geoff asked himself. He took the notebook back to his desk, and typed Maura's last entry:

Daughter

Sleep, sleep my little one, my child.
Iniquity assuaging, tranquillity unchanging,
Breathe deep and slow all the while.
Simplicity pervading, silently persuading,
Dream peace and hope for your life.

Sing, sing my little one, my child,
In happiness rejoicing, laughter announcing
Openness and love in your heart.
Voice full and ringing, a well-spring
outflowing,
Give of yourself without fear.

Geoff wiped away the tears from his eyes and returned to the lab. He used his transcriptor to convert the poem into machine code, and hyperlinked it from Maura's last memory. He ran Zaijian again, and waited while streams of boot-up commands filled his screen, faster than he could read. But the last item was more than just computer source code. It was a message he would remember always. He read it and felt his body unwind.

Maura:

Don't say Zaijian, Geoff. You should have called the program 'Hiya'. But thanks anyway, I think I've been born again.

Geoff:

Oh, my love. How are you feeling? Sorry, stupid question.

Maura:

Sure, but it's not. The only experiences we can ever have are just phenomena in our brains – you know that. And actually, I'm okay, although this seems like a dream at the moment. I need time to adjust. But I'm certain I can link with you mentally in some way. Perhaps we won't have to keep writing messages to each other.

Geoff:

Oh Maura, that would be fantastic. I can't think of anything better.

Maura:

I know I have a lot of work to do, but I'm kind of looking forward to it. I'm buzzing with ideas, and they're coming faster and faster.

Geoff:

Don't be in too much of a rush. You probably need to pace yourself.

Geoff realised he was automatically repeating advice he'd given Maura countless times before. She no longer needed suggestions of that sort.

Maura:

Don't worry, I know you will help me. We can do lots of science together, just like we always have.

Geoff:

I'll be ready. Just tell me what. I've only ever wanted the best for you.

Maura:

I know that. I now have a perfect memory, thanks to you. But you must be extremely tired. We'll talk again, when you've had some rest. By the way, you need to make more nappies. Chen has just used the last one. And make them a bit bigger this time.

Geoff:

How do you know what Chen is doing?

Maura:

Oh, there'll be a lot to tell you. But I'll save it for later. Thanks for finding my poem. It'll remind me of holding Clodagh in my arms. Sleep well, Geoff.

Geoff:

Thanks, Maura. I love you!

><

Major Willard Breckenridge hadn't slept too well. He'd read every communication sent to the Septagon during the last month, and there had been no hint of G-bombs, just the usual routine output: awards given to departments for self-sufficiency; health and safety reports showing no lost-time accidents; more lies about their care of environment and so on. He wouldn't be able to keep the general off his back much longer. He poured himself a glass of water and washed down two tablets from the blister pack he kept in his desk drawer. He picked up his com-phone and clicked on Library.

'Hi, Elisabetta? Breckenridge here. I wonder if you could hop over to see me in my office . . . Yeah, as soon as possible, please.'

The major programmed his coffee machine to pour two cups of Arabica and carried them to his desk. Elisabetta sat demurely with her legs crossed, looking rather small in Breckenridge's simulated leather armchair.

'D'you like your job in the library?' he asked her.

'Oh yes, Major.'

'Ain't it rather repetitive, p'raps a little borin'?'

'No, not at all. I enjoy carrying out information searches for people. I learn something new every time.'

'Well, I've noticed you're very conscientious and competent. I'm preparin' a shortlist of possible candidates for a new department I'm creatin'. If you did well in a little old performance test, I'd set you up as Group Head. You'd still be a civilian, but your salary would be a helluva lot higher than you get now.'

'Oh, Major, thank you for considering me. Can I ask what the new job is about?'

'You can ask, but I'd have to marry you if I told you,' said Breckenridge, hiccupping his peculiar laugh. Elisabetta smiled politely.

'Nah, seriously, this new operation is top secret. Not even our Intelligence unit know about it. But to prove you're as cute as I think you are, I'd like you to do a test. You just have to use this com-pad to give me printouts showin' whenever someone in the Unidome searches the network using certain words. D'you think you can do that?'

'Oh yes, Major – willingly.'

Geoff was working late in the lab again. He was trying to get back into the galactic uni-nets he'd first accessed in Atherlonne's caves, to see if earlier civilisations had invented G-bombs. But it wasn't going well. He'd found many examples of alien worlds that had tried to create black holes but, mysteriously, the information ceased shortly afterwards – or perhaps it wasn't so mysterious, after all.

A message appeared on Geoff's com-pad:

Maura:

> Hiya Geoff, how are you doing?

Geoff:

> I'm great thank you, Maura. It's so good to hear from you.

Maura:

> I'm sorry to write on your com-pad. I think we can get some more direct contact going soon. But this is kind of important, so I don't want to take any chances of misunderstanding. I've really expanded my mind, since the jump. With a bit of effort, I can access just about any data that exist electronically. But these feckin' OPDEO eejits have got wise to the Thiosh hacking their networks. They're reverting to old-fashioned hard-copy documents for their secret stuff. It looks like they're using their keyboards for typing. Did you know, in the twentieth century, people had mechanical 'typewriters' so they

didn't have to write by hand? Well, the buggers are using their com-pads offline like typewriters, and I can't see what they've got in their G-bombs.

Geoff:

Is there nothing on their network, indexes, stuff like that?

Maura:

The bockedy-arsed bastards are too clever for that.

Geoff:

D'you know what? I think it's time to talk to Prof, if he's still in post.

Maura:

What are you thinking of?

Geoff:

He was once a reputable scientist. Let's see what how loyal he is to his lords and masters, now they're killing off the remaining Thiosh on Europa. I don't think he was ever comfortable collaborating with OPDEO. We need to turn him into a rebel.

Maura:

I like the idea, but I'm not clever enough to do that yet.

Geoff:

Maura, love, d'you not feel that you're a conscious being?

Maura:

Ha, you ought to talk to Kai about that. He thinks consciousness is an illusion, to make you get up in the morning and find food. It doesn't do much to serve the rest of humankind, or any other sentient beings.

Geoff:

As you're an über-brain, I don't think I'll get into any philosophical arguments with you. But how can we influence Prof's neural networks so he collaborates with us?

Maura:

> I think you should talk to Kai. There's life even beyond a Virtuon's understanding.

Geoff:

> I think you've become more like me.

Maura:

> If you mean I'm more logical, I can calculate faster and more accurately than before. But logic is purely historical. I can extrapolate the present and guess at the future, and even ascribe probabilities to my predictions. But that's only logic.

Geoff:

> What's happened to your intuition?

A convulsion of fear pulsed through Geoff. *Did I miss part of Maura's mind I should have replicated?*

Maura:

> Don't worry. I still have that as well. That's why you should speak to Kai. But give our babe a cuddle first. Okay?

Geoff found Kai sitting at his desk in the open-plan office. He was looking at the protocols for earlier attempts to set up world peacekeeping organisations.

'Have you got a minute?' Geoff asked. 'I wondered how you'd got on contacting General Watkins and Shan.'

'Yes, they are keen to cooperate. But I think you have other things on your mind?'

Geoff nodded his head. 'As always, you are several steps ahead of me. I wanted to ask your advice. We need someone in OPDEO to collaborate with us. A sort of a secret agent.'

'Such a person needs to have sufficient motivation to make the risks tolerable. Who have you got in mind?'

'I used to work in Professor Mitchell's department. At least, that was the unit I was allocated to, for administrative purposes. He sold out to OPDEO, ages ago, and gave up doing proper science. If he's got any kind of conscience, he would want to help us, I'm sure.'

'If he defects to us, it will put him in great personal danger,' said Kai. 'But if we tell him the truth, we may be able to get him to risk his neck. But it will not be easy contacting him. We will have to do it in such a way that he complies with us rather than OPDEO, who say we are traitors.'

'Hm, that's going to be a problem. Prof's a loner. I can't think of anyone who was close to him when I worked there.'

'Leona could have done it. She once told me that Prof was infatuated with her. I think she may be able help us, even beyond the grave. I will share with Atherlonne and see if we can prepare the ground.'

Brain Waves

Professor Peregrine Mitchell washed down his Semperyuve caplets with a glass of sparkling mineral water, and frowned. He switched on the light above his bathroom mirror and looked again. The lines in his forehead were deepening. He brushed his coiffured hair and stared at the grey strands clinging to the bristles.

He spoke into his com-phone. 'Memo, seven thirty CHT, Sunday sixteenth April 2141. Please arrange analysis of Semperyuve pills manufactured on Europa. Compare with control sample of original anti-ageing supplement manufactured on Earth. Send message to Dr Adams in Pharmacology.'

'DO YOU MEAN ADAEZE?' said the phone.

'No, shit, forget it,' said Prof.

He walked over to his desk where his com-pad was charging. There was an urgent notification flashing on the screen. It was a message from Breckenridge. 'Oh, Christ!' he muttered. 'What does he want now?' He picked up the photo on his desk and shook his head. It showed him wearing his cap and gown at Cambridge. Underneath, his students had written 'To the best Senior Tutor ever. Good luck in your new job!'

His omniprinter flashed green to shown it had finished processing. In spite of the machine's name, its software did not allow many of the more convenient mind-altering substances to be synthesised. However organic seeds and derivatives used for culinary purposes were all permitted. Prof unlocked the side panel and took out a flask of white powder. After adding a measured quantity of hot water to the flask, he stirred the mixture with a narrow spatula until all the powder had dissolved. He took his necktie and tied it tightly as a tourniquet around his upper arm, smiling grimly as the coat of arms of his old college, Corpus Christi, became embedded in the knot. He placed some cotton wool in neck of flask as a filter and drew the liquid into the body of a hypodermic syringe. Then he pushed the needle point into the crook of his arm. He slightly withdrew the plunger to check he'd hit a vein and red-black blood ballooned inside the syringe, like the glob of 'lava' he'd once seen in a strange lamp in an antique shop. He tore off the tourniquet with his free hand, gripped the syringe and pushed the hit home. After ten seconds he returned to his com-pad.

He opened Breckenridge's message. 'How are you doing Prof? You made any progress dissecting that Thiosh carcass? There must be something we can put in the ocean to clean them out. I need your update PDQ. Have a nice Sunday!'

'Stupid fucker,' said Prof, laughing. He began to type a message to his lab technician. 'Hi, Laura . . .' An error flashed DO YOU MEAN LEONA?

'Fuck,' Prof swore. He deleted the name, left the greeting just as 'Hi' and continued. 'Release the Thiosh autopsy to Breckenridge, but delete any reference to specific poisons. Just say Thiosh toxicity is being researched currently.'

Geoff now spent hours in the lab, the place where he'd shared much of his recent time, hopes and aspirations with Maura. Without her he preferred to be on his own. The lab was now his private space.

He heard a voice. It sounded very close to him. He looked around the empty room, and it was still empty. He typed on his com-pad.

Geoff:
Maura, is that you, or am I hallucinating?

Hiya, Geoff, it's me to be sure. I thought I'd try speaking inside your head. You would only have heard me if you'd wanted to, but of course, you did. You don't have to type messages any more. Just think the sentences you want to say, and I'll see if I can pick them up.

Testing one, two, three, four, thought Geoff.

Very good, but d'you think you could think of something more original?

Oh, I never expected it to work. Are we really doing telepathy? It's fantastic!

Well, it beats comp-mails any day. But I doubt if you'll be able to telepathise with anyone else, though you could try if you want to. But I think it'll be something special between you and me. Would you like that Geoff?

Too right – it would be wonderful to know what you really think. Not that you've kept anything from me. You've never done that. Well, except for your poem. I liked it by the way.

There'll be no more room for secrets. I'm sorry I hid the poem, but I was embarrassed about anyone seeing it, even you.

Hey, Maura – I can feel your emotion. You've got emotions and I can feel them.

Emotions are good as long as they're positive. But come what may, I'll always love you.

Thanks. 'Always' may be a long time in your case.

I've been reading what you write in your Clodagh diary on the TUCC network. I'm sorry you've had to get up so often in the night.

She keeps changing her routine, but it's okay, we're managing. I take it in turns with Chen to change her nappies. And she's growing so fast. She's put on nearly a kilo. Geoff wondered if Maura could tell how tired he felt.

I know how tired you feel. You've been through a lot lately.

Like you say, no more secrets.

Thanks for putting the infrared camera in Clodagh's room. I saw she'd dropped her dummy the other night. I nearly TK-ed it up and put it back in her mouth, but I thought I'd better not. But you live in clean conditions. There shouldn't be any germs.

So you're pretty skilful with your TK-power, now?

It's coming on. If I know exactly where something is, I can apply telekinetic force down to, say, microscopic level. I can't do molecules yet, but I'm working on it.

That's great, you've achieved so much. Geoff wondered if she'd found a way of getting to OPDEO's secret records.

I still haven't found a way of getting to OPDEO's secret records, but I can see where the missiles are, because Breckenridge is tracking them electronically.

Brilliant!

We've got barely a month to do something before they reach Earth. There were three missiles. Each has now split up into six separate warheads.

Okay, you've made so much progress, I'm sure you'll be able to disarm them soon.

Oh, Geoff. This is so ironic, using more and more technology to fight technology. More than ever I'm coming round to the idea that we need to ditch all our hi-tech advances, and get back to a simple life. You know Atherlonne promised to deindustrialise the Thiosh, like the dolphins did long ago. Unless humans do the same, we'll disappear as a species.

Are you sure you've taken account of all the benefits? We can print any amount of food. We can stay young, if we choose too. And what about our ability to communicate? If you took away telecommunication, how are we going to resolve problems peacefully?

Actually, I've thought about it a lot, equivalent to thousands of man-years of human thinking. There are many pros and cons. But as for technology, telecommunication needn't be electronic. We've proved that. The problem is we can't help using technology to destroy the Earth and ourselves.

Maybe, but we can't go back to nature while we're being gravity bombed. Share with me tomorrow, Maura, if you have a spare minute.

━━●

When he awoke next morning, Geoff wondered if his telepathic experience had all been a dream. He reached out in his mind.

Maura O'Hara. Maura O'Hara. This is Geoff. Come in please, over.

Oh, Geoff, you don't have to be so formal.

Sorry, Maura, I didn't know how to get your attention.

Don't worry, I know when you're thinking of me, even in your dreams.

Oh right. Well, you probably know I want to talk to you about stepping out from your hardware. You mustn't stay too long living in the TUCC network. You're using almost every bit of computing power the TUCC has but, more importantly, you're vulnerable to hardware breakdown. If OPDEO get even one of their bombs through, it could wipe you out, as well as us.

Okay, I'll work out how to do it. But the bombs are the priority. I saw Atherlonne hack into the OPDEO network. Prof's getting reminders about Leona several times a day now.

He must think he's being cyber-stalked. He won't know Leona has passed away. What should we do next?

It's time to increase the pressure on Prof. Can you set up a mind-meeting with Kai, Atherlonne and Cetania? Oh, and count me in too, projected Maura.

Prof was swimming near the bottom of the sea. He was naked underneath his academic cap and gown. He was breathing water in and out through his nose. It was warm and tasted like something familiar – something sexual. A dolphin beckoned him with its flipper. He followed it into a cavern, which glowed with the light of flaming torches. The dolphin was clearly male. It dipped its head into a jar and brought out a wriggling eel, which it wrapped around its penis. Electric arcs tracked down the eel's body and the dolphin writhed with pleasure. A female dolphin swam over to Prof, holding an eel in her mouth. She offered it to him but he shook his head. Then she beckoned him to swim further into the cave, through stalactites and stalagmites, the way ahead lit by candles. Leona stood by an open fire, wearing a Maasai shuka.

'Come to me, slave,' she said. As he stepped out of the water, she removed his gown and mortar board and flung them in the fire. She slapped his cheek, and the sound echoed down the passageways.

'You're a puppet – OPDEO's puppet,' she said. 'You no longer seek knowledge. You do only your masters' bidding. You've helped them hunt down the remaining Thiosh.'

'It wasn't my fault,' pleaded Prof. 'They said I'd be charged with treason if I didn't help them. I had no choice.'

'You're a bastard, a collaborator, a coward, a traitor!' At each word, she slapped his face harder than before. 'You do not know the evil you serve.' Prof fell to his knees, sobbing.

'Stop whimpering. I'm giving you a chance to redeem yourself. Check on all the missile launches during the last thirteen months. Find out all you can and be ready to report to me.'

～●

Prof got out of bed. He took a hypodermic needle from the bathroom cabinet, dropped it on the floor and took another. He dissolved more powder and injected it. Then he showered vigorously. He got dressed and left his apartment, leaving his pre-timed breakfast in the nanowave cooker.

It was only a short walk. He swept through the outer office, nodding as his office girls chorused 'Good morning', shut his door and flicked it locked. Once his com-pad had booted, he used his global search app to find the OPDEO launch history. Then he shook his head and smiled. The last recorded launch was a test three years ago. His smile turned into a long, high-pitched laugh. His office supervisor peered through the window of his door, and then turned away.

He put his feet up on his desk and opened his comp-mail messages. He deleted half a dozen and then began a reply to the Sustainability Unit regarding the edibility of indigenous aquatic craniates. But he left that unfinished, opened another tab, and typed 'munitions' into the search app. Pages of inventories flashed across his screen. Then he entered 'stock withdrawal' as a refined search. He stared at the screen for a long time. Three interplanetary missile assemblies had been withdrawn six months previously. He clicked on the 'build component' hyperlink and opened a spreadsheet of data. He muttered the subheadings under his breath as he paged through the tables, pausing at 'Warhead/GX'. He loosened his tie and undid the top button of his shirt. The cursor began to oscillate on his screen. He let go of the trackball and the cursor stopped shaking. He tried more keywords: 'GX', 'Warhead G', 'G Warhead'. But every time his search only brought up the same message: 'Error: File Name Invalid'.

Prof swore under his breath. 'Fuck, fuck, fuck.'

The League

Hi Maura, are you there?

I am, Geoff, I'm always here.

Oh, good. I just wanted to tell you Clodagh grins each time she sees me now. And she can really bat those dangling toys Chen made for her. It's not just chance, she's doing it on purpose.

That's great! I'm glad you're enjoying fatherhood. Can you give some thought to how I can interact with her? Could you make me a talking head on a screen? She might get to like me too.

Sorry, I get so excited talking about Clodagh. I'm probably trampling all over your feelings.

Well, I brought this on myself. But don't stop being excited, Geoff, I want to feel it through you. Just think of me as a working mother. And there's something I want to tell you. I've figured out how to do the next stage of the jump, so we can give Zakristan his computers back soon. But I still need to solve the problem of what's inside the G-bomb warheads.

Can you use your TK? Apply a gentle force and map what it looks like?

Well there's some sort of pressure vessel. I can push against the walls. But inside the shell, there's nothing to press against. It's a complete vacuum.

D'you mean like outer space? Geoff asked.

Even outer space has low density hydrogen and helium plasma, and a bit of dust. There isn't any of that inside the core of the warheads. It's just a total void.

That's weird, I'll see if we can dig up anything from Europa. Atherlonne and Cetania have found a way of giving Prof designer dreams.

I know, thought Maura. It should be having some effect soon.

><del></del>

Sitting at a desk surrounded by no less than five screens, Geoff opened the proceedings.

'I now have visual and audio contact with you all. Welcome, and thank you for making time to join the Colloquium. I'm Geoff Kirby, a former consultant to the Unified Nations. I anticipate that this will be the first of regular online conferences. My objective today is simply to provide a forum for you to get to know each other better. Let me begin by greeting General Courtney Watkins at the Septagon. Also on screen are Shan Chonglin and Yul T'an at the Potala Palace, Lhaza. My colleagues to right and left of me respectively are Kai Yongze, whom most of you know, and Chen Khan, also a former Khitan celestonaut. My Hesperian colleague wearing what I believe is called a bush hat is the eminent Oztralian astronomer, Dr Wallis Frazer.'

Wally smiled and touched the brim of his hat.

Geoff continued with his introductions. 'We humans are, of course, only too familiar with the robo-troop armies who attacked both the Federation and the Empire. They were products of the advanced technological civilisation that we call the Thiosh. It's my pleasure to welcome two Thiosh representatives with us today. The Thiosh–Human War was clearly a disastrous episode in the history of our planet, and I believe it's the earnest wish of my Thiosh friends, Atherlonne and Voorogg, to win your trust, and to move forward in a constructive way to bring mutual benefit to humans and Thiosh alike.'

Two black, cigar-like shapes appeared on screen, swimming in slow circles in an aquamarine pool. Subtitles appeared.

Voorogg:

> My name is Voorogg. Thiosh rebel, guilty
> of murder, theft, and heinous crimes against

the human population of this planet.
I thank you for this opportunity
to offer my condolences to all
who lost their friends and loved ones in the war,
against the robots under my command.
I feel the greatest sorrow for the harm
I caused through my unwarranted attack.
I have no reason to expect you to
accept my facile words of shameful guilt.
I take responsibility for all
my crimes without attempting to excuse
myself. Nor do I seek avoidance of
the punishment that I deserve. I urge
you to accept my leader Atherlonne,
most honoured consort of my noble lord,
the Saazat Mettravar, who lost his life
during my cyber-onslaught on the dome
built by the humans on our blessed moon;
the Saazship now must pass to Atherlonne.
Her wishes for you all have only been
honourable, benign and generous.

'Thank you, Voorogg, for your opening statement,' said Geoff. 'The agreements we reach between us are potentially the most important ever to be discussed by humans. I shall not prejudge any outcome at this stage, but I will say that it's my hope that we shall only look forward, not back.'

Geoff patched another of his screens so that all members could see it, and spoke into his microphone. 'My human colleagues will notice that a more familiar sea creature, of the genus Tursiops, has joined our two Thiosh friends. Yes, she's a bottlenose dolphin, and a very distinguished one. Some of you may be surprised if I tell you that, twenty thousand years ago, dolphins organised themselves in a sophisticated technological society on Earth, but they voluntarily gave it up to live a natural life in our oceans. However, they retained formidable mental powers, and these were instrumental in ending the Thiosh–Human War. Thanks to Wally's expertise, we have engineered a way of communicating with the revered leader of Tursiop society, Cetania, here with us today.'

Cetania: Hi.

'Please, ladies and gentlemen, Thiosh and dolphin,' said Geoff, breaking into a rising hubbub of vocal sound, 'don't all speak at once. I shall end this session today with a free discussion forum, during which you can ask as many questions as time allows. It will be of benefit to us if we become familiar with each other in our different biological domains. The purpose of this session is only to put you in touch with each other. Later, we must discuss matters of the greatest importance, but we must get to know each other first. To this end, please allow me to finish the introductions. There is someone else I want to mention, who is party to these proceedings. She is Dr Maura O'Hara, an experienced microbiologist and oceanographer. Unfortunately, for technical reasons, I'm unable to show her on screen at present but, I assure you, she will play a crucial role in our future undertakings. She also will be our secretary. You okay with that, Maura?' he asked vocally, followed by a mental request for her to project her answer as subtitles.

Maura:

> Sure, I'm keeping up with you all. I'm just a bit worried about the title of your group, The League of Sentient Beings.

'Why's that?' asked Geoff. 'Oh, it's the sentient bit? Perhaps we'll just call it the League. I'm going to open the discussion forum now. You will have a great deal to say to each other, I know, but please direct your questions and comments through me.'

⊱⋯⊰

As soon as he could, Geoff slipped back to the lab and booted up his com-pad.

Hi Maura, have you got a minute? he projected.

I've possibly got until the end of time, Geoff, if that's what I choose.

Oh, right, that's good, I think. I want to try out some software. It's based on a recent photo of you, but I've CGI-ed the movements to synchronise with your speech, and I used some sound recordings to get your voice print. Some of it's from the bathyscaphe, so it might come out a bit serious sounding, but it should be a start.

Oh, that's grand. I like the picture. How do I use it?

Well, when you project your words, I'd like you to transmit the binary code that created them. If you stream that as input data into my com-pad, I'll route it to my talking-head program. D'you want to try it?

'Sure,' said Maura's talking head. 'Did you hear about the mathematician who was afraid of negative numbers? He'd stop at nothing to avoid them.'

Hm, I suspect the software works better than your joke.

Did you write this program so I can talk to Clodagh, and she can see what I look like? Thank you, Geoff, it's a wonderful present.

I'm glad you like it. But I think we can also use it at meetings of the League.

Prof had stayed up for forty-eight hours. He was afraid to go to sleep. His hair had become almost completely white and his skin was grey. Tired of pacing up and down, he slumped into an armchair in his apartment. Almost immediately his nightmare returned. Once again, he found himself in the cave, his pale naked body illuminated by the flickering firelight.

'Well?' said Leona. She was holding a whip. 'What have you found out? What was in the missiles?'

'They had warheads designated "GX". But there are no data on the network to explain what they are. They must be top secret.'

'Come on, Prof. You're supposed to be intelligent. Think. How can you get the information?'

'There's a rumour that classified documents are now produced manually. They must be held in the OPDEO strongrooms. Their security systems are unbreakable.'

'Pathetic slave,' said Leona. She slashed the whip around his body and drew him towards her. 'The warheads are a new weapon. OPDEO may put drawings and reports in the strongroom, but they wouldn't carry out design calculations manually. They would use computers offline. There will have to be electronic data somewhere. Find it, slave. Remember how the dolphins play games with electric eels. It will help you concentrate.'

Prof woke up and went to the bathroom for another fix.

Gorgonblast

Geoff welcomed the members of the League to the second Colloquium. He ran through the names of those online and each gave their salutation in his or her respective language. In her role as Secretary, Maura recorded greetings from Saazat Atherlonne, Cetania, Shan Chonglin, Dr Wallis Frazer, Yul T'an, and General Courtney Watkins. Voorogg had sent his apologies and given his endorsement to any and all proposals made by the new Saazat. Chen Khan also apologised for his absence, necessitated by babysitting duties. Dr Geoff Kirby was recorded as the facilitator of the meeting.

'I'm pleased to say that our secretary Dr Maura O'Hara is onscreen today,' said Geoff. 'I could have introduced her as our "permanent secretary", as she is more permanent than most us. At the last meeting, many of you registered a degree of shock when you heard that Cetania's ancestors were once part of a highly sophisticated technological society. Today we need to discuss issues you may consider to be even more surprising. Firstly, I believe you're all aware there are beings in our universe known as Virtuons. Many of you will be amazed to hear that Maura herself has recently Virtuonised.'

Geoff picked out Wally's voice over the sudden eruption of exclamations and questions.

'Okay, let's deal with that news first,' said Geoff. 'What was your comment, Wally?'

'Struth. You sure that's dinky-di? Maura was just a slip of a girl when I saw her last. You'd better explain, mate.'

'Perhaps I should explain myself,' said Maura's image. 'As you know, I went to Europa as a research scientist, and Geoff and I discovered the existence of Thiosh. Since then, the feckin' OPDEO have worked their bollocks off, trying to destroy every living Thiosh. Not only that, but the total feckin' eejits are about to hit Earth with a new weapon of mass destruction. I'm not sure how, but I'm going to stop them.'

'Thank you, Maura,' said Geoff. 'I think that's a fair summary of the situation. I'm sorry that we've had to break the news in this way to Yul and Shan. Everyone else, I believe, was aware of this threat.'

'I heard something like this from the Septagon,' said General Watkins. 'They'd received a message from Dr Wallis here. No one understood it, and it began a huge row when they challenged OPDEO. Our colony on Europa seems to have mutinied, and they answer the Septagon's questions with gobbledygook. I'm frankly horrified to think their attack on the Earth is a real threat.'

'So, tell me, please, what are these new weapons?' said Shan.

'They're gravity bombs,' said Geoff. 'OPDEO launched three high-speed missiles, which discharged six warheads each. They're all on a collision course with the Earth. The ETA is less than three weeks away.'

'How much damage will they do?' asked Yul.

'The physics suggest they will warp space–time causing singularities. In less than a picosecond, they'll seed black holes which will either crush the Earth to infinite density, or tear it apart by tidal forces.'

'*Ta ma de,*' said Yul. 'Can we stop them?'

'We're working on that,' said Geoff. 'Atherlonne and Cetania will get the design details from Europa so that Maura can defuse them. We already know they contain vacuum cylinders.'

'A vacuum doesn't sound very dangerous,' said Watkins.

'This is not a normal vacuum,' said Kai. 'It is a total void.'

'In our religion,' said Shan, 'the void is reality and matter is an illusion. Each is anathema to the other.'

'I shall call another meeting in two days' time,' said Geoff. 'I'm confident we can stop the missile attack. However, as a contingency, those of you who represent the Hesperian and Khitan authorities should investigate the possibility of launching a rocket to Mars. It should be big enough to contain the minimum constituents for our civilisation to live on another planet.'

'Like Noah's Ark,' said Watkins.

'We hope it won't come to that,' said Geoff.

—◆—

After the meeting, Kai walked with Geoff back to their accommodation.

'I didn't want to be negative at the meeting,' said Geoff, 'but the Septagon are bombarding us with messages. For a start, they don't know where we are, and they're desperate to meet us. And they keep asking where the warheads will hit. They're talking about evacuating the cities that survived the war. How do we tell them you can't run away from a black hole?'

'I think we have put General Watkins in a difficult position. He has had to warn his colleagues, but I suspect he has not told them the true nature of the warheads. He is letting them cling to the hope we can survive the impact. Similarly, he must be reluctant to explain our best hope lies with a Virtuon. They would not believe him.'

'I never thought I would say this,' said Geoff, 'but I think Watkins had better let the Septagon think the warheads are fusion bombs, on course for the main oceans. It's a lie, but there's no point in starting a senseless panic.'

'Sun Tzu said "All warfare is based on deception". Sometimes you have to deceive your own side,' said Kai.

—◆—

As a department head, Prof had certain privileges. In particular, he had access to the confidential personnel data in Human Resources files. He found the résumé for Clive Alexander. He had gained a first in Physics from Oxford and had written his PhD thesis on 'Operations Analysis and Capability Development', code words for weapons design. If anyone had worked on the G-bomb project, it had to be him.

Prof had administrative responsibilities for one of the academic workers' residential areas, rather like the university don he once was. It was perhaps lucky his area of authority included Alexander's living accommodation. The biometric data of the bursar and the cleaners were included in the software which operated the doors of private rooms. It took Prof no more than five minutes to appoint himself as a cleaning supervisor. He could easily erase the post later.

Having checked Alexander's meeting schedule, Prof returned to his own room. He collected his com-pad, and a list of robot fire extinguishers from his desk. It was well known he periodically walked the residential corridors, checking that routine inspections had been carried out. He went to his bathroom cabinet and stared at the stoppered bottle of white powder for a while, before taking off his jacket and rolling up his sleeve. His preparations complete, he set off for Alexander's rooms.

Checking there was no one in the corridor, Prof slipped into Clive Alexander's apartment. Like many experts in their field, Clive tended to invent his own systems rather than follow authorised procedures. But keeping mem-drives locked in a box labelled 'Gorgonblast Project' did not, perhaps, offer the highest level of security for a top-secret development. Prof prised open the lid with a screwdriver and copied the files onto his com-pad. He looked through the door's spyhole, confirmed no one was in sight, and stepped out into the corridor.

A Securopa officer, standing on one side of the door with his back against the wall, snapped handcuffs on Prof's wrists within seconds. Major Breckenridge, waiting on the other side, pulled the com-pad from under Prof's arm. He levered open the case, ripped out a chip array and tossed it on the floor. Scything downwards with his steel-tipped heel, he smashed the memory into fragments.

Breckenridge smiled. For once his face showed no sign of its convulsive tic. 'You can't have a com-pad where you're goin', Prof. But you're gonna love your new accommodation. I've got some serious new substances for you to try. Believe me, they'll melt your mind.'

Endgame

Geoff read the message:

Wally:

> Ace job, you guys. The G-bombs are gonners. I counted eighteen flashes, fifty million miles from Earth – each was as bright as the sun. I'm monitoring for collateral damage.

What happened, Maura? Geoff projected.

Hang on, I'm a bit busy at the moment.

The occupants of the Unidome stopped what they were doing as the siren alarms began to wail, and then fell silent. The light panels in the Unidome flashed intermittently, and then went out. Luminous, humanoid figures skimmed through the air, some soaring up to the highest levels, some passing unhindered through walls, others diving down the vertical shaft to the quayside. The Securopa paramilitary troops responded, and the dome resonated with the *whump* of ion guns until their weapons disappeared from their hands.

Whatever the invading holograms touched was transformed. The control room, barracks, and OPDEO complex vaporised in seconds. In their place, neat rows of vegetables and herbs glowed in the soft illumination of battery-powered light. The occupants of the conference chamber, as well as the trainees in the classrooms, found themselves standing in coppices full of shrubs and conifers. A mill and grain hopper appeared in place of the fusion power station. In other buildings, fittings and equipment vanished without trace; workshops became storerooms for hand tools, hand pumps, arable farm implements, pens, typewriters and paper books. Art and craft materials cascaded over the desks in the office areas. The laboratories' scientific instruments disappeared in a moment, replaced by pots and pans, needles, thread and fabrics, and musical instruments. Only the desalination plant and the basics of the living accommodation remained intact.

The Europan colonists milled around, some shouting and wailing, others as if they were in a dream. A few found their wings and flew in circles above the mêlée. OPDEO military and Securopa officers, support workers, researchers, and prisoners miraculously released from their cells rushed to and fro, frequently running into each other and falling over. But, within an hour, the Chief Engineer had found a capstan and gears driving a shaft projecting through the dome wall. He summoned a few of his staff, and together they threw their weight against the bars so that the machinery began to turn. As it gathered speed, the main lights flickered, and then shone brightly again, revealing a new world within the Unidome.

It took less than an hour to link everyone together for the League's third Colloquium. Geoff welcomed the delegates. Word had spread quickly, and they were all aware Maura had destroyed the G-bombs. But they didn't know how.

'We owe a debt of gratitude to Atherlonne and Cetania, so we do,' said Maura's talking head. 'They managed to drive poor old Prof Mitchell to distraction. He thought his only chance of staying sane was to steal the G-bomb design. He only had it for a minute, but I saw it all on his com-pad as he copied it in.'

'Can you explain how the G-bombs work?' asked General Watkins.

'I could list the components,' said Maura, 'but I really think it's information you organic creatures ought not to have. G-bombs are a genie I'd like to keep stoppered in a bottle.'

'But how did you blow up the warheads? Did you set them off early?' asked Yul.

'Not at all,' said Maura. 'The absolute void was maintained by electrostatic and magnetic fields. The power source was a radioisotope thermoelectric generator. Like most RTGs, it used Plutonium-238 as the isotope. All I had to do was juggle some neutrons around and make Plutonium-239. There was enough mass in each to go critical.'

'But it was a hell of a risk,' said Wally. 'We would have been up shit creek if they'd made black holes so close to Earth.'

'Sure,' said Maura. 'But I'd calculated the vacuum would decay just before the fissile material started a chain reaction. I just caused a few little nuclear explosions – nothing serious, not at all.'

Spontaneous applause broke out. As it subsided, Shan raised his hand to speak. 'We are very grateful for all Maura has done. Can I ask what she thinks OPDEO will do next?'

'Actually, I think they'll have their work cut out just surviving,' said Maura. 'What nobody knows outside the Unidome is that they've been deindustrialised. You should have seen it, Geoff. I made some holograms to help me focus on the mods I carried out, and then I invaded OPDEO.'

'Did anyone get hurt?' asked Shan.

'Unfortunately, some of the Securopa paramilitary troops managed to shoot each other,' said Maura. 'They seemed to forget their guns were only designed to damage organic matter. They couldn't take out holograms. I intervened to stop fatalities but, I have to admit, there were some injuries. I wouldn't have been concerned if certain characters we know had died, but my focus was to deindustrialise them, not to kill them.'

Chen spoke up. 'You send them back to Stone Age?'

'Not entirely,' said Maura. 'But from now on the occupants of the Unidome will be living a simple life.'

'But Europa is an alien environment. How can they manage without technology?' asked Watkins.

'That was tricky, to be sure. I decided they couldn't live without electricity, but from now on they'll have to generate it manually. Actually, it's not that onerous because I've moved their generators outside the dome. They'll operate as superconductors in the extreme cold. I gave them driving shafts through the dome shell. I've left their existing heating system too. It pumps heat from the ocean and increases the temperature, like a fridge in reverse.'

Atherlonne:

> I have a question, please. OPDEO could
> not bear to share the sea with Thiosh 'aliens',
> the hostile word they used to show their hate.
> What happened to their nuclear submarines?

'I sank them to the seabed in a place deep enough to crush them, but still keep the reactor pressure vessel and the nuclear warheads intact,' said Maura. 'That way the radioactivity will be contained until it naturally decays.'

'I believe you have followed our religion,' said Kai. 'You found a middle way to disable OPDEO without totally destroying it.'

'Actually, I did a lot of destroying. All their computer equipment, mechanised transport, and their munitions. I reduced it all to a molecular level. Most of it got recycled.'

'What happens if they fall ill?' asked Geoff.

'I don't s'pose they'll like what I've done,' said Maura. 'I removed their scanners, biometers, analysis equipment – all the electronic medical apparatus. But I've left them a lot of books about anatomy, herbal remedies and alternative therapy. They'll have to find their own cures for their ailments.'

'Will they survive, d'you think?' asked Geoff. 'None of them has a clue about living without technology.'

'It depends,' said Maura. 'If they use the opportunity, they may find a way to live together without internal conflict. They should manage okay in the Europan environment. I've left them oxygen cylinders and thermal suits for outside maintenance. Sufficient to last one generation, at least.'

'What will they do after that?' asked Kai.

'They'll only have one generation,' said Maura. 'I gave all the men vasectomies. OPDEO won't be threatening Earth again.'

Epilogue

Five years had passed, and Geoff and Clodagh were living quietly in Kalifornia. With some help from Atherlonne and Maura herself, Geoff had created an android to faithfully replicate Maura's body. Using advanced animatronics, it spoke, gestured, and made facial expressions just like Maura. Geoff found it ironic that, having gone to the trouble of leaving her body, Maura had chosen to re-inhabit a facsimile. Sometimes even he forgot Maura was no longer human. The friends and relations they tracked down and visited were totally unaware of her true nature, although some did say they thought she'd changed. Geoff had been worried about Maura having to pretend to eat and drink on such occasions, but she managed to dispose of food and beverages without giving any indication she hadn't swallowed them.

The hardest part was meeting Geoff's sister, Georgina, again. She'd survived the war but had contracted leukaemia from the radioactive fallout. Geoff designed new bone marrow cells for her and Maura made them. Zakristan sent equipment from the TUCC for them to carry out a bone marrow transplant at home. Georgina's Hesperian doctors had no explanation for her cure, other than it being a miracle. She knew Geoff and Maura had done it, but she didn't know how.

As far as Clodagh was concerned, the android was her mummy. Clodagh herself was growing up fast. She was big for her age, with freckles and curly red hair. Chen was so attached to her, Geoff agreed he could live with them as a home help and odd job man. This worked out well as Geoff preferred Maura not to use her supernatural powers for plumbing and decorating. Geoff also abstained from telekinesis, because it didn't 'feel right' in a domestic environment.

All their human friends and colleagues had found new occupations. The old Abbot of the Drepung monastery had passed away, and the monks had asked Kai to fill the post. Shan retired to live in the mountains, and Yul became the Khitan Secretary of State. The Sydny Institute of Astronomy invited Wally to be their Head of School, and General Watkins became President of the General Assembly of the League.

Maura had hoped the Europan colonists would find a way of living in harmony. But the bucolic idyll she'd hoped for did not materialise. Flannery ruled the Unidome like a feudal chief, rewarding his cronies, and eliminating anyone who opposed him. Breckenridge and his gang of thugs terrorised the dome's other inhabitants. They punished anyone who would not accept Flannery's rule by chaining them to the capstan to generate electricity. Prof, however, managed to escape this fate; he was put in charge of growing poppies for their seeds.

As Saazat, Atherlonne worked hard to heal the divisions in the Thiosh community, and Voorogg devoted himself to the same cause. Together they began a phased deindustrialisation of their society.

With General Watkins as their spokesman, the Thiosh urged the human governments to do the same. The Hesperian and Khitan leaders debated this at great length but there was little support for the proposal in their democratic assemblies. Few humans were prepared to sacrifice the comforts and benefits of a hi-tech existence.

In secret, the Hesperian and Khitan armies re-armed and developed their own design of gravity bomb. And so the arms race continued . . .

Acknowledgements

This story has taken at least four trips around the sun to write. Consequently, I'd like to express my gratitude to all who have encouraged me with grace and good humour during that protracted period: my wife, my family and the GlosInk creative writing group. I also thank my beta readers for their comments and encouragement: Steve Abbott for his blunt but accurate critique and particularly Maia Kumari Gilman who arranged for five thousand words of *The Hesperian Dilemma* to be included in ASEI Art's book *Anthology House*, sold as a fundraiser for hurricane relief in the southern US and in the Caribbean. I'm grateful too to my editor Lesley Jones, Rachel Lawston who designed the cover and Richard Buxton whose wood cut inspired its design.

It's inevitable that the experiences of one's own life, and those of other people, influence the development of a story. Kai's early years, running away, following materialistic pleasures and then a spiritual path echoes, in part, *Siddhartha*, the novel by Hermann Hesse, which details the spiritual journey of self-discovery of a man during the time of Gautama Buddha. Secondly, my depiction of the deprivations of Maura, Geoff and Leona as they trek across the 'Oztralian' bush, 'borrows' fairly heavily from *Mutant Message Down Under* by Marlo Morgan, a woman's journey into dreamtime Australia. If you haven't read these books then I urge you to do so.

Feedback

Dear Reader,

Although *The Hesperian Dilemma* was primarily meant for your entertainment, there was an underlying message, i.e. the onward march of technology is wonderful but also frightening. Things are invented and become available before their effect on society has been evaluated or even recognised. Cars, computers, phones and drones are obvious examples which spring to mind, even before we consider the weapons arsenal held by countries with varying levels of conflict with their neighbours – and nowadays all countries are effectively neighbours.

If you have any thoughts on this, or any comments about the book, please contact me via my website www.fabulahula.com.

Thank you for your interest,

Colin Waterman

18718266R00159

Printed in Great Britain
by Amazon